CW01501356

A Witchy Christmas

Bea St. Clair

A Witchy Christmas

Copyright © 2025 Bea St.Clair

All rights reserved.

ISBN: 978-1-916989-16-0

DEDICATION

For all the witchlings, great and small. May your Yule logs rise, your charms hold true, and your hot chocolate never run out of marshmallows. This book is for you, whether you call it Christmas, Witchmas, Yule or simply an excellent excuse to eat too many biscuits by candlelight.

Bright blessings, merry mischief, and love to you all.

CONTENTS

ACKNOWLEDGMENTS

To my children, who have grown used to finding glitter in their sandwiches
and pine needles in their socks. You are the true heroes of this book

To the readers of this book, if you're reading this instead of untangling
fairy lights, you've already made the right choice.

CHAPTER ONE

The Roots of Yule - Mistletoe Mischief

Let me begin with a confession: the first time I celebrated the Winter Solstice properly without the assistance of my parents, I accidentally set fire to my tea towel. In fairness, it was hanging a little too close to the Yule log I'd enthusiastically (and perhaps overzealously) anointed with cinnamon oil, frankincense resin, and a frankly unsafe quantity of rosemary. The whole kitchen smelled like a festive apothecary had exploded... which, to be honest, is precisely the sort of ambience I was going for.

You see, as a green witch, I've long held a deeply affectionate relationship with Yule. It's the time of year when everything goes quiet, the hedgerows freeze, the birds stop squabbling, and even the foxes seem to pad around more reverently, like they've remembered they're sacred animals and not just bin burglars in fur coats. It's the pause before the turning. The still breath of the earth before it exhales again.

While the modern world hurtles toward Christmas with its shopping centres glowing like nuclear reactors and its carol singers aggressively jingling bells in four-part harmony, we witches tend to walk a little slower. We gather herbs and stories, light candles rather than strip malls, and mark the solstice not with debt but with gratitude. (yes, occasionally, minor kitchen fires.)

But it hasn't always been easy to explain this to people. Mention Yule, and half the room thinks you're talking about a Scandinavian furniture store. Mention witchcraft, and the other half discreetly checks you for goats or bubbling cauldrons. Which, is fair. I do have a cauldron and a goat. Maybe I look like I do! (no comments please!)

So, I thought I'd begin this first chapter, by doing what all witches are historically known for: telling stories. Or, more specifically, digging up the muddy, moss-covered roots of the midwinter season and giving them a good rinse under the tap so we can all get a clearer look at just how much of what we now call "Christmas" is, in fact, deeply, and very deliciously pagan.

Take, for instance, the Winter Solstice, the astronomical moment when the earth tilts as far from the sun as it dares, plunging us into the longest night of the year. Ancient peoples didn't have clocks or Black Friday sales to mark the season, but they *did* have an intimate relationship with the sky. They noticed the sun slipping lower, the shadows growing longer, the days shorter and colder, until one day... the light began to return.

This moment, this cosmic turning point, was cause for celebration across cultures. Bonfires were lit on hilltops. Trees were brought inside to remind everyone that life, stubborn and green, continued even in the heart of winter. (Yes, that tree in your lounge today, festooned in baubles and LED lights, is a direct descendant of that same sacred tree.)

In the Norse and Germanic traditions, Yule was a time of fire and feasting, of storytelling and spirit-walking. The Wild Hunt rode through the skies, a ghostly procession of the dead and the divine, and households lit fires to ward off unwanted visitors (or to guide in the right ones, depending on your mood). People exchanged gifts, burned the Yule log (ideally without also burning the kitchen), and told tales to one another as the snow piled up outside.

Then there was Saturnalia, Rome's answer to "Let's Eat and Be Weird for a Week." The festival of Saturn involved public feasting, role reversals, gift-giving, and general revelry. Masters served slaves. Everyone wore silly hats. Gambling was legal. If this sounds suspiciously like your office Christmas party, congratulations: you're already halfway to being pagan.

But what fascinates me most is how all these traditions, sun worship, tree decorating, light festivals, feasting, got wrapped up, rebranded, and reissued under the label of Christmas. Christianity, not one to let a good party go to waste, absorbed a buffet of pre-existing customs and gave them a new spin. The result is a holiday that's as much druid as it is divine.

Through it all, the witches, quietly, stubbornly, joyfully, kept the old ways alive. In whispered stories. In recipes passed down through smoky kitchens. In candles lit for the returning sun. In dried orange slices and clove-studded pomanders. In mulled wine and midwinter blessings whispered over sleeping gardens.

I wrote this book, and this chapter in particular, because I believe understanding the roots of our celebrations makes them all the more meaningful (...and delightful). Knowing that your gingerbread has ancestors in ancient solstice bread, or that your wreath mirrors a wheel of the year older than any Victorian greeting card, adds layers to the season that no plastic tinsel ever could.

So before we dive into modern recipes and magical rituals, before we craft charms and hang enchanted ornaments, let's take a moment to honour where it all began. With stars in cold skies. With the hush of

3

snow over soil. With the flicker of a fire against the darkness and the age-old promise:

The light will return.

Just mind your tea towel.

Bea

The Longest Night: Understanding the Winter Solstice

Ah, the winter solstice. Or as I like to call it: Nature's dramatic pause. It's the day she gathers herself, sighs deeply, and quietly begins turning the whole world back toward the sun while we're all distracted by mince pies and seasonal existential dread.

Now, the technical bit, which I promise I'll keep brief and only moderately confusing. The winter solstice occurs when the Earth's axial tilt is farthest from the sun, which means it's the shortest day and longest night of the year in the northern hemisphere. Astronomers mark it with precise instruments and complicated star maps. Witches, however, tend to notice it when the birds stop singing at four in the afternoon.

But here's the magical thing: the solstice isn't an ending. It's a beginning. From this point forward, the light slowly returns. Not that you'd notice immediately, of course. The sun still sulks off-stage for several weeks, rising at a frankly unreasonable hour and disappearing by tea time. But imperceptibly, secretly, the world is shifting. The soil remembers. The roots stir. Those of us who've been paying attention start lighting candles, not to mourn the dark, but to welcome the light back in.

Ancient peoples didn't just survive the solstice. They celebrated it, and they did it without central heating, Wi-Fi, or delivery apps that bring you cinnamon rolls in under 30 minutes. They built stone circles aligned with the sunrise. They decorated trees, not because John Lewis or Macy's told them to, but because evergreens were a reminder that life continued, even in the harshest months. They feasted and told stories and sang songs, some of which we still hum today, even if we've long since forgotten they were originally about the sun returning, not Santa arriving.

One of my favourite examples is Newgrange in Ireland, older than Stonehenge, older even than your gran's gravy boat. It's a passage tomb, carefully constructed so that, on the morning of the winter solstice, a beam of sunlight travels down the narrow stone corridor and illuminates the inner chamber. Just once a year. Just for a few minutes. Imagine the wonder. The joy. The sense that, yes, the sun is coming back. The wheel is turning. We made it through.

We still do. Even if our rituals now involve thermal leggings, battery-powered fairy lights, and that one awkward relative who insists on debating politics over roast potatoes.

For witches, the solstice is sacred precisely because it reminds us that even the darkest night ends. That light returns. That rebirth is not just possible but inevitable. It's a time for reflection, yes, but also for hope. For spellwork centred on new beginnings, for letting go of what no longer serves, and for gently coaxing our sleepy souls back toward the warmth.

I always do a simple ritual on solstice night. I light a candle, just one, and sit with it in silence. No TV, no music, no Golden Retriever demanding treats, no husband reminding me to bring another bottle of wine back from the lounge. I breathe. I listen. I write on a scrap of paper the one thing I most want to let go of. Then I burn it in the flame and watch it curl into ash. It's a tiny act. But somehow it feels like speaking the same language as the earth. We both release something. We both begin again.

So yes, the solstice is astronomy. It's planetary tilts and solar declination and other things that make your eyes glaze over. But it's also *poetry.* It's the story of a planet that remembers how to turn toward the light... and of people, witches, druids, modern mystics, and curious souls, who mark that turning with herbs, with fire, and with the soft, persistent belief that life endures.

If that's not worth celebrating, I don't know what is.

Yule Before Christmas: Yule Laugh, You'll Cry, You'll Sacrifice a Goat

Let us begin with a truth that might unsettle some: long before the jingle bells jingled or Santa climbed down his first chimney, winter celebrations across northern Europe were already in full swing. The Norse and Germanic peoples, far from sitting quietly in the snow with polite carols, were engaging in a riotous, fiery, occasionally spectral celebration known as Yule.

Yule, or *Jól*, as the old Norse would have it, was not so much a holiday as a full-bodied experience. Picture this: long nights, frozen fields, animals huddled together for warmth, and a community determined not to let the season swallow them. In a time before thermostats and corner shops, celebration wasn't optional, it was a matter of survival, or at least sanity. You either made merry with what you had, or you stared moodily into the hearth while chewing stale roots and contemplating the brevity of life.

So they made merry. Yule was twelve days (or more, depending on who was doing the counting) of drinking, feasting, storytelling, sacrifice, ritual, and a not-insignificant amount of singing around the fire. It was the time to honour ancestors, toast the gods, and burn things, lots of things, with dramatic flair.

Central to all of this was the Yule log. Now, I know what you're thinking: that delightful chocolate confection rolled up with cream and topped with powdered sugar snowflakes. Lovely, but not quite what the Norse had in mind. Their Yule log was a massive chunk of oak, sometimes a whole tree, that was dragged into the hearth, lit with a piece of last year's embers, and meant to burn for the entire festival. If it went out prematurely, it was considered terribly unlucky, possibly even a bad omen, and definitely the sort of thing that would prompt a lot of nervous muttering into one's mead.

The Yule log wasn't just a heat source; it was a symbol of the returning sun, a talisman of protection, and a focal point for magical intentions. Charred fragments were kept throughout the year to protect the home from lightning, illness, and in-laws. Modern witches (myself included) still burn Yule logs, albeit on a smaller, less tree-consuming scale. Some of us even bake the chocolate version and call it a spell for joy.

No discussion of Yule would be complete without mentioning the Wild Hunt. Imagine, if you will, being tucked in bed under a mound of woolen blankets when you hear it: a howling wind, the sound of hooves on snow, ghostly laughter echoing through the trees. That, my friends, was the Wild Hunt, a spectral procession of gods, dead warriors, and occasionally witches, who tore through the night sky in midwinter, led by Odin himself.

To see the Hunt was a mixed blessing. It meant you were sensitive to the unseen, sure, but it also meant you risked being swept away with them. People left offerings outside their doors, bread, mead, or bits of meat, to appease the riders. Fires were lit not just for warmth, but to keep the spectral host at bay. Even today, in parts of Europe, stories persist of a ghostly hunt that rides through the woods on stormy nights.

Let's take a moment to appreciate the sheer theatricality of it all. These weren't timid spiritual beliefs. These were traditions that flung open the doors to the numinous and said, "Come on in, just don't knock over the ale." The Norse were not afraid of the dark. They knew it intimately. They also knew how to light it up with story, with fire, and with the insistence that community and ritual could see you through even the most bone-chilling of nights.

Evergreens were another key piece of the Yule celebration. In a world of barren trees and withered fields, the sight of green boughs held deep symbolic power. They were cut, hung over doorways, wrapped around banisters (or whatever the 8th-century equivalent was), and used to remind everyone that life persisted. Today's wreaths and garlands are spiritual descendants of those early winter charms. My own home tends to look like an enthusiastic hedge which went mad in a pine forest by mid-December.

Mistletoe deserves its own paragraph. This peculiar, parasitic plant was revered by the druids and respected by the Norse, particularly after a rather tragic incident involving the god Baldr. The story goes that Baldr was invincible to all things, except mistletoe. A bit of trickery, a rogue arrow, and a devastating death later, and mistletoe was never looked at the same way again. Eventually, it became a symbol of peace and reconciliation. Hanging mistletoe was said to ward off lightning and evil spirits. The kissing bit came later, because apparently us humans just can't help ourselves.

Now, let's talk feasting. The Yule feast was a sacred and strategic act. The livestock that wouldn't survive the winter was slaughtered, and that meat, salted, smoked, or roasted, formed the centrepiece of the celebration. Ale was brewed. Bread was baked. Spices, if one was lucky enough to have them, were used liberally. People toasted to health, to ancestors, to gods, and to the land itself. A well-made toast could bless the crops for the year to come. A poorly made one could invite mockery from your neighbour and possibly a hex.

Yule wasn't merely a festival; it was a reminder. That warmth could be found in the cold. That the darkness had an end. That death and life were part of the same sacred cycle. It wasn't polished or sentimental. It was raw, and wild, and full of fire.

As a modern witch, I find myself both enchanted and comforted by these older traditions. We may not chase pigs through snowy fields or leave bread out for spectral horsemen (although I do often leave out a slice of sourdough for a fox who may or may not be a minor forest deity), but the essence remains. We gather. We honour. We light candles. We feast. We tell stories that stretch back through time, all the way to snowy hilltops where ancestors once sang to the stars.

When you hang up your wreath this year, or slice into that chocolate Yule log, know that you are participating in something ancient and powerful. Yule is not just the quiet prelude to Christmas. It is a season unto itself, rooted in frost and fire, howling wind and evergreen hope.

So raise a glass. Whisper a blessing. Watch the firelight dance. The hunt may ride, the sun may sleep, but you, dear witch, are part of the turning of the world.

When in Rome… Party Like It's Saturnalia"

Somewhere between the solemnity of solstice rituals and the chaos of the Wild Hunt, sits Rome, toga-clad and wine-soaked, belting out a drinking song and enthusiastically declaring a week-long holiday. If the Norse celebrated the season with roaring fires and starlit sacrifices, the Romans responded with something between a street party and a philosophical experiment gone delightfully rogue.

Saturnalia, named for the god Saturn, was held in mid-to-late December, right around the time people started grumbling that the days were too short and the wine was too cold. Saturn was a god of agriculture, abundance, and time, a bit of a cosmic all-rounder, really, and the festival in his honour was both a farewell to the old sun and a bit of wishful cheerleading for the new one.

The first rule of Saturnalia was simple: everything was upside down. Social order? Reversed. Slaves dined like kings, and sometimes their masters served them. The head of the household might don a silly cap and play the fool for a day. Business shut down, courts closed, schools paused, and gambling, normally frowned upon, was joyfully embraced. The whole city leaned into chaos, which for a civilization famous for aqueducts and straight roads was no small feat.

At the heart of it all was joy. Or at least, sanctioned merriment. It was as if the Romans had collectively agreed that, once a year, everyone could take a break from being serious and just be wonderfully, gloriously human. There were feasts, yes, and drinking, of course, but also games, performances, song, dance, and gifts, mostly small, symbolic things like candles, dice, or little figurines called sigillaria. (If that sounds like stocking fillers to you, you're not wrong. Saturnalia was the original Secret Santa.)

Gift-giving wasn't just about generosity. It carried a touch of sympathetic magic, the idea that giving light (like candles) or abundance (like tokens of food or fortune) could invoke real warmth and prosperity. The very act of giving, of turning outward in a season that turned inward, was its own kind of spell.

There is something incredibly modern about Saturnalia. The idea that we should loosen our grip on routine, laugh at ourselves, play games, overeat, and pretend… just for a moment… that the world is upside down… well, tell me that doesn't sound like December in any Western household right now.

One cannot mention Roman winter holidays without meeting Sol Invictus, the Unconquered Sun. While Saturnalia basked in earthly chaos, Sol Invictus was a celestial campaign of hope. Celebrated on December 25th, this newer Roman festival honoured the rebirth of the sun, freshly triumphant after its lowest point in the sky.

The temple to Sol Invictus stood gleaming in Rome, and his cult blended well with just about anything, he was the deity equivalent of a nice chardonnay: adaptable, bright, and immensely popular. Soldiers loved him. Emperors endorsed him. People lifted their faces to the pale December sky and offered praise for the light's slow return.

This is where things get historically delicious. Early Christians, looking to establish the birthday of Jesus, needed a date that made symbolic sense and already had a celebratory vibe. December 25th, with its existing festival of divine solar rebirth, fit like a well-stitched sandal. So sorry to pour a little cold water on your religious fireworks (and yes, I know that's a very un-Christmassy image), but the Bible itself gives us a rather big seasonal clue that Jesus probably wasn't born on December 25th. In Luke 2:8, it says shepherds were out in the fields at night when the angels popped in with their birth announcement. Lovely image, isn't it? Except in Bethlehem, by late December, nights are cold, damp, and about as inviting as a wet sock. Sensible shepherds would have had their sheep tucked up under shelter long before the frost set in. Most scholars agree that this scene fits far better with springtime, just after lambing, or early autumn, when both shepherd and sheep could actually survive a night outdoors without frostbite or the sort of cough that ends with a hot toddy. The December 25th date? That came along a few centuries later, when the early Church, with all the subtlety of a modern marketing department, merged the celebration with Sol Invictus, the Roman festival of the Unconquered Sun. Light returning, Son arriving, tidy bit of symbolism, really, and it saved everyone from having to invent a whole new winter holiday. So the birthday of Sol Invictus and the birthday of Christ gently fused, creating the foundations of Christmas as we now know it. The feast remained. The light persisted. The poetry of rebirth endured.

From a witch's perspective, this all tracks. The mingling of traditions, the layering of symbolism, the way sacred meanings are carried forward like candles through the ages, it's exactly how magic works. Nothing is lost. It is reinterpreted, reshaped, re-enchanted. The Saturnalian reversal becomes the Twelve Days of Christmas. Sol Invictus becomes the light of the world. The feasts stay feasts. The candles still burn.

Even today, when I light my solstice candles, I imagine myself joining an unbroken line of celebrants stretching from a smoky Roman alleyway to my own modest kitchen. I may not wear a toga (flattering on very few people, frankly), but I do wear an apron and a wry smile. I pour spiced wine, bake honey cakes, and leave a small offering of fruit and fire for the spirits of the season.

It's hard not to feel connected to the past when you do this. Not in a dusty, academic sense, but in a deeply sensory one. The scent of citrus and clove. The flicker of flame. The echo of laughter as someone tries to win at an ill-advised parlour game. These are the threads that tie us to ancient Rome more intimately than any textbook ever could. If you have read my first book *The Witch's Botanical Apothecary,* you will know how close my family home feels to those ancient Romans.

Saturnalia teaches us that sometimes joy is the ritual. That revelry can be sacred. That letting go, for a moment, of all the serious business of being human is not only acceptable, it is, perhaps, necessary.

When I explain this to non-witch friends, they often look bewildered. Isn't magic about solemn chants and black robes and doing something terribly complicated with a crystal and a bell? Yes, occasionally. But more often, it's about lighting a candle, drinking wine with friends and laughing until your belly hurts. It's about making cake with intention. It's about toasting to the sun and remembering that life has always been a bit ridiculous.

So this season, if you feel the urge to throw on a party hat and drink something with too much nutmeg, know that you are honouring Saturn. If you light a candle and whisper a prayer for the light's return, you are invoking Sol Invictus. If you gather with loved ones and exchange tokens, sing songs, and eat until you need a nap, you are, knowingly or not, keeping the old fires burning.

History is not just something that happened. It's something we still do.

The Witch's Solstice: Frost, Fire, and a Little Bit of Witchery

Some witches inherit their craft through family bloodlines. Some are drawn to it by books, dreams, or that one oddly powerful moment in a garden centre when they lock eyes with a particularly judgmental crow. I came to witchcraft through my bloodline, yes, a family of witches, but everyone has a personal journey. Mine came by way of soup. More specifically, a winter root stew brewed during the solstice of my twenty-second year, which, despite being mostly parsnips and indecision, somehow summoned an epiphany.

That solstice evening was cold enough to make the stars blink. I sat beside a half-lit fire with a mug of dubious mulled cider, watching the candlelight flicker against sprigs of rosemary I'd tied into a circle and called a "wreath." There was no ceremonial script, no coven, no dramatic cloak. Only me, a wooden spoon, and a feeling that I was participating in something very old.

It turns out I was.

Witches, in all their guises, have been marking the winter solstice long before we had the luxury of scented candles or electric kettles. In medieval Europe, before the word "witch" got you dunked in a pond or invited to a spontaneous village bonfire, cunning folk quietly practiced seasonal magic tied to the rhythms of the land. They were the local healers, midwives, charm-weavers, and weather-watchers. While bishops fretted over the Devil's whereabouts, these folk were busy drying hawthorn berries and preparing salves.

For them, the solstice wasn't abstract. It was a necessary signal. The days were darkest, the food was thinning, and spirits, of the dead, of the forest, of one's great aunt who never entirely left, were closer than usual. Cunning folk lit fires, offered bread or ale at the edge of the woods, and muttered charms for protection and endurance. These weren't spells for spectacle; they were spells for survival.

In the coldest months, folklore wrapped around the hearth like a second shawl. Farmers told tales of animals speaking at midnight. Mothers whispered warnings of frost spirits who crept through cracked doorways. Children were taught to leave an offering, not a glass of milk and cookies for Santa, but because the old gods remembered who gave back.

Even under the weight of Christianisation, much of this seasonal magic endured. It adapted. It found new names and forms, as magic often does. Holly and ivy kept their protective status, tucked into doorways and fireplaces to ward off ill will. Wassailing, once a pagan toast to the orchard spirits, became a cheerful carol service, though the mulled cider stayed impressively consistent.

Later, when Wicca emerged in the mid-20th century, the solstice was officially folded into the Wheel of the Year as Yule. It gained ceremony and structure: rituals of candle-lighting, invocations of the Holly King and Oak King, chants in circle. This was a revival and a reinvention, much like the holiday itself. The old bones remained, but they were dressed in new robes, often velvet, occasionally glittery.

Personally, I've always favoured the green witch's approach, earthy, improvised, rooted in the practical magic of daily life. For me, the solstice is less about formal rites and more about presence. Lighting a single candle in the dark. Brewing tea with intention. Thanking the bare trees and the buried bulbs. Not because I expect the snow to answer back (though once on the way back from the pub, I swear it nodded), but because magic is made in the act of noticing.

Over the years, I've developed my own seasonal rituals. I hang a bundle of cinnamon and clove over my door, not just for the scent, but to welcome warmth and sweet fortune. I walk the garden with a lantern and murmur thanks to the skeletal hedgerow. I tuck handwritten blessings into the woodpile. On solstice night, I stir a stew or bake a seed cake, whispering hope into the dough like it's an ancestor who's come for tea.

This isn't flashy magic. It doesn't come with thunderclaps or Instagram filters. It's quieter, like snowfall or moss growing in moonlight. But it is, in its own way, revolutionary. In a world built for speed and spectacle, choosing to honour slowness, darkness, and return is its own kind of spell.

Of course, witches today are a wonderfully varied bunch. Some gather in covens and dance beneath the stars. Some craft elaborate solstice altars with quartz grids and meticulously placed runes. Others toss a cinnamon stick in their coffee and call it a seasonal charm. All are valid. Magic isn't measured in ritual complexity... but in sincerity.

What unites us, across centuries, borders, and brewing styles, is the solstice itself. The still point. The sacred pause. Whether you're a medieval herb-wife, a Victorian spiritualist, or a woman in wellies stirring soup by candlelight, the moment is the same: the longest night, the turning of the wheel, the breath before the sun returns.

Sometimes I imagine a long table, stretching through time. At one end, a Saxon wise woman knots ivy into a charm. Next to her, a 17th-century bearded man lifts a cup of warmed ale in a silent toast. Across from him, a 1920s spiritualist checks her crystal ball, while a barefoot Wiccan adjusts her flower crown. Somewhere down the line sits me, with flour on my apron and my cat stealing the Yule loaf.

We are all there. We are all watching the same stars.

This, I think, is the real magic of the witch's solstice. It is not confined by time or geography. It is an inheritance, passed down in scent and song, in gesture and guesswork. It is the lighting of one candle in the dark and trusting that it matters before lighting the candle of the person next to you.

So this year, however you celebrate, whether with incense and invocation or with mulled wine and murmured thanks, know that you are part of something ancient. Something holy. Something defiantly warm.

The sun will return. The wheel will turn. The witches are watching.

Theological Compromise: When Pagans and Priests Share the Eggnog

Let us begin, as so many things do, with a bishop trying to solve a PR problem. Imagine the early Church, newly gaining ground in the Roman Empire, a bit of a start-up, looking out across the snowy fields of Northern Europe and realising, with some dismay, that the locals were still enthusiastically setting fire to logs, exchanging fertility symbols under mistletoe, and toasting Odin with spiced beer.

This, understandably, required a response.

Now, the early Christian Church wasn't without its charms, but it had a real knack for practical solutions. It saw no need to invent new holidays when perfectly good ones already existed. So rather than ban these popular midwinter customs outright (which, let's face it, would have gone down like a frostbitten turnip), the Church did what any resourceful institution might: it rebranded them. Can you image your dad coming home one dark night and saying "we've cancelled Christmas", well the exact same reaction would have been received about cancelling all the other fun bits of Yule life.

Thus, Saturnalia became the Twelve Days of Christmas. The solstice fire became the Christ candle. Yule became Christmas. The sacred grove became the nativity pine. You get the idea.

Christianity was less an aggressive replacement and more a spiritual overlay, like placing a lace cloth over a weathered table. You could still see the grains beneath. In many cases, you still can. Those baubles on your tree? Ancient charms. That star? A solstice sun. Even the jolly man in red has roots in pre-Christian folklore, though I'll save Krampus and his goatish pals for another chapter entirely.

Take holly, for example. The prickly plant with blood-red berries has been used since ancient times to ward off evil spirits and attract prosperity. Druids believed it remained green to offer shelter to woodland spirits during the cold months. The Church, ever keen on symbolism, declared holly's sharp leaves to represent Christ's crown of thorns, and the berries his blood. Meaning was not erased, just rewritten.

Mistletoe also made the leap, albeit more reluctantly. The Norse had their own complicated love-hate relationship with the plant (see: tragic death of Baldr, previously discussed). It was revered by druids and banned from churches. Yet somehow, it wormed its way into parlours and poetry, dangling above thresholds like a botanical dare.

Then there's the fire. Always the fire. In every ancient midwinter festival, from Yule to Saturnalia to Celtic solstice vigils, flame played a central role. It was life, light, warmth, protection, transformation. When Christianity arrived, it did not extinguish these flames. Instead, it relit them in the form of candles: the Advent wreath, the Christingle orange with its fiery spike, the rows of tiny tapers in stained-glass chapels. Same flicker, different context.

From a witch's point of view, this adaptation isn't theft, it's continuity. Seasonal magic has always been syncretic. It borrows, blends, evolves. It survives by being porous. The rituals of the solstice slipped neatly into Christmas because they were already rooted in the same soil: a desire for light, warmth, togetherness, and meaning in the depths of winter.

Of course, there were bumps along the way. The medieval Church did crack down on some more unruly elements. Wassailing sometimes got a bit too rowdy. Mummers' plays became less moral tale and more pre-panto chaos. But by and large, the bones of old festivals remained. To this day, we gather pine branches, hang ornaments, light candles, and bake things shaped like suns and stars, often without quite knowing why.

I once had a neighbour, bless her, who proudly informed me she didn't "believe in any of that pagan nonsense," while standing under a wreath she'd made entirely of ivy and hawthorn berries. I offered her a slice of solstice seed cake and didn't say a word.

What matters, ultimately, is that we're still doing it. Still pausing in the cold to bring greenery indoors. Still telling stories. Still lighting fires. Still giving. Still hoping.

Some witches celebrate both Yule and Christmas, with varying levels of theological negotiation. I am indeed one. Some pick one and leave the other to the department stores. I say: do what feels true. If singing carols fills you with joy, sing them. If you want to light a solstice lantern and whisper a blessing to the ancestors while your neighbours roast turkeys, light away.

Magic is not diminished by sharing space. It thrives there.

Each year I write Christmas cards with sigils hidden in the loops of my calligraphy. I bake gingerbread in sunwheel shapes. I hang garlands of rosemary and bay leaves next to the tinsel. My nativity scene includes a ceramic owl. The lines blur. That's the beauty of it.

Christmas, in its tangled, layered way, is a palimpsest, a manuscript overwritten but never fully erased. Beneath the carols, the shopping, the velvet-and-gold pageantry, you'll find the bones of something older, wilder, and deeply magical. Look closely at the lights on the tree. They're stars. They always have been.

Globally Toasted: Burn, Baby, Burn - A Yule Disco Inferno

If there's one thing humanity excels at, it's coming up with increasingly creative ways to fight off the existential dread of winter. Somewhere in every corner of the globe, people have decided that when the nights grow long and the air begins to bite, the best course of action is to light something on fire and tell stories about how it'll all be alright. Possibly with snacks.

Let's begin with the Celts, those fine mist-draped mystics of the British Isles. The Celtic midwinter festivals were less about orderly ceremony and more about elemental theatre. Fire, of course, was central. Giant bonfires were lit on hilltops to honour the rebirth of the sun and to scare off anything unsavoury that might be lurking in the dark (spirits, Saxons, your ex, it was all up for interpretation). Holly, ivy, and mistletoe were gathered not as mere decorations, but as protective charms. Mistletoe in particular was harvested with great reverence, preferably with a golden sickle, ideally while chanting, and never, under any circumstances, letting it touch the ground. Think of it as the herbal equivalent of catching a sacred bridal bouquet.

In Slavic traditions, things get frosty in the most charmingly dramatic way. Enter Ded Moroz - Grandfather Frost, a figure who delivers gifts, ushers in winter, and occasionally drags misbehaving children off in a sack. Unlike our jolly Santa, Ded Moroz is accompanied by his granddaughter Snegurochka, the Snow Princess, who is inexplicably cheerful despite being made of ice. (hey, Walt Disney Pictures, there could be a movie in that!) In rural communities, bonfires were often lit during Kolyada festivals to symbolise the rebirth of the sun, and carolers would go door-to-door in animal masks, singing blessings (and occasionally mildly threatening songs) in exchange for food. As seasonal extortion schemes go, it was delightfully folkloric.

Wander further east and you'll find yourself soaking in a warm bath at the Japanese festival of Toji. Celebrated on or around the solstice, Toji is all about banishing illness and restoring balance. One steps into a steaming yuzu-scented bath (yes, actual citrus fruits floating in the tub) to purify the body and spirit. People eat kabocha squash for health and visit temples to light candles and give thanks for the return of the sun. It's less about spectacle and more about serenity. I've tried it myself, though substituting a clawfoot tub for a wood-fired bathhouse and swapping yuzu for a couple of tangerines. The cat was horrified. I felt marvellous.

Meanwhile in India, Diwali, the festival of lights, technically occurs earlier in the autumn but deserves an honorary mention for its sheer luminous splendour. Households are adorned with oil lamps, fireworks light up the night, and families gather to celebrate light overcoming darkness. Though not strictly a winter solstice festival, Diwali resonates with many of the same themes: fire, renewal, abundance, and an overwhelming desire to drive away the metaphorical shadows.

Let us not forget Hanukkah, the Jewish Festival of Lights. Rooted in the miraculous endurance of a single day's oil lasting eight full nights, it is a celebration of resilience, faith, and illumination, literally and metaphorically. Families gather each night to light another candle on the menorah, each flame a testament to endurance. Add in spinning tops, fried foods, and heartfelt songs, and you have all the ingredients of a warm winter ritual with soul.

A little closer to my own hearth, Scottish Hogmanay deserves a mention, not only because of its joyful chaos but because it involves something known as "first footing." The first person to cross your threshold after midnight (ideally a tall, dark-haired man bearing coal and whisky) is believed to bring good fortune for the year ahead. There's fire too, naturally, torchlight processions and bonfires to burn away the old and light the path for the new. Once, after a particularly enthusiastic Hogmanay visiting friends in Edinburgh, I ended up wrapped in a tartan scarf I didn't own, singing Auld Lang Syne with a coven of pensioners who could summon tears with a single verse.

In Scandinavian countries, where the darkness gets ambitious, the Feast of St. Lucia shines through with its candle-crowned maidens and warm saffron buns. Originally rooted in pagan solstice rites, the celebration was absorbed into Christianity but retained its luminous core. Children dressed in white carry candles and sing in processions, honouring light's return through song and sugar. It's gentle, heartfelt magic, with a carbohydrate centre.

All these traditions, fiery, watery, noisy, serene, circle around the same yearning: to honour the turning point, to kindle hope, to remind ourselves that the dark doesn't last forever. Whether with citrus baths or goat masks or gingerbread moons, we are all, in our own way, keeping the light.

What strikes me most is not the difference, but the repetition. Every culture, in its own poetic language, says: here is the dark, here is our flame, and here is how we carry it forward. The tools differ, but the spell is the same.

These global rituals remind me that magic isn't confined to a single tradition. It moves. It adapts. It lights a candle in Kyoto and a bonfire in Cornwall and calls it sacred in both places. As witches, this is our inheritance: the shared impulse to mark the seasons, to greet the sun with a full heart, and to make beauty in the bleak.

So wherever you find yourself this solstice, under a snowy sky or in a steamy citrus bath, know that you are part of a vast, twinkling web of celebration. Light your fire. Sing your song. Offer your bread. Dance your goat dance.

We are all holding the same flame.

CHAPTER TWO

The Turning of the Wheel

Broomsticks and Snowdrifts: The Slippery, Sparkly Bit

If you've ever stood in the frozen garden with a mug of something steaming, wearing seven layers of wool, trying to decide whether the frost on your rosemary bush is magical or just mildly alarming, congratulations: you've already begun observing the winter quarter of the Wheel of the Year.

There is something deliciously unhurried about this time of year, something that says, "No need to bloom, dear, just rest." The birds have stopped singing anything ambitious. The sun can barely be bothered to roll over the horizon. Even the dog seems contemplative. It's as if the whole world has exhaled, pulled the blanket up to its chin, and is waiting for someone to bring biscuits.

This, witches know, is not laziness… it's sacred dormancy.

Winter on the witch's calendar begins with Samhain (Halloween to the uninitiated) and deepens into Yule, which we've thoroughly explored already and I'm sure you'll agree includes just the right balance of ghost stories, cinnamon, and mild pyromania. But Yule is not the end of something, it's the midpoint of winter's magic. It's the candle in the middle of the cake, the ember under the ash. The spark that reminds us the world is still turning, even if it's doing so in thermal socks.

We call it the Wheel of the Year, this grand cosmic carousel of sabbats and seasons, and it turns with an elegance that never fails to impress me. Spring, summer, autumn, winter. Birth, bloom, harvest, rest. Every season has its gifts, but winter asks us to receive them slowly.

Of course, this doesn't always align with modern life. Society, in its infinite wisdom, has decided that December is the time to achieve everything, see everyone, and spend one's weight in gift wrap. But the witch's calendar says otherwise. It says: hush darlings. Breathe. Hibernate a little. Stir your soup clockwise and whisper your wishes into the steam.

That might sound terribly poetic (it is), but it's also intensely practical. Winter is when you gather your energies, rather than scattering them like pine needles on a supermarket floor. It's a time for visioning, for dreaming, for watching your Golden Retriever behave suspiciously in the moonlight and deciding that, yes, this is definitely a good time to start a new spell journal.

Ritually, winter invites us inward. Not just into our homes, but into ourselves. It is the time of root work, both literal and magical. Herbs that survive the frost carry potent energies. Dreams tend to be more vivid. Spellwork done in this season leans toward protection, release, and the planting of psychic seeds. You might not see results just yet, but something under the surface is always growing.

Yule, as the seasonal focal point, offers a moment to honour this liminal space. The days begin to lengthen again, but imperceptibly, like a shy guest creeping back into a party. That shift, gentle but profound, marks the promise of return. In rituals, we mirror it. We light candles. We bless our hearths. We reflect on what we've let go of, and what we might begin to call back in.

You don't need elaborate ceremonies (though if you enjoy them, by all means, do light the twelve-symbol solstice grid and chant in your best ceremonial robes). Often, the most powerful winter rituals are the simplest: a moment of silence by the fire, a breath in the snow-sparkled air, the act of choosing rest over endless motion.

This chapter will guide you through how winter fits into the greater rhythm of the witch's year. We'll look at the magical correspondences of the season, the symbols that survive the freeze, and the small, steady ways we honour winter's wisdom. We'll talk about fire and stillness, dreams and roots, cold earth and warm bread.

It's a chapter best read with a thick blanket, a hot drink, and something gently herbal wafting in the background. Because winter is not a pause in the magic. It's the magic of the pause.

Welcome to the quiet season, dear witch.

Let's listen in.

Bea

The Wheel of the Year: Like a Clock, But Prettier

Every witch I know has, at some point, stood in the middle of their kitchen and declared something like, "Is Mercury in retrograde again?" or "It's Imbolc soon, isn't it?" while holding a spoon and staring suspiciously at a burned pan of porridge. We do this because time, for us, is not a straight line, but a circle. Or rather, a spiral. A corkscrew of days and energies that loop and deepen each year. Welcome, dear witchy person, to the Wheel of the Year.

The Wheel is not a calendar you pin to your wall and forget about by mid-January. It is a living, breathing rhythm. It is how witches track the tides of the earth, the moon, and our own moods. There are eight major festivals, or sabbats, spaced evenly through the year. Four solar events, two solstices and two equinoxes, and four cross-quarter days that mark the midway points between them. These are the spokes on the Wheel: Yule, Imbolc, Ostara, Beltane, Litha, Lammas (or Lughnasadh), Mabon, and Samhain.

Each one holds a unique energy, a different flavour of magic, a changing light. Yule, where we find ourselves now, is the rebirth of the sun. It is the hinge of darkness into light. The spark in the cold. Imbolc follows, bringing early signs of life, lambing and snowdrops and the quiet stirrings beneath frozen ground. Ostara is the spring equinox, a balance of day and night, eggs and fertility and sprouting possibility.

By Beltane, the world is wide awake. Fires blaze, maypoles rise, and the earth is flushed with desire and abundance. Litha, the summer solstice, crowns the sun at its peak. Longest day, shortest night. The height of power, but also the tipping point. After Litha, the light begins to wane.

Lammas is the first harvest. The grain is cut, the bread is baked, the work begins to slow. Mabon, the autumn equinox, balances light and dark once more. It is the witch's Thanksgiving, a time of gratitude and gathering. Then comes Samhain, the most whispered of sabbats. The veil thins, the ancestors stir, and the year begins to fold in on itself.

Then we return to Yule. Round and round it goes.

But this is not just a historical exercise or a poetic way of marking the seasons. It is a framework for living. A guide for aligning your energy, your intentions, your magic, and even your grocery list with the natural flow of things. It is a way of remembering that you are not separate from nature, you are stitched into it. You are one part of this living planet.

Each sabbat speaks to a different part of the self. Yule is the inner light. Imbolc is the hopeful heart. Ostara is the curious mind. Beltane is the wild body. Litha is the bold spirit. Lammas is the wise hands. Mabon is the reflective soul. Samhain is the quiet depths.

Let's say you're feeling burnt out and a bit crispy by July. That would be Litha energy at its most intense. You are standing in full sunlight, but maybe you've forgotten to rest. The Wheel reminds you that the sun is not meant to blaze forever. It must set. It must give way to shade. This is not failure. This is rhythm.

Or perhaps you feel melancholic around Samhain, unsure why the fading light makes you nostalgic and sleepy. The Wheel shows you that this, too, is sacred. It is the season of remembering. Of pulling the blanket closer. Of listening inward.

You begin to notice things. The way your energy dips or lifts at certain points. The way your creativity blooms in spring or how your dreams grow wilder in autumn. The Wheel teaches you to listen to your own tides, and in doing so, become your own kind of wise.

Living with the Wheel does not mean holding full moon ceremonies every fortnight or dancing naked in the woods at every sabbat (though no judgment if you do, in fact, don't forget to send the invite next time). It means knowing where you are in time. It means eating root vegetables in winter because your body wants grounding. It means setting intentions in spring because the air smells like possibility. It means letting go in autumn because the trees guide us to.

I keep a Wheel of the Year chart above my desk. It's scribbled on parchment, a bit tea-stained, and slightly inaccurate because I dropped a jam tart on it last Lammas. But it helps. It helps me remember that I am not stuck. I am turning. I am moving. Even in stillness, the wheel turns beneath me.

Some witches track the sabbats with rituals. Others with recipes. Some with garden notes or moon journals or playlists that match the season. However you do it, the point is not to be perfect. The point is to be *present*. The wheel does not care how tidy your altar is. It only asks that you pay attention.

At Yule, you may light a single candle. At Imbolc, you may sweep the floor and bless it. At Ostara, you may plant one hopeful seed. Each act, no matter how small, is a turning. Each choice is a spell. Each moment is a step forward on the spiral path.

This is the joy of the Wheel. It teaches you to see the magic in the mundane. To honour the seasons not with performance, but with presence. To remember that time is not a to-do list. It is a dance.

So dance my darlings. In your kitchen. In your heart. With your mismatched socks and your root vegetable stew. The Wheel is turning. You are turning with it. You are *exactly* where you are meant to be.

Rest, Reflection, and Renewal: Blankets, Brews, and Brilliant Ideas

I used to think winter was just something to survive. A long, slow shuffle from Halloween to the first snowdrops, punctuated only by too many emails and far too much stew. Then I began paying attention, not just to the weather, but to the energy of the season itself. It didn't whisper "productivity." It whispered, quite insistently, "nap."

You see, the natural world is astonishingly good at knowing when to stop. Trees don't apologise for losing their leaves. Hedgehogs don't feel guilty for sleeping through January. Even the garden, that relentlessly cheerful overachiever, packs it in and quietly returns its energy to the soil. It's only humans, and let's be honest, mostly the over-caffeinated ones, who try to pretend that winter is just summer with a scarf.

But witches know better. We are students of rhythm, watchers of the wheel, celebrants of cycles. We know there is sacred power in the pause.

Winter is the season of stillness. Not the sterile, do-nothing kind of stillness that gets mistaken for idleness, but a deep, potent, womb-like stillness. A space where ideas germinate, where healing begins, where visions are brewed slowly like a good root tea. It's the part of the spell where the herbs steep, the moon rises, and you stop stirring long enough to listen.

There's a reason so many winter rituals focus on release. As the year darkens, we're invited to let go of what no longer serves. Think of it as magical composting. The old grudges, the worn-out intentions, the "why did I say yes to that" obligations, into the cauldron they go. Burn them. Bury them. Write them down and toss them into the fire with a cackle that would make Baba Yaga proud. The cold earth will take them, and from that decay, something new can grow.

But we don't leap straight from compost to cornucopia. Winter insists on a lull. It offers the witch a gift: time.

Time to reflect. To re-read the notes from last summer's rituals and realise, with amusement, that half of them were about becoming a forest-dwelling yogi. (Maybe next year.) Time to write, not with urgency, but with curiosity. To trace the shape of the year in your journal and ask yourself where your energy wants to go when the thaw comes. Time to look up at the stars and remember that you are made of the same stuff, but considerably less combustible.

Reflection in winter isn't just introspection, it's reclamation. In the hush of the cold months, we retrieve the pieces of ourselves scattered by busier seasons. We dream vividly, journal strangely, and notice patterns in the tea leaves that we swear weren't there before. Some witches keep dream diaries during this season, swearing that messages come clearer through the long nights. I once dreamed an entire spell for banishing unwanted houseguests using only a broom and three cloves of garlic. It worked. Co-incidence maybe but use with caution.

Rest, too, becomes ritual. Not "I'll rest after I finish everything" rest. Not "binge-watching under duress" rest. But real, sacred, intentional rest. A bath with rosemary and sea salt. A nap after divination. A day spent in silence, just listening to the wind shake the bare branches.

Witches sometimes get caught up in the glamour of high energy. We love the summer sabbats, the blazing bonfires, the ecstatic rites. But winter asks: what if your most powerful magic is done under a blanket, holding a cup of mugwort tea, listening to your breath? What if rest is the spell? What if sleep is the ritual?

Animals understand this. Bears disappear into caves. Bees huddle in tight clusters. Even frogs, frogs! slow their hearts down to barely a beat beneath frozen leaves. We are animals too, despite the Wi-Fi and the woolly socks. When we sync with nature's rhythms, we remember that we don't need to push. We just need to be.

Healing, another gift of the season, thrives in stillness. There's something profoundly medicinal about winter's quiet. The long exhale after the year's chaos. The gentle reset of shorter days. This is the season of salves and broths, of slow rituals with no flashy finish. Take time to anoint, to sip, to wrap yourself in intention and let the magic mend you.

I once attempted as a teenager to spend an entire January doing only three things (other than School): drinking nettle tea, writing one sentence spells, and watching the frost form on my windowpane. I emerged in February feeling like I'd been gently reassembled. The world hadn't changed, but I had. That's winter magic: quiet transformation. Subtle alchemy. True, it drove my mother slightly bananas, which at the time, forgive me but I was a teenager, was an upside. Sorry mother.

In the witch's year, this season is governed by the element of earth. Deep, cold, nourishing earth. It teaches us to root, to wait, to trust in the unseen. It's also the season of the crone, wise, wrinkled, and thoroughly unimpressed by your to-do list. The crone doesn't rush. She sits by the fire with a crooked grin and waits for you to stop fussing. Then, and only then, does she offer you the truth you weren't ready to hear in midsummer.

This is also when ancestral magic stirs strongest. The veil doesn't just thin at Samhain, it lingers, subtle but present, through the darkest months. Winter is a time to tend to the ancestral hearth. Light candles for those who came before. Cook their recipes. Wear their jewellery. Tell their stories. Leave a chair empty for them at the table. Feel how their lives loop into yours, how their dreams shaped the world you now stand in, preferably in boots with good grip.

So, dear witch, if the season finds you yawning more than usual, if your bones crave silence and your soul aches for soup... listen. Don't rush to fix it. Don't caffeinate it away. Let it be. Let the frost write poems on your windows. Let the wind sweep your thoughts clean. *Let yourself be wintered.*

Because in winter, we don't stop. We deepen.

We dream not in spite of the dark, but because of it.

In the hush between solstice and spring, magic finds us waiting, not idle... but ready.

From Flicker to Flame: Warming Yule the Witchy Way

If winter is a lullaby whispered by frost, then Yule is the drumbeat heard beneath it. Not a deafening, festival sort of rhythm, but a warm, steady thump. The kind you feel in your bones when you're near something burning with purpose.

The truth is, witches have always been a bit obsessed with fire. Not in the "let's set the village on fire" way, at least not anymore, but more in the "we understand that fire is life, death, and transformation" kind of way. Especially at Yule, when the sun itself seems to be sputtering, when our ancestors feared it might never return. What do you do when the world feels like it's turning off the lights? *You strike a match.*

Fire at Yule isn't just warmth. It's a promise.

This is the time of year when we gather around hearths, candles, and bonfires, not just because it's cold, though that certainly helps, but because it answers something ancient inside us. Fire in the dark is more than practical. It's sacred. It's storytelling and spellwork and sanctuary all at once.

Let's begin with the hearth, the original altar. Before we had Pinterest-worthy shrines and Instagrammable cauldrons, we had hearths. The centre of the home. The source of heat and food and survival. Witches still tend their hearths with reverence at Yule. Even those of us with gas stoves and electric kettles can light a candle and whisper a blessing. Fire magic doesn't care how you ignite it... only that you do so with intention.

Many witches light a Yule candle at sunset on the solstice and let it burn through the longest night (safely, please, with supervision and probably a fire extinguisher somewhere nearby). This flame becomes a spell in itself, one of endurance, of kindled hope. You can whisper wishes into it. You can write them on slips of paper and feed them to the flame, one by one, like offerings to the returning sun.

Bonfires, too, are central to the Yule tradition. If you've ever stood in a field at midnight in midwinter, your toes frozen and your fingers numb, watching flames leap into the night sky while someone in a cloak chants to the elements, congratulations, you've probably wandered into a very good solstice celebration. There's nothing quite like it. The fire crackles. The stars blink overhead. Your breath becomes visible magic. In that moment, you realise that the cold isn't just something to escape. It's something to honour, so that the fire feels even more alive.

Candle magic also shines brightest at Yule. Choose your candles with care. Red for strength and passion. Gold for sun and abundance. White for peace and purification. Dress them with herbs if you like, cinnamon, rosemary, or pine resin are my favourites, and carve symbols into the wax. Light them with words. Let the flame reflect something you're calling in: courage, clarity, a better relationship with your bank account. Flame-gazing, where you stare into a candle until visions come, is surprisingly effective, especially if you let yourself slip into the trance of flickering light, but be careful with your eyesight.

Of course, fire magic isn't all solemn ceremony. Sometimes it's as simple as baking. Your oven becomes an altar. Your hands stirring dough are hands stirring spells. I've enchanted everything from honey cakes to spicy nuts this way. The secret is to whisper your intentions while you mix, to sing a charm into the rising steam. It doesn't have to be fancy. Magic rarely is. A rosemary loaf baked with love can carry more power than a crystal grid you found on TikTok.

Yule also invites us to examine the shadow cast by the flame. Fire, after all, consumes. It reveals, but it also transforms. What do you need to burn away? What habits, fears, or expectations are ready for the pyre? I like to write mine on bay leaves and toss them into a small cauldron. They curl, spark, vanish. There's something exquisitely satisfying about watching your anxiety turn into ash.

If you're lucky enough to have a fireplace, you might want to revive the tradition of the Yule log, not the chocolate one, though that's also a fine and noble tradition. I'm talking about a real log, chosen with care, maybe carved with runes or symbols, dressed in ribbons, herbs, and wishes. The log is burned slowly across Yule night, and the ashes are often saved for future protection spells. Some witches keep a piece of the log to light the fire the following year, a bridge between solstices, a reminder that the wheel always turns.

Then there's the practical magic of fire, the kind that brings people together. Lighting a fire has always been an invitation. Come in. Sit. Tell me a yarn. Let's warm ourselves and speak of dreams. It is community magic. I've hosted many a Yule night where we gathered not to cast elaborate circles, but to sip cider and laugh until the candles guttered. That too is spellwork: joy in the dark.

Of course, fire is also wild. It doesn't belong to us, not really. It allows us to use it, but never quite trusts us with full control. That's part of its charm. It's the element that won't be boxed in. It dances. It devours. It transforms. That's why we work with it, to channel a force that's equal parts danger and delight.

Yule is the moment we remember this. We remember that we are not the masters of the sun, only its admirers. We light our candles not to command the light, but to honour it. To say, "We see you. We miss you. Come back when you're ready."

The sun, being a somewhat dramatic celestial body, takes its time. It lingers below the horizon. It sulks. Then, eventually, it returns.

Just like us.

Because we, too, are fire. We flicker, we wane, we flare up at the wrong times. We throw off sparks and sometimes forget what we were supposed to be burning for. But deep down, beneath the weariness and the wool, the flame is still there.

Yule is when we feed it. Tenderly. Joyfully. Without expectation.

So gather your matches. Dress your candles. Watch the flames and see what they say. Because at Yule, every flicker is a promise: the light is coming back.

… and until it does, we'll keep the fire.

Seasonal Sorcery: Like Strawberries, but More Magical

There's a peculiar magic that clings to the days around the solstice. It's not the glitter-and-gin kind of magic that gets splashed across greeting cards, but something quieter and infinitely more powerful. Yule, sitting right at the hinge of the year, holds a potent kind of liminality. The old has not quite ended. The new has not quite begun. This is the in-between. The space between breaths. The pause between incantation and result.

Witches have always been particularly fond of thresholds. We understand that transformation rarely happens in broad daylight with everything neat and labelled. It happens in the cracks. The dark moon. The changing tide. The moment just before the sun returns. That is Yule's gift. It gives us a moment where we can plant something in the deepest soil of time and trust it will take root.

This is the time to set intentions. Not resolutions, which, let's be honest, often come with the enthusiasm of a half-written gym membership. Intentions are *very* different. They are chosen with care, nurtured in sacred space, and allowed to unfold organically. While resolutions whisper, "You should," intentions ask, "What do you long for?" Think about it. It is very different. What do **you** long for?

Crafting an intention at Yule begins with stillness. Sit in the dark, quite literally if you like, with nothing but a candle and a warm blanket. Let the silence stretch out. Feel your thoughts drift like smoke. Ask yourself what you are truly ready to leave behind in the old year. What have you outgrown? What no longer fits the shape of your spirit?

Once that's clear, write it down. Write it slowly, with a pen that feels nice and paper that doesn't come from your recycling pile. Make it ceremonial. You can burn this list in a fire-safe bowl (or the fireplace, if you're feeling dramatic) with a pinch of rosemary or bay. Watch the flames. Feel the release. You have made space.

Now turn to the year ahead. Not the version society insists upon, full of detoxes and inbox-zero fantasies, but your own version. What do you want to grow into? What kind of energy do you want to walk in? Who are you becoming, one small, magical step at a time?

Write those thoughts down, too. Some witches create intention scrolls, tiny parchment bundles tied with red thread and tucked into a jar with herbs. Others make vision candles, carving symbols or words into a fresh candle and lighting it once a week through January as a way of returning to the spell. I keep a little "dream seed" pouch under my pillow, with lavender, mugwort, and a slip of paper containing a single sentence: my intention, whispered into fabric.

Timing matters, too. Astrologically, Yule aligns with the entry of the sun into Capricorn, a grounded, no-nonsense sign that asks us to commit. If you can align your spellwork with this energy, it can lend a sturdy foundation to your dreams. New moons near Yule are also ideal for intention-setting, while the waxing moon helps amplify those goals into something more tangible.

Of course, no witch worth her nettles sets an intention without checking it with her bones. This is intuitive work. Let your body guide you. If you light a candle and feel the urge to dance, do it. If your hands ache to braid herbs into a charm, do that instead. *Rituals only work when they feel alive.* They are not homework. They are invitations.

If this is your first time, here's a simple solstice ritual you can try: on the evening of Yule, light a single candle in a dark room. Sit with it and breathe. On a piece of paper, write three things you release and three things you call in. Read them aloud. Fold the paper and pass it through the candle's smoke (not flame), saying:

"By flame's truth and winter's breath, I shed the old and call the new. So it is, and so it shall be."

Tuck the paper into a jar or box you keep on your altar, windowsill or bedside table. Open it at the spring equinox to see how your magic has begun to unfold.

You may also find it helpful to link your intentions to the sabbats that follow. If Yule is the seed, then Imbolc is the sprout, Ostara the first leaf, Beltane the bloom. Let each sabbat be a check-in. How is your intention growing? What needs tending? What might be pruned or redirected?

Intentions also love to be anchored in the real. Pair them with action. If your spell is for creative inspiration, spend time journaling or drawing, even badly. If it's for healing, make the appointments. Drink the tea. Take the nap. I have heard some speak as if Magic somehow replaces effort, it doesn't. *It illuminates the path.*

Personalising your spellwork is essential. If you're a kitchen witch, stir your intention into a winter stew, clockwise for drawing in, widdershins for releasing. (don't you love that word – widdershins? It means anticlockwise, but we hardly ever use it.) If you're more of a tech witch (and yes, that's a thing, stop moaning, you probably bought this book online!), you can make your phone background a sigil for your goal or set reminders on moon phases.

This season also offers rich dreamwork potential. Some witches create "dream boards" using images, herbs, and handwritten goals and sleep with them nearby. Others anoint their temples with essential oils like clary sage or frankincense to open the psychic channels. I find mugwort tea or a mugwort sachet under my pillow to be remarkably effective at prompting dream clarity but do your research and always check contraindications. (Yes, that is a legal word in scrabble)

There's no single way to do it. That's the point. Yule reminds us that we are not cookie cutters. Our magic is as individual as our breath. Your intention might be poetic, like "to walk with wild grace," or practical, like "to pay off that cursed credit card." Both are valid. Both deserve firelight and reverence.

It helps to speak your intention aloud. There's something in the vibration of the voice that roots the spell deeper. Try standing at your window on the solstice morning, breath fogging the glass, and declaring to the rising sun what you are choosing. Not what you are hoping but what you are choosing. It is very different. The sun doesn't hope to rise. It chooses to rise, every day, regardless of clouds.

As you continue through winter, return to your intention like a stone in your pocket. Touch it. Turn it over. Let it evolve. A good intention is a living thing. It grows. It surprises you. Sometimes it drops you off in a completely different place than you expected, and you realise the magic knew better than you did.

That's the delight of seasonal spellwork. It connects us not only to nature, but to the rhythm of our own becoming. You don't have to get it perfect. You only have to begin.

So this Yule, light your candle. Whisper your truths. Write the letter. Stir the soup. Sleep deeply. Dream wildly. Trust the fire in your belly and the frost on your windows.

Something beautiful is about to grow.

Mint, Mugwort, and Mittens: Sage Advice for Frosty Days

Some witches dream of summer roses and lavender fields. I, however, find my magic under frost-covered leaves and in the sharp scent of pine. Winter is often dismissed as barren, a time when the earth goes quiet and green things sleep. But to the observant witch, this is the season when our true herbal allies emerge, resilient, pungent, hardy plants that laugh in the face of a hard frost.

Let's begin with rosemary. Rosemary is many things, culinary darling, protective powerhouse, and symbol of remembrance. At Yule, when we look back on the year that's been, rosemary becomes a botanical companion for grief, gratitude, and clarity. A few sprigs in a simmer pot, or tucked into a wreath above the hearth, help sharpen the mind and draw in ancestral wisdom. I always place rosemary beneath my pillow during the solstice week. It brings dreams of the past, yes, but also glimpses of what may yet bloom.

Then there's cinnamon, warm, sweet, spicy, and wildly misunderstood. Cinnamon isn't just for lattes and mince pies. It's fire magic in bark form. This humble kitchen staple is brilliant for charm bags, prosperity spells, and drawing warmth, physical and emotional, into your space. I often grind cinnamon sticks and blend them with orange peel, cloves, and star anise into a winter powder I sprinkle on the doorstep. It smells like holiday cheer and keeps the spiritual drafts out.

Pine, meanwhile, might just be the most overlooked witch's ally in winter. We haul entire pine trees into our homes, string them with lights, and call it festive. But pine's energy is far deeper than decoration. It's about resilience, endurance, survival, the kind of magic that says, "You can lose every leaf and still be green." Burning a bit of pine resin (or frankincense, its sunnier cousin) on a charcoal disk fills the house with strength and solar energy. It's also antimicrobial, in case you need a magical justification for airing out a home that's been closed for weeks.

Bay leaves are another must-have. They're sharp, aromatic, and surprisingly versatile. Ancient Greeks crowned victors with bay, and witches have been using them for centuries in vision work and spell craft. I write intentions on mine with ink (sometimes glitter gel pen, because, because why not), then toss them into the fire with a prayer. Bay also makes a marvellous addition to winter stews, just remember to remove it before serving, unless you fancy explaining divination by dental emergency.

Don't forget about juniper. Its berries are fierce and purple, its scent peppery and ancient. Juniper clears energy like a cranky grandmother with a broom. It protects. It banishes. It reminds you not to dither. I love placing dried juniper branches above the front door at Yule, tied with red string and a small bell, to ward off negativity and ring in good spirits. Sometimes I add a drop of juniper essential oil to a cloth sachet and tuck it in my coat pocket for extra magical armour on winter errands.

Simmer pots, those bubbling cauldrons of scent and spell, are particularly potent this time of year. Combine water with cinnamon sticks, cloves, orange slices, rosemary, bay, and a few pine needles. Let it simmer gently on the stove, and as the fragrance unfurls, let it become a moving spell. Stir clockwise while speaking your intentions. Breathe deeply. Invite warmth into the bones of your home. Even the cat will start acting slightly more benevolent.

For altar work, I bring in sprigs of holly and ivy, not just for tradition's sake, but because they represent endurance and intertwining. Holly protects; ivy persists. Together, they form a shield and a lifeline. Wrap them around your Yule candles or place them in a cauldron beside your written spells.

Crystals may not be herbs, but in winter, they deserve a mention. My favourites at this time are garnet for vitality, smoky quartz for grounding, and clear quartz for clarity in ritual. Tuck one beside your herbal charm or hold one in hand during winter meditations. Let the stone remind you that just like seeds under snow, you too hold untapped strength.

Even mundane tools become magical in winter. Your kettle becomes a cauldron. Your teapot a vessel of enchantment. I like to blend a winter tea of chamomile, rose hips, lemon balm, and a hint of cinnamon. It calms, heals, and stirs the spirit. You can infuse your intentions as the herbs steep, whispering over the steam and sipping with purpose.

Don't forget about salt. In a season where everything can feel a bit too sugared, salt remains grounding. Sprinkle black salt at doorways for protection. Add a pinch of sea salt to bath rituals to cleanse and reset. Mix with dried sage and pine needles for a powerful winter floor sweep. Sometimes magic is less sparkle, more sweep and scrub.

The lesson of winter's herbal allies is this, simplicity is not weakness. These are not fragile hothouse blooms. These are plants that survive. That thrive. That laugh in the face of snow and stretch stubborn roots beneath frozen ground. When you work with them, you're not just making a spell, you're forging an alliance.

So gather what you can. Walk the hedgerows with pockets for pinecones. Trim your rosemary bush and speak to it kindly. Honour the bay in your cupboard, the cinnamon on your shelf. These herbs are not waiting for summer. They are here. Now. Ready to help you remember that magic, like nature, never truly sleeps.

This winter, let your spells be steeped in bark and needle, in resin and root. Let your charms smell like the hearth. Let your work be stitched with the wisdom of things that grow slow and strong. Let the plants guide you, not with a shout, but with a whisper.

Living the Magic Without the *Ta-Da* Moment

When I was a baby witch, I thought ritual meant big things. Elaborate things. Things with robes and incantations and a dozen candles that wouldn't stay upright no matter how many wax drips I stacked beneath them. It was theatrical, a bit chaotic, and rather stressful if I'm honest.

These days, my rituals are quieter. Less of a performance, more of a practice. In fact, I've grown quite fond of the subtle magic that hides in plain sight. Blessing the logs before placing them in the wood burner. Whispering gratitude into my tea. None of it would impress a coven of showy ceremonial witches, but I like to think the earth notices. I like to think the soil, the snow, and the stars give a little nod of approval.

This is what Yule has taught me. It is not about grandeur, it is about rhythm. It is the art of syncing your life with the seasons, of moving inward when the world grows cold. It is about walking the dog while silently releasing the thoughts that no longer serve you. It is the act of tidying your kitchen as if you were clearing a temple. Magic is not separate from daily life. It is embedded in it, stitched into every breath if you let it be.

One of my favourite Yule practices is journaling in the dark. I do not mean metaphorically, although that works too. I literally turn off the lights and sit by candle glow, scribbling down what the year has taught me. Sometimes it's a messy tangle of half-thoughts and overgrown feelings. Sometimes it's a single sentence that rings out like a bell. Last year's was, "You cannot water everyone else's garden if your own roots are dry." I promptly brewed a pot of root tea and made a pact to nap more. That counts as spiritual growth!

Cooking, too, becomes a spell at this time of year. Not the "eye of newt" variety, unless you count the rogue sprout you forgot to chop. I mean stirring your soup clockwise while thinking of love. I mean grinding herbs with your wishes. I mean baking gingerbread with the intention to bring joy to whoever bites the head off the first biscuit. The oven becomes a hearth. The mixing bowl becomes a cauldron. You become a kitchen witch, even if you're just making toast.

One Yule I ran out of cinnamon and accidentally discovered that cardamom has a peculiar affinity for healing spells. It's how I learned that kitchen disasters are often magical interventions in disguise. I now keep both on hand, along with a small jar labelled "emergency courage" which is mostly just nutmeg and optimism.

Let's talk about firewood. Not a topic most spiritual books cover, but I believe it should be. When you stack your logs with intention, when you bless them for warmth and light, you're performing one of the oldest rituals known to humankind. Fire was the original altar. It was the first circle of safety, the first hearth of communion. When you place a log on the fire at Yule, you're feeding a flame that burns back through centuries. You're joining every witch who ever warmed her hands and muttered prayers to the crackling kindling.

I like to carve little symbols into my firewood, just a star, a spiral, or a word that means something only to me. Then, as the flame takes it, I imagine the energy being released. Some logs are for letting go. Others are for inviting in. It is not ceremonial. It is barely noticeable to anyone else. But it changes the way I greet the dark.

There is also the matter of socks. Yes, socks. Hear me out. Choosing your Yule socks is a form of sympathetic magic. Do you wear green for growth, red for vitality, gold for courage? Do you select the pair with tiny pine trees because you want to feel rooted? Do you choose the ones with pink unicorns to remind you that you are still really just a child in bigger clothing? These small decisions, made in softness and warmth, are not trivial. They are how we cast daily spells without even thinking.

I once did a full moon ritual in stripy socks and a tea-stained jumper, and it was one of the most potent experiences I've ever had. No robes, no incantations. Just me, a candle, the moonlight, and my intention. The universe, it turns out, does not care what you're wearing. It only listens to what's in your heart. Who knew? Well actually I think we all knew really, just need reminding sometimes.

Yule reminds us that not everything needs fixing. Not everything needs fanfare. Sometimes what is needed is stillness. Sometimes what is needed is presence. This is the season of long nights and soft voices, of dreams half-formed and seeds still sleeping. It is the pause before the song, the breath before the spell.

You do not need to decorate every surface. You do not need to bake sixteen varieties of enchanted biscuits. You do not need to document your altar for social media. Sorry TikTokers but no, just no. What you need is to honour the moment, however it shows up. Maybe it is a single candle lit in memory. Maybe it is a quiet walk in the woods. Maybe it is a whispered promise to yourself that you will rest more this year.

An alternative to fire, is taking a piece of paper and writing down three things you are letting go of. Maybe the same ones you brushed through a candle flame of burnt in a bowl. Then I fold it up and tuck it under a stone in the garden. Come spring, I dig it up, if I find it, sometimes by chance, and see if I've changed. It is messy, unglamorous magic. But it works. Sometime the notes are legible, other times not. That in itself may be telling me something, but what I haven't worked out yet.

Sometimes I bless the laundry. Sometimes I whisper affirmations to the cat and dog. Sometimes I fall asleep mid-meditation and consider it divine intervention. The point is not perfection. The point is presence. The wheel does not demand performance. It simply turns. Our job is to notice it, to greet it, to live in step with it.

This Yule, may you find your rhythm. May your rituals be messy, your spells heartfelt, and your socks delightfully mismatched. May you walk the dog like a priestess on pilgrimage. May you bless the woodpile with laughter. May you sip your tea like it holds the secret to everything.

Magic lives here, in these ordinary sacred things. In your breath, your hearth, your quiet smile at the morning frost. That is the heart of Yule. That is the gift. That is the spell.

CHAPTER THREE

The Magical Home

Broom Cupboard to Winter Wonderland

Ah, the house at Yule. The very phrase makes me feel like I ought to be clutching a warm mug of spiced cider in one hand and a broom in the other. Because while some people spend December racing around shopping centres and fretting about string lights, a witch knows that the real magic of the season begins at home. The hearth. The altar. The scent of clove and pine carried on the steam from a simmer pot.

This chapter is not about Pinterest-worthy perfection. It is about enchantment stitched into the very corners of your home. You see, every witch's dwelling becomes a seasonal temple at Yule, whether you live in a cottage in the woods, a city flat with questionable plumbing, or a caravan parked beneath a skeletal oak. When the light begins to return, we prepare not with stress but with spellwork.

We begin with the hearth, the ancient heart of the home. Whether you have a roaring fireplace or simply a stovetop that tries its best, this sacred space is where warmth gathers and magic rests. The first section explores fire blessings, candle rituals, and how simply lighting a flame can welcome spirit into your space.

Next, we move to wreaths and windowsills, those unsung heroes of seasonal symbolism. A circle of evergreen isn't just festive, it's protective. It is the wheel of the year woven from pine, ivy, and intention. This section offers ideas for blessing your wreath, charging it with energy, and turning your windows into quiet altars that invite in light and keep out mischief.

Then comes the enchanted altar. A witch's altar is never more magical than at Yule. Whether it is a shelf, a table, or a stone outside that nobody else notices, this is where the season's power gathers. With pinecones, cinnamon sticks, dried orange slices, and golden cloth, we create a space to meditate, to speak, to be still, and to remember.

We will also explore the language of candlelight. Each colour sings its own tune. Gold for the returning sun. Red for courage and bloodline. Green for growth and the promise of spring. White for clarity and the sacred unknown. Lighting candles becomes more than ambience. It becomes invocation. This chapter will show you how.

Of course, Yule is a season of scent. Nothing whisks the soul into sacred space faster than the smell of clove, star anise, and woodsmoke. In the section on magical scents, we will explore simmer pots, essential oil blends, and incense recipes that turn the mundane into the mystical. When your home smells like spellwork, you cannot help but remember who you are.

Then, we come to the art of everyday enchantment. The way a witch sweeps the floor with intention. The way she stirs her cocoa while whispering a blessing. The way a simple act becomes sacred when you show up fully. This section reminds us that presence, not perfection, is what we are here for. Magic lives in tea bags and tangled tinsel when seen through the right eyes.

Finally, we arrive at the tree. That glorious green beacon standing in the corner, covered in lights and charms. For a witch, a Christmas tree is no mere decoration. It is an altar. A living spell. The last section of this chapter guides you through crafting a tree that holds stories, wishes, protections, and ancestral whispers in its branches. From dried orange garlands to cinnamon bundles and protective sigils tied with red thread, the tree becomes a magical map of the season's heart.

So welcome to your magical home, dear reader. Whether you are dusting off last year's ornaments or crafting a brand new ritual from pine and purpose, this is your invitation to bring magic into every drawer, curtain fold, and candle flame. The season does not demand perfection. It asks for presence. Let the transformation begin with your space.

The Hearth as Heart: Where Toasty Toes Meet Toasted Spells

There is something ancient about sitting near a fire in the dead of winter. The flicker of flame seems to tap on the bones and whisper stories that have been passed down in embers and ash for thousands of years. Children feel it instinctively. Give them a candle, even one of those battery-powered ones, and they will cradle it like a treasure. Fire is memory. Fire is transformation. Fire is home.

The hearth, in whatever form it takes, is the beating heart of a witch's house at Yule. Maybe yours is a glorious Victorian fireplace with tiles depicting suspiciously witchy-looking ladies. Maybe it is a battered wood stove that smells of resin and adventure. Maybe it is a gas hob that hisses like an annoyed dragon every time you try to light it. It does not matter. What matters is the reverence you give it.

I bless my hearth each December with a mix of bay, rosemary, and a sprinkle of salt. I whisper to it, thanking it for its warmth, its steadiness, and its endless appetite for toast. I light the first Yule candle on the stove itself, watching the match flare and thinking of all the fires lit in celebration, in sorrow, and in story before mine.

Children absolutely adore hearth rituals. Especially if they are allowed to hold something that sparkles. My six-year-old daughter declared that the hearth was where Santa's reindeer come to nap between houses. My eight-year-old solemnly informed me that her, clearly uninformed little sister, was incorrect and that the flames were actually "sun dragons" stretching before flying back up to make dawn. I did not correct either of them.

One of my favourite Yule traditions is the Blessing Flame. It is deceptively simple. You light a single candle on the evening of the solstice and invite each person in the house to light their own candle from it, one by one, sharing a wish or a word for the new year. The room glows brighter with each flame. The words settle like stardust on the mantel. Then we place all the candles around the hearth and sit in a golden hush.

Even if you live alone, the Blessing Flame can be a powerful ritual. Light your candle and speak aloud to those who came before you. Speak to those you have yet to meet. Speak to yourself. Fire listens in a way that few things do.

Food, of course, becomes a kind of fire offering. Stews bubble. Biscuits brown. Chestnuts roast, or in my opinion spit angrily at you at the afront of being roasted. One year I tried to toast chestnuts directly on the wood stove and ended up summoning the spirit of burnt sugar and disappointment. Now I stick to cinnamon apples, simmering gently and making the entire room smell like an orchard dreaming of pie.

For those with no literal hearth, candles are your allies. Place them on your kitchen counter, or in jars by the window. The flicker and shadows are the important part. It is the movement. The reminder that even the smallest light moves darkness back an inch at a time.

Children love to make hearth charms. A bundle of cinnamon, a little salt pouch for protection, a twig of pine, all tied with red thread. Let them hang it near the fireplace (not too near) or tuck it under the logs. Tell them it keeps the warmth in and the goblins out. They will believe you. That belief, by the way, is the magic. Children do not worry about whether the spell is scientifically sound. They feel it in their toes.

I once had a tiny cauldron filled with bay leaves, each marked with a word: joy, peace, courage, biscuits. Guests could take one and throw it into the fire as an offering or intention. My cousin took "biscuits" and said it was both a wish and a promise. She meant it. She baked twenty-six gingerbread owls the next day.

The hearth becomes the anchor point for the season. When the world outside is mad with tinsel and postal deadlines, the hearth is the place where you sit with a cup of something warm and remember what matters. The flicker. The hush. The crackle of logs or the squeaky tick of the radiator. It grounds you. It reminds you to stay home in yourself.

Even cleaning the hearth is sacred. I sweep the ashes dropping a few crumbs of lavender in, and say, something along the lines of "Old year out, new year near, clear this space for joy and cheer." It helps that it rhymes. Magic loves rhyme. Children love rhyme. Dogs are indifferent but tend to wag along anyway.

Decorating the hearth for Yule is a delight. Drape evergreen garlands across the mantle. Tuck sprigs of rosemary into picture frames. Place oranges studded with cloves in little bowls that seem to multiply overnight. If you have fairy lights, wind them like spell-thread through the greenery. If you have nothing else, a single candle and your breath will do.

One year when I was living in Portland, I used only what I found in the garden, partly because I was a student and broke. Ivy, some fallen holly, a pinecone stolen from the neighbour's tree (apologies, Judith), and a crooked stick that looked suspiciously wand-like. It was one of the most magical hearths I have ever created. Judith's daughter insisted we leave a saucer of milk for the household spirits. Their cat drank it. Spirits seemed unbothered. For the little girl she had just witnessed the magic of Christmas.

The hearth is where stories are told. It is where children sit cross-legged and demand tales of snow witches and fire foxes. It is where adults sip mulled wine and slowly unwind the tension of the year. It is where your magic gathers, one log at a time, one flame at a time, until the whole house breathes slower and deeper.

So, dear witch, however your hearth looks this Yule, honour it. Clean it. Light it. Sit by it. Let it tell you stories. Let it teach you how to hold light gently in your hands

Wreaths and Windowsills: Tiny Altars for the Outside World

There is a curious power in the circle. Children understand it instinctively. They gather in circles, dance in them, pass snacks in spirals, and rarely question why it feels so right. The grown-up world calls it sacred geometry. The witch just calls it a wreath.

Wreaths are not merely seasonal decor. They are protective spells in circular disguise. When we weave one from evergreen boughs and red berries, we are not copying department store catalogues. We are reenacting an ancient act of reverence for life that endures. That is what evergreen means, it stays green even when the world turns white. That resilience is not just botanical. It is magical.

The circle of a wreath is the wheel of the year. It is no beginning, no end, just the ever-turning spiral of seasons and self. Some witches make their wreaths to mirror this cycle. Dried lavender from Litha, oak leaves from Samhain, holly for Yule. A story told in twigs and scent.

Children love to help. Give them clove-studded oranges or cinnamon sticks wrapped in red thread, and they will construct something between a wreath and a magical hedgehog. One year my son tied his spell-intention to a wreath in the form of a purple plastic unicorn. It stayed there all winter, and we all had excellent luck. Coincidence? Perhaps. Or perhaps unicorns know something we don't.

When crafting a wreath, start with what you have. Ivy, rosemary, bay leaves, pinecones. Twist them together with patience and a little muttering. The muttering is important. It lets the magic know you are serious. If you wish to charge the wreath, hold it in both hands and speak your blessing into it. Something simple like, "Circle of green, strong and true, bring protection, love and joy through."

Hang the wreath on the front door, and you have done more than decorate. You have set a magical boundary. It welcomes in the good, the true, the neighbour who brings shortbread. It nudges away the chaos, the coldness, and the sales flyers for things nobody wants.

Now we drift toward the windowsills. These are like the eyebrows of the house. Always watching. Always needing a bit of sprucing. For witches, they are thresholds. Places where inside meets outside. Where spirit meets sight. A windowsill at Yule can be more than a ledge for baubles. It can be an altar.

Lay a row of cinnamon sticks or a bundle of herbs tied with red or gold thread. Sprinkle a pinch of salt across the wood and whisper a charm for peace. Hang small charms from the curtain rod, snowflakes, pentacles, stars... each one a shimmering message to whatever energies peer in.

Herbal bundles work well here. A sachet of rosemary for remembrance, sage for cleansing, bay for clarity. Children can make them too. Let them choose a word and find a herb to match. Curiosity, for example, is marjoram. Courage is ginger. Mischief is probably mint.

In my home, the kitchen windowsill always receives the grandest treatment. It holds a little row of spell jars, one with star anise and cloves, one with sugar and nutmeg, one with tiny bells and ribbon. They clink softly when the wind rattles the panes, which I like to think means they are talking about me. Hopefully in a good way.

At night, I place a single candle in each windowsill, usually white or gold. It is a beacon, a welcome, a small flame against the dark. Last year, an Amazon delivery driver asked if I was signaling UFOs. I smiled and said, "Only the benevolent ones."

Window charms can also reflect what you need. Feeling scattered? A quartz crystal will catch the light and remind you to breathe. Seeking love? A rose quartz heart in the corner invites sweetness. Guarding your peace? A sprig of juniper will quietly bristle at the door of trouble and tell it to move along.

If you want to be subtle, use festive garlands. Wrap rosemary and eucalyptus around your curtain pole. Tuck orange peel stars into the greenery. Let your home smell like a spell before you have even begun one.

The most beautiful part of decorating this way is how much of it comes from the earth. No plastic. No glitter trails that haunt you until April. Just twine, herbs, intention, and breath. It is sustainable. It is sacred. It is deeply satisfying to know your house is not just trimmed — it is enchanted.

Children pick this up faster than adults. I have seen a four-year-old bless a doorknob by gently booping it with a cinnamon stick. Another made a garland entirely out of popcorn and buttons. It looked bonkers. It also radiated joy.

Of course, the best part of these decorations is that they do something. Unlike tinsel, which only sits there and gathers dust, your wreath and window charms are working. They are protecting. Inviting. Whispering. Remembering.

At the end of the season, you can offer them back to the earth. Take down the wreath, say thank you, and burn it (safely) or bury it with a handful of oats or wine. The herbs from your window bundles can go into your compost, or better yet, into your bath.

Sometimes I forget to take mine down until February. That is all right. The magic does not mind. It lingers until we are ready to turn the wheel again.

So gather your garlands, dear witch. Wind your herbs with love. Place your intentions like lanterns in every window. Let your home become the spell it has always wanted to be.

From Solstice to Santa - One Tree to Rule Them All

Now let us turn to that most iconic of holiday emblems, the Christmas tree. Or, as I like to call it, the towering evergreen altar of seasonal magic. For witches who grew up trimming trees with baubles and tinsel, the idea of blending Christmas tradition with Yule practice can feel as natural as cinnamon in cocoa. After all, the tree itself is a symbol drawn from ancient winter rites, a nod to evergreens' enduring life and the promise of renewal in the darkest season.

How does a witch decorate her tree? With intention, of course. (sounds a bit like a Christmas cracker joke!) Every ornament can become a charm, every light a flame of hope. Strings of cranberries and dried orange slices spiral sunwise around the branches, invoking vitality and solar return. Small bundles of herbs, rosemary for remembrance, pine for protection, cinnamon for warmth, are tied with red ribbon and tucked among the boughs. Tiny bells ward off stagnant energy and echo joy through the room.

Some witches hang handmade sigils written on bay leaves or wooden discs, charged with wishes for the year to come. Others weave charms into the tree itself: feathers for messages, small crystals for clarity, a star anointed with oil to crown the top, not just as a nod to Bethlehem, but as a symbol of inner guidance.

Lights are chosen with care. Soft golden tones evoke the returning sun and are kinder to the senses than flashing technicolour strobe-fests. Beeswax candles may be placed nearby (never on the tree unless you live wildly) to create a sacred circle of warmth and flickering magic. I once tried to place a beeswax candle in a hollowed apple and nestle it safely on the tree (yes I saw it on Pinterest). It ended with some dramatic smoldering and our dog wouldn't come in the room for two days. Use caution, fellow witches.

The base of the tree becomes sacred space. Some place offerings beneath it, nuts, coins, handwritten intentions, or ancestral photos, so that the gifts wrapped in paper sit beside gifts of spirit. My own tree always shelters a tiny cauldron filled with cloves and star anise, a quiet spell for harmony and abundance. There is something comforting about knowing that beneath all the glitter and tinsel, there is intention, memory, and magic tucked into the roots.

Decorating a witch's tree does not require expensive ornaments or a Pinterest board. It requires thoughtfulness. It requires that moment when you pause, herb bundle in one hand and a ribbon in the other, and think, "What do I want to call into my home this season?" That question becomes a guiding star.

Garlands of popcorn and juniper are wonderful for draping intention along branches. The popcorn represents simplicity, nourishment, and joy. Juniper brings protection and clarity, its sharp scent reminding us to keep boundaries clear during bustling social seasons. A friend of mine strings whole cinnamon sticks like tiny wands and lets them dangle near the base, a literal circle of warmth.

Do not forget the tree skirt. A witch's tree skirt is not just there to catch needles. It is a foundation. Consider weaving protective symbols into its design or tucking herbs and crystals into the folds. Mine has a little pouch sewn underneath it that I fill with slips of paper, each one bearing a word or blessing I hope to grow through the season.

Music is part of the ritual too. While you trim your tree, sing. Or hum. Or play carols that make your bones feel sparkly. Sound is vibration, and vibration is spellwork. I often play old folk tunes with minor keys and strange harmonies, the sort of music that feels like mistletoe and mist together. If nothing else, it keeps the cats intrigued.

You might also choose a theme for your magical tree. One year I dedicated mine entirely to the elements. Feathers for air, seashells for water, acorns and stones for earth, candles for fire. It created a powerful energy in the house that winter, as though the tree was whispering balance and blessing into every room.

I went to a good friends' house for pre-Christmas drinks last year, she isn't a witch, but I loved her tree. It really captivated me. It focussed on her ancestors. Tiny framed black and white photos, antique lace, and really small charms from her grandmother's old charm bracelet. I loved it. Each time I passed the tree, I felt as though I was walking by a gathering of quiet, loving spirits, all watching over the solstice fire. I will have a go this year. She said she got a batch of the silver frames from Ebay. (Note to self: I will have to look.)

Children make brilliant tree magicians. Let them craft charms, choose colours, hang trinkets that mean something only to them. This is how tradition roots itself, not in rules, but in stories. My son and I once made a clay gingerbread witch with glittery green eyes. He insisted it protected the biscuits from the goblins. We still hang it every year. We created a tradition.

The act of decorating is a spell. Whether you're alone with a pot of tea and soft music or surrounded by chatter and cinnamon-scented chaos, it is a rite of beauty and intention. A moment of sacred making. A reclaiming of joy.

Tinsel, when used with purpose, becomes shimmering threads of light magic. Ornaments can be programmed like talismans. Even the act of fluffing the tree's branches becomes a kind of energetic cleansing. You are shaping space. You are casting warmth into every needle and bauble.

For those who prefer living trees in pots, this becomes an even deeper connection. The tree will return to the earth after Yule, carrying the energy of your season back into soil. Offer it a drink laced with herbs or sing a blessing when you plant it. Its roots will carry your magic onward.

If a tree is not part of your tradition or space, consider decorating a branch. A Yule branch set in a vase, adorned with charms and lights, carries all the symbolism in miniature. The size does not matter. The spell is in the intention.

Finally, when the season ends and the ornaments return to their boxes, do so with ceremony. Cleanse them with smoke or song. Thank them. Store them with lavender or cedar for protection. This way, when next winter rolls around, the magic will still hum from each ribbon and sprig.

A witch's Christmas tree is more than a festive decoration. It is an altar of light. A gathering place for wishes. A forest spirit invited into the home to remind us that even in the deep cold, there is life. There is green. There is something evergreen in all of us.

The Enchanted Altar: Holly, Ivy, and a Bit of Glitter Glue

Every witch needs an altar. Some have vast surfaces covered in ancient relics and exotic incense holders, while others operate from the top of a chest of drawers wedged between a laundry basket and a houseplant who is trying its best. What matters is not size or grandeur. What matters is attention. Presence. Intention. That, and maybe a good cloth.

At Yule, your altar becomes the centre of everything. It is where your breath slows, where your tea cools beside a candle, where your magic gathers like frost on the windowsill. It does not need to be a shrine to Instagram perfection. It needs to feel like yours.

I begin by choosing a cloth. Gold, deep green, or red always feel right. Something with a bit of texture. Velvet if I'm feeling fancy. Burlap if I'm embracing "peasant witchcore." Lay it down with care. Smooth it with your hands like you're tucking a child in for a nap. Whisper to it. That part is optional but strongly encouraged.

Next, bring in the elements. Earth might be represented by pinecones, cinnamon sticks, or a little dish of salt. Air could be a bundle of dried herbs, or feathers, or bells that jingle like gossip. Water could be snowmelt in a jar, or a seashell filled with rosewater. Fire, of course, is the candle, always present, always flickering like a heartbeat.

Then come the seasonal gifts. Dried orange slices strung with cloves. Little pouches of star anise and nutmeg. Bits of holly (careful of the prickles) or ivy trailing like a slow spell. I love to include things gathered on winter walks; acorns, twigs, the occasional perfectly shaped stone that looks like it might remember something older than me.

This altar is not just decorative. It is interactive. Children can make mini versions, their own sacred spaces with buttons and marbles and tiny cups of glitter that will never fully come out of the carpet, but which radiate pure intention. Invite them to leave wishes there. Or draw pictures of what they want to grow in the next year. My eldest once offered his altar a slice of toast, because "spirits get peckish too." She wasn't wrong.

The altar is a place for ritual. On solstice night, I light every candle on mine. I speak my intentions for the year, not goals or resolutions, but words like nourish, laugh, create, heal. They sit there all season, humming quietly, until spring comes to stretch them awake.

Offerings on the altar can be anything. Honey for sweetness. Coins for abundance. A handwritten note to your ancestors. A ribbon from a gift that made you cry (in a good way). I once placed a single hazelnut in a bowl after reading a myth about wisdom hiding in small things. It stayed there until Imbolc, and then went to the birds.

Deities, spirits, and guides are welcome guests here. You do not need to have statues or icons unless you want them. A stone shaped like a goddess. A feather for the spirits of air. A cup of cider left out for whoever walks softly through your house at night. Say their names if you know them. Say "thank you" if you don't.

Some witches change their altar daily through Yule. Others build it slowly like a snowdrift, adding one piece each day. You can light a single candle every morning with a word of gratitude, or you can simply pass by it on the way to feed the cat and nod solemnly. The altar knows when it is seen.

Incense can transform the space, though beware of setting off the smoke alarm. I like frankincense at Yule. It smells ancient. Like something that would make a wise man blink and say, "Now that's proper scent." My neighbour prefers fir and peppermint, which makes her house smell like a candy cane forest. Both are valid.

Music helps too. Soft harp, wind chimes, a playlist of instrumental winter songs. Or children's laughter. Or the silence that wraps itself around candlelight and stays for tea. Your altar responds to what you bring it. Joy, sorrow, uncertainty, it holds them all.

You might find, after a while, that your altar begins to speak. Not with words. But with nudges. You will suddenly feel the need to add a stone you've ignored for years. Or light a candle at a certain hour. Or replace the red cloth with something silver, just because. This is not nonsense. This is intuition. Trust it.

Sometimes the altar becomes crowded. Let it. Sometimes it is sparse and empty. That is all right too. Your altar is not a performance. It is a dialogue. An invitation. A mirror. A little hearth of its own, glowing quietly in the corner, saying, "You are home."

So gather your pinecones. Arrange your cinnamon. Lay down that cloth like a prayer. Light a candle and exhale. You have made a space for magic to land.

The Art of Looking Mystical While Fumbling with Matches

There is something about candlelight that makes everything feel like a story. Not the kind with dragons necessarily, although those are wonderful, but the kind where something important is happening quietly in the corner of your kitchen. Maybe it is the flicker, that little dance of flame. Maybe it is the way shadows play along the walls like bashful spirits. Whatever the reason, a candle is not just wax and wick. It is a spell waiting to happen.

At Yule candles do more than light up the room. They carry us. Through long nights. Through quiet fears. Through the deep stretch of winter where the trees sleep and the birds dream in their feathers. Candlelight reminds us that the sun is returning. Even if it feels very far away.

Now, let's talk colour. Because as any child with a box of crayons knows, colour matters. Witches understand this instinctively. A green candle hums differently than a red one. A gold candle does not just shine, it sings.

Gold is for the sun. The returning light. The brilliance we are calling back from the long shadows. When you light a gold candle on solstice night, you are joining every hearth that ever called out to dawn.

Red is for the life force. The blood that keeps us warm. The courage that gets us through winter. Red candles burn hot and sure. They do not whisper. They proclaim. Use red for passion, for protection, for a very firm wish. Children adore red candles. Something about their vibrancy makes them irresistible. If you let them help, make sure they know which end to light. Or, better yet, do it together.

Green, of course, is for renewal. For the first shoots beneath the snow. For the promise that the earth has not forgotten us. Green candles are gentle companions. They are the ones you light while journaling, while tending your plants, while stirring soup with a wooden spoon that has seen many winters. Green is a friend. Trust it.

White candles are for clarity. For peace. For the sacred breath that happens when you finally sit down and stop cleaning. White is winter snow, ancestral bones, the pause between words. It holds space. It calms. It asks nothing but presence.

Now, how to use these flames? Begin with intention. Before lighting, speak your need or your offering aloud. Something simple like, "For joy" or "For the strength to finish what I started." You can carve a word into the wax with a pin, or anoint the candle with oil; rosemary, orange, or cinnamon are lovely choices at Yule.

Place the candle in a safe holder, preferably one that makes you smile. I have one shaped like a toadstool and another that looks like a tiny cauldron. Yes, they're slightly ridiculous. I adore them. Light the candle and sit for a moment. Let the flame pull you into stillness.

This is where flame-gazing begins. Not staring, not zoning out entirely, although that might happen too. But looking into the fire with soft eyes, and letting it show you what you need to see. It might be memories. It might be colours. It might be a sudden idea that pops in and insists you plant lavender next spring. Take notes, if you like. Or just feel.

Flame-gazing is one of the oldest forms of divination. It is like speaking with the universe through the language of flicker and glow. Children are naturals at it. Whether it's a candle or embers, they will see dragons, dancers, messages from Santa. All valid. All magical. I wrote another book called The Witch's Botanical Apothecary. In that book I cover this in a lot more detail, especially smoke-grazing with Dittany of Crete. I recommend it, of course I would.

Sometimes I light a candle and just talk to it. Not like I expect it to answer, although I wouldn't be entirely surprised if it did. I tell it my worries, my wishes, my grocery list. Something about the act of speaking into fire makes the words feel heard. Understood. Blessed. Some people openly talk to plants, like King Charles, I talk to candles (and plants). Does that make me less weird?

You can also use multiple candles in a grid. Four corners. One for each element. Or seven for each day of the week, lit in a spiral from dark to light. Let children choose their candle colours and explain why. One might choose purple because "it smells like mystery." Another might pick blue because "the snow fairy told me to." Trust them.

Some witches create candle jars, layers of herbs and salt and wishes, topped with a tea light. Others use floating candles in bowls of water with flower petals. All are beautiful. All work.

My favourite solstice ritual is the Candle Walk. Bundle up, take a lantern or a jarred candle, and walk through the garden or down the street in your village. Greet the trees. Whisper your gratitude to the stars. Let the candle guide your way. Once, a fox walked beside me for six whole steps before disappearing into the hedge. I am convinced it approved.

Candle magic is simple. Profound. Inexpensive. You can buy a hundred tealights for less than the cost of a celebrity coffee. You can turn off every light in your house and navigate by flicker. It feels ancient. It feels right.

In the end, what matters is that you light the candle. That you let it burn. That you remember, in its glow, who you are becoming.

So gather your matches. Choose your colours. Whisper your wish into the wick. Light the flame. Watch it dance. Let it warm you.

Yule is coming my friend. Let your house glow like hope itself.

Seasonal Scents: Myrrh, Frankincense, and Why Is the Cat Sneezing?

There is a kind of alchemy in scent. You know it the moment a whiff of pine hits your nose and you're six years old again, buried under a tangle of tinsel and grand expectations. Or when the spicy snap of clove whirls you back to your grandmother's kitchen, where something ancient was always bubbling away and someone was always telling you not to touch it.

At Yule, scent is not just nostalgia. It is magic. Real, potent, aromatic magic. It gathers memories like old photographs and stirs them into the air, turning ordinary spaces into sacred ground. Unlike the more elusive aspects of witchcraft, astral travel, for example, or locating your second cousin's missing aura, this magic is very accessible. It lives on your stove. It simmers in your pot. It perfumes your jumper long after the ritual is done.

Let us begin with the mighty simmer pot. There is nothing more satisfyingly witchy than a bubbling cauldron of citrus and spice, sending up fragrant steam like a kitchen incantation. You do not need anything fancy. A saucepan will do. Start with orange peels, for joy, for light, for the sun returning. Add star anise for protection and a touch of the mysterious. Throw in cloves, which might be the most festive of all spices, smelling like every winter holiday rolled into one sharp, spicy bundle.

Rosemary joins the party next. She is grounding, wise, a little prickly in personality but very good company. Cinnamon sticks follow for warmth, for wealth, for good cheer. If you are feeling bold, a few slices of fresh ginger add fire. If you're feeling traditional, a sprig of pine ties everything back to the season.

Cover it all with water and let it simmer gently. Your house will smell like the inside of a magical bakery inside a forest cathedral. Visitors will arrive and ask what you're cooking. You can say, "Hope."

Simmer pots can be adapted endlessly. Lavender and lemon balm for calm. Apple slices and nutmeg for love. Add a bay leaf with those wishes written on it. Stir clockwise to bring something in. Stir widdershins if you're trying to let something go. Children adore helping with this, mostly because they love throwing things into pots. That, and the thrill of being told they're "making a potion."

Essential oils are another route. These tiny bottles are like potion flasks in their own right. A few drops of fir or spruce oil on a cloth will fill your home with woodland energy. Orange oil uplifts. Cinnamon and clove energise. Frankincense grounds. Myrrh is moody, in a good way. A blend of rosemary, pine, and orange oil is my personal favourite at Christmas, it smells like an enchanted orchard got lost in a forest and decided to stay.

Diffusers are lovely. Oil burners are classic. Even placing a few drops on a tissue near a heater will do the trick. You can also make a witch's Yule spray. Mix water with a splash of vodka (to help it disperse), then add your chosen oils. Mist your rooms with it. Mist yourself with it. Mist your cat if it consents. Everything smells better with a little intention.

Now, let us talk incense. There's something very primal about watching smoke curl into the air, carrying your thoughts, prayers, and a bit of accidental glitter into the ether. You can use stick incense, cone incense, or make your own loose blends if you are feeling particularly crafty.

Start with a base, dried herbs like rosemary or sage. Add spices; crushed cinnamon, cardamom, or even a pinch of pepper. Toss in dried citrus peel, bits of resin like frankincense or copal, and a dash of magic. Grind it all together with a mortar and pestle or bash it about with enthusiasm. Burn a pinch on a charcoal disc in a heat-safe dish and let it do its work.

Loose incense has the advantage of being completely customisable. You can tailor blends to different days, moods, or spellwork. A calming blend might include lavender, chamomile, and rose petals. A more energising one could mix orange peel, juniper berries, and ginger. Children can help with this too, though supervise them closely unless you enjoy cleaning glitter from your walls.

Scent can also be worn. Anoint yourself with a drop of oil before meditation. Dab it on your wrists, your third eye, your heart. It becomes a signal to your body and spirit: "We are entering sacred space now." You can also dress candles with scented oils or rub them into wooden tools and altar surfaces. We have a wooden fire surround which I always rub some oil into.

I once crafted a perfume oil for Yule using vanilla, orange, and clove. It smelled like a memory you could wear. People asked what I was wearing. I told them, "The ghosts of every happy winter I've ever had." They did eye me a bit weirdly, but if you're reading this book I guess you're used to that look already yourselves.

Scents have stories. That is why they matter. That is why they are magic. A sprig of pine by the door says, "You are safe here." A bowl of cloves in the kitchen says, "This house remembers love." A simmering pot says, "We are together, even in the dark."

So light your incense. Blend your potions. Let the steam rise and the air shimmer. This is how a witch prepares her home for Yule, not just with spells, but with spice.

Everyday Enchantments: Putting the 'Hex' in Your Grocery List

Let us now turn to the smallest magics, the ones you hardly notice until you realise your entire life is laced with them. Because while grand rituals and seasonal altars are glorious, the real magic of Yule, the kind that roots deep and lingers long after the mistletoe is gone, happens in the quietest corners of the day.

Take, for example, the broom. Yes, the humble broom. Often maligned as a mere cleaning tool or cartoon witchy transportation device, it is in fact a fine magical ally. Before you sweep the floor for guests or clear out pine needles that have made a break for the kitchen, pause. Trace a small rune with the handle. Whisper a thank you to the bristles. You are not just tidying; you are banishing stale energy, making space for blessings to arrive. Sweep clockwise for attracting joy. Sweep widdershins if you're clearing out the ghosts of last year's awkward Christmas conversation with Uncle Derek.

When it comes time to stir your cocoa, do not rush. This is no mere beverage. This is molten comfort in a mug, and it deserves to be stirred with purpose. Clockwise for joy, for sweetness, for warmth that wraps around your soul like a woolly jumper. Add cinnamon for love. A pinch of chilli for courage. Marshmallows for whimsy. Whispers optional but highly recommended. Especially the kind that says, "This year, I will be kinder to myself."

Even putting up the tree becomes a ritual when done with intention. Before stringing the lights, pause. Hold them in your hands and imagine joy coursing through every bulb. Picture laughter, kindness, soft music and safe spaces glowing in every colour. Then, as you drape them, speak your wishes out loud. "Let this house be a home." "Let this season be gentle." "Let the cat please not climb the tree this year."

Children are marvellous at this sort of magic. Give them a ribbon and tell them to tie a wish onto a branch. Watch as they create enchantments with sticky fingers and wide eyes. They know something we forget, that wonder lives in moments. That magic doesn't need an audience. That a cookie offered to the night sky is a perfectly valid offering before eating.

Take your morning tea. Before the kettle boils, set an intention. Let the steam bless your face (from afar). Let the clink of the spoon be a charm. Say thank you to the leaves or the bag. Say thank you to the moment. Magic, you see, does not always shout. Sometimes it just sits with you, in wool socks, breathing slow.

I keep little charms tucked everywhere this time of year. A sprig of rosemary above the sink. A chestnut in my coat pocket. Not because I think disaster lurks in the cutlery drawer, but because these things anchor me. They remind me that the sacred lives here, in this house, in these rooms, even when the dishes pile up and the dog has eaten the advent calendar.

Music is a spell, too. A carol sung from the belly, a hum while you hang laundry, a little whistle while folding napkins. Sound shifts energy. Sound invites the spirits in. I have one playlist for joy, one for reflection, and one entirely composed of medieval songs about wassailing that make no sense whatsoever but fill the room with mirth.

Bless your shoes before going out. Tap them three times and say, "Carry me well." Sprinkle a little salt by the doorway. Place a pinecone in the hallway to catch blessings as they enter. These are not grand gestures. These are stitches in the great tapestry of your season. They are how a witch weaves her life into the wheel. You may look back on some of these things and say "what AM I doing!" and allow a small giggle to slip. No you're not losing your marbles, at least no more than me.

Even the act of wrapping presents becomes magical. Knot the ribbon with love. Write sigils into the fold of the paper. Whisper, "May this bring joy" as you tape the edges. Wrapping gifts is spellwork in disguise, you're binding intention into beauty, hope into ribbon, laughter into twine.

So bless the mundane. Stir the soup with love. Fold the laundry with a lullaby. Tuck wishes into your slippers. Sweep out last year's sadness. Invite in quiet joy. Let your home be a cauldron, your day a charm, your every breath a spell.

This is Yule. This is the magic of ordinary days, dressed in fir and frost and cinnamon steam. No grand proclamations needed. Just presence. Just heart. Just the sacred breath of everyday enchantment.

CHAPTER FOUR

The Green Witch's Pantry

Keeping Spirits High and the Wine Rack Full

It is a truth universally acknowledged (or at least cheerfully mumbled over the cauldron by most witches of good sense) that winter will sneak up on you faster than a hedgehog on moonshine. One minute, you're basking under the golden haze of Samhain, smugly drying apples and muttering hexes for the neighbours' roses; the next, you're frantically rummaging through your cupboards in the dead of December and discovering nothing but three crumbling bay leaves and a suspiciously soft onion.

Let this, dear witch, be your wake-up call. Or as I like to think of it: the winter pantry equivalent of a slap from a wet birch twig. It is time, long past time, perhaps, to stock your enchanted larder.

Now, before you panic and sprint off to your local witchy co-op or start hyperventilating over the herb jars at the back of Holland & Barrett, rest assured: we are not talking about doomsday prepping. This is not a competition to see who can survive the longest in a blizzard with only a jar of pickled mushrooms and a smug attitude. This is about preparing, with magic and intent, the kind of pantry that feels like an embrace every time you open the door. A space filled with possibility, protection, nourishment, and the quiet, persistent hum of winter enchantment.

Let's Begin with a Shelf

Or a cupboard. Or a lovingly hand-carved walnut dresser that once belonged to your great-aunt Hilda and smells faintly of elderflower and snuff. The container matters less than the intent. Your larder is an altar of sorts, only instead of candles and chalices, you have cinnamon sticks and rather bossy jars of pickled red cabbage.

The first rule: Do not let your magical ingredients sulk in chaos. No good spell was ever brewed with a teaspoon of "I think this might be oregano?" and a cupboard that resembles the inside of a dragon's sock drawer. Label your jars. Honour your herbs. Give your spices room to breathe and stack your dried orange slices like little suns on the darkest days of the year.

The Core Components of a Winter Witch's Pantry

Now, to the heart of the matter: what goes in the pantry. You may think you know the answer to this already. "Tea," you say confidently. "... and biscuits, obviously" ... and while you're not wrong (no witch worth her wand scorns a good biscuit), allow me to walk you through the full winter arsenal.

Dried Herbs: The Green Heart of Winter

Fresh herbs are lovely. They also die in the cold like overly dramatic fairies. Hence the need to dry them in advance, ideally during the waxing moon of late summer or early autumn, when their magic is peaking and their chlorophyll is doing a little happy dance.

Every winter pantry should have at least:

- **Rosemary** – for remembrance, clarity, and keeping out the sort of guests who say things like "I don't believe in energy."

- **Thyme** – courage, protection, and an excellent addition to anything vaguely stew-adjacent.

- **Sage** – wisdom, purification, and the ultimate "get out, bad vibes" herb.

- **Oregano and Marjoram** – for joy, digestive support, and putting a mildly enchanted twist on Tuesday's pasta bake.

Dry these herbs by tying them in bundles and hanging them somewhere dry, airy, and pleasantly dramatic. Your pantry should look like a very sensible herbalist has moved in, or at the very least, someone who might charm the village vicar with a well-placed infusion.

Once dried, crumble them into clearly labelled jars. Add a small bay leaf or a rune-charged coin to the bottom of each jar to keep the energy fresh. Store them away from direct sunlight and curious cats.

Honey: Liquid Gold with a Sting

If you are not already using honey as a magical staple, I must politely ask: what are you doing with your life?

Honey is prosperity. It is attraction. It is sticky, glowing, ancient magic in a jar. Raw honey (the cloudier and more assertively bee-like the better) contains the energy of a thousand flowers and the tiny memory of sunlight, stored up for winter use.

Use it to:

- Sweeten spells, especially those involving love, peace, and neighbourly tolerance.

- Glaze roasted roots or winter fruits for a golden-crusted protective charm you can eat.

- Add to tea when your throat is scratchy and your patience is thinner than a fairy's nightgown.

I keep three types on hand in winter: wildflower for cheer, lavender for calm, and a dark buckwheat honey that tastes like burnt toast and old mysteries.

Bonus tip: stir your honey sunwise (clockwise) while whispering a line of intent, something like, "Warmth within, sweetness without, as the hearth glows, let love pour out."

Roots and Preserved Things

If you've never stared lovingly at a shelf full of glass jars containing slightly menacing vegetables, have you even wintered properly?

Pickled carrots. Fermented garlic. Beets that bleed like dramatic theatre queens. These are the soul of your witch's pantry, dear one. They are the things you made when the garden was full, and now they whisper to you from the dark: "Look, you are clever. You planned for this. You are fed."

Magical uses of common root cellar fare:

- **Beets**: Grounding, love, and slow courage. Slice thinly and lay out like heart runes.

- **Garlic**: Protection, banishment, and deeply satisfying pasta. Hang it braided or brined.

- **Onions**: Wisdom, transformation, and the occasional ghost deterrent.

- **Potatoes**: Pure earth energy. You may laugh, but the humble spud is the anchor of a hearth-witch's feast.

Preserving is its own spell. You're bottling time. You're capturing summer under seal. Label your jars with not just contents but intention: "Chilli relish – bottled joy. Sept. Waxing Moon."

Berries: Jewels of the Wild

Berries are wild magic. They stain your fingers, whisper through the hedgerows, and contain that flash of abundance that says, "Yes, the land loves you still."

By winter, the berries are dried or syruped or sitting smugly in cordials. Keep:

- **Elderberries**: For protection and immunity. Make them into syrup with cinnamon and clove.

- **Hawthorn berries**: Heart-healing, both magical and literal.

- **Juniper berries**: Warding, cleansing, and flavouring that one regrettable gin experiment.

- **Rowan (Mountain Ash)**: A witch's shield, best used in charms or winter wreaths (do not eat raw).

A handful of dried berries in a tea or cake transforms it from a snack to a spell.

Spice Blends: The Pantry's Fire

This is the part where your larder earns its scent. Winter spices are not just for flavour, they're magic disguised as flavour. I keep mine in small glass jars with handwritten labels and great ceremony. (Tip: Never store magical spices in plastic. The energy sulks.)

Your foundational spice rack should include:

- **Cinnamon** – Love, warmth, money. Also a handy disguise for culinary sins.

- **Clove** – Protection, clarity, spirit connection.

- **Nutmeg** – Luck, joy, and sleep. Also, irrational confidence.

- **Allspice** – Healing and courage.

- **Star anise** – Intuition and mystery. Looks like a tiny witch's wheel, tastes like prophecy.

Make up your own **Winter Solstice Blend**: 2 parts cinnamon, 1 part clove, 1 part nutmeg, pinch of dried orange peel. Bless it under a full moon and whisper your hopes into it. Use it in everything from porridge to mulled wine to spell sachets.

Storing and Organising with the Moon

This is the part most witches skip. Don't be most witches.

Your pantry's energy is shaped not just by what's in it, but when it was placed there. The moon has moods, you know. She has opinions. You wouldn't want to pickle beetroot under a waning moon unless you want your guests to sob into their shepherd's pie.

Here's the basic pantry-moon guide:

- **New Moon** – Begin preserves and drying. Plant new magical intentions.

- **Waxing Moon** – Stock and gather. Anything added now gains in strength.

- **Full Moon** – Bless and label. Charge items with lunar energy (leave jars on the sill!).

- **Waning Moon** – Clean out expired goods. Compost the things you've been "meaning to use." Release stagnant energy and restock intentionally.

Put a small moon phase calendar on the inside of your pantry door. It doesn't need to be fancy. Just enough to remind you that the universe has a rhythm, and so should your soup.

Warming Winter Teas – Steep Dreams Are Made of Tea

Fact: There is no situation in life that cannot be improved by a well-made cup of tea. Illness, heartbreak, spiritual crisis, snowstorm, full-blown hexing accident, tea. Tea is the answer. Now unless you haven't guessed by my spelling, yes I am British. The possibility of a British person writing a book that doesn't include a) The weather or b) Tea, would be un-natural…. rude and simply wrong on so many levels I can't describe.

I am going to borrow a couple of paragraphs from a friend of mine's book "Rudely Interrupted" by David Ivell. I did ask his permission.

"Now, I could write an entire volume on the subject of British tea. Not just a chapter. A volume. Possibly with footnotes, appendices, and a bonus fold-out timeline charting the psychological significance of 'tea o'clock' as a national coping strategy. Because tea in Britain is not a beverage. It is not even a concept. It is a response.

You see, when an English person offers you tea, they are not merely suggesting hydration. No, no. What they are really saying is, "The world is on fire, my emotions are all trying to sit in the same chair, and someone's just reversed into my dustbin, but if I can put the kettle on, something <u>can</u> still be done."

In other words - tea is the national emotional duct tape. It is Britain's go-to tool for addressing grief, stress, awkward silences, diplomatic incidents, mild inconvenience, and the recurring national crisis that is British weather. If you stub your toe, make tea. If someone dies, make tea. If a foreign dignitary says something vaguely insulting about crumpets, definitely make tea. If there's an alien invasion, rest assured someone, somewhere, will be filling the kettle and muttering, "Well, better get the good mugs out, then."

The point, I realised, was not the tea. It never had been. It was the performance of calm. The illusion of control. The quiet statement that no matter how strange, how unsettling, or how catastrophically absurd life, or in this case, afterlife became, one could still boil water, pour it over something dried and crumbling, and declare with great national pride: this will help."

Now, a witch's winter pantry without a tea shelf is like a cauldron without a handle, deeply inconvenient and liable to scald someone. Winter teas are more than just deliciously steamy beverages; they're gentle potions in porcelain, healing spells in mugs, mood stabilisers with steam. They are the closest thing we have to drinkable hugs.

But before we get into blends and brew times, let us begin, as all proper things do, with a kettle and a bit of reverence.

Tea as Ritual, Not Just Beverage

Let's be clear: you are not merely "making a cup of tea." You are performing **kitchen witchery**. You are conjuring a mood, setting intention, aligning spirit with leaf. You are, essentially, communing with plant spirits over boiling water. (Which sounds far more impressive when you say it aloud. Do try it at parties.)

So make the act sacred:

- **Choose your cup like a wand**: Every witch has a favourite mug. It's usually chipped, oddly shaped, and looks as though it survived a minor explosion. Perfect. That cup holds memory. Use it.

- **Boil with purpose**: Whisper your intention to the water as it heats. Protection. Peace. Energy. A clear head. A clean house. A partner who understands how to fold towels properly.

- **Stir sunwise (clockwise)** for drawing in; stir widdershins (counterclockwise) for banishing. This includes things like anxiety, fatigue, and passive-aggressive WhatsApp messages.

- **Bless with breath**: Blow gently over your cup before sipping and imagine your spell carried on the steam.

There you go. A five-minute potion, lovingly disguised as Earl Grey.

Foundational Herbs for Winter Blends

Before you can mix like a magician, you'll need a small apothecary of dried herbs. These can be wildcrafted (with permission and practical boots), purchased from a reputable herbalist (preferably someone with at least one cat and suspiciously accurate weather predictions), or harvested from your own enchanted garden.

Some staples:

- **Peppermint** – Energetic reset, digestive aid, and clarity-bringer. Think of it as the verbal slap your soul sometimes needs.

- **Chamomile** – Calm, comfort, and childlike joy. Good for sleep and not yelling at the news.

- **Rosemary** – Memory, strength, and psychic shielding. Pair with lemon for a "why yes, I *do* know what I'm doing" blend.

- **Elderflower** – Immune support, gentle protection, ancestral connection. Useful during both cold season and unexpected hauntings.

- **Ginger** – Heat, courage, and vitality. Also good for sore throats and romantic courage.

- **Cinnamon** – Attraction, joy, and abundance. Also smells like every good winter memory you've ever had.

- **Hibiscus** – Heart magic, beauty, and blood flow. Also, it turns everything bright crimson, which is always fun.

- **Lavender** – Peace, dream enhancement, and slight smugness. Use sparingly, lest everything taste like soap.

Store your herbs in glass jars. Label them not only with names but also with moon phase harvested, date, and intention. Bonus points if you tie a little ribbon or dried sprig around the neck and pretend you run an Etsy shop.

Signature Witchy Winter Blends

Here are five magical winter tea blends that will warm your belly, bolster your magic, and possibly keep you from strangling a relative over board games.

1. Hearth & Home

For: Comfort, protection, and surviving winter with your sanity intact.

- 2 parts chamomile

- 1 part cinnamon bark

- 1 part dried apple

- A pinch of nutmeg

Spell tip: Stir while envisioning your home bathed in golden light. Whisper:

"Peace within these walls I weave, warmth and safety I believe."

2. Solstice Sunrise

For: Energy, brightness, and banishing winter blues.

- 2 parts hibiscus

- 1 part dried orange peel

- 1 part ginger

- 1 part rosemary

- A few rosehips for beauty

Spell tip: Brew at sunrise and drink while facing east. Imagine the sun returning through your bones.

3. Dreamer's Brew

For: Deep rest, dream magic, and a night without existential dread.

- 2 parts chamomile

- 1 part lavender

- 1 part mugwort (half if you're sensitive)

- A sliver of vanilla bean

Spell tip: Sip in bed, notebook at hand. Speak aloud:
"May dreams be safe, may visions stay, through moonlit path and shadowed way."

4. Witch's Resilience

For: Cold-fighting, energy boosting, immune-shielding brilliance.

- 2 parts elderflower
- 1 part peppermint
- 1 part dried lemon balm
- A few slices of dried ginger
- Optional: pinch of cayenne (if you're brave)

Spell tip: Drink under a waning moon. Say firmly:
"From root to crown, health flow down. Ill winds pass, strength shall last."

5. Yuletide Blessing Tea

For: Festive ritual, family harmony, and being marginally more patient.

- 2 parts cinnamon
- 1 part clove
- 1 part dried cranberry
- 1 part sage
- Tiny bit of honey stirred in clockwise

Spell tip: Pour into a shared pot and serve with blessings for all present. Best served before everyone's had too much sherry.

Brewing with the Moon (Again, Because It Matters)

Moon phase tea brewing is like planetary microdosing. Trust me, it makes a difference. Even muggle guests will say, "Wow, this is really good. What's in it?" and you can answer, "Waxing crescent and mild psychic optimism."

- **New Moon**: Herbal detox blends. Clarity and setting intentions. Great time to start a new blend.

- **Waxing Moon**: Strengthening and energising teas. Blend for goals, motivation, and vitality.

- **Full Moon**: Dream teas, love infusions, or ancestral blends. Best for tea ceremonies or group rituals.

- **Waning Moon**: Healing, releasing, and banishing blends. Excellent for colds, grief, or post-holiday fatigue.

Tools of the Tea Witch

It's not just about what's in the cup. The tools you use carry their own magic. Here are my essentials:

- **A well-loved teapot**: Preferably ceramic or cast iron. Must have personality. (Mine isn't shaped like one but somehow reminds me of a badger. No regrets.)

- **A wooden spoon**: For stirring with intention. Never metal, it can muddle the energy unless you're brewing a sass spell.

- **A tea strainer or infuser ball**: No one likes floaty bits. No-one. Bonus points if it's shaped like a moon, cat, or something entirely ridiculous.

- **A tea towel embroidered with profanity**: Not strictly magical but deeply satisfying.

- **A small journal**: For recording blends, effects, dreams, and thoughts. Title it "The Book of Teas and Other Cures" if you're feeling dramatic.

Tea as Spellcraft

Don't underestimate the power of tea as spell. Unlike candles or complex rituals, tea can be done quietly, gently, under the nose of even the most skeptical houseguest.

- Feeling ungrounded? Brew with roots, ginger, dandelion, chicory.

- Need courage? Add cinnamon and clove.

- Need to speak your truth? Peppermint and thyme.

- Want to seduce someone very specific? Rose petals and honey. (But get consent, for heaven's sake.)

You can also write a sigil on the bottom of your cup with edible ink or inscribe words into a sugar cube. When the tea melts it, the spell is released. Very sneaky. Very fun.

Seasonal Serving Rituals

Consider hosting a **Midwinter Tea Ritual**. Invite a few kindred spirits. Lay out mugs, a single candle, a plate of enchanted biscuits (see previous section), and let each person choose their blend. Have them speak their intention while the water boils. Pour, stir, bless, sip. Talk if you like. Or don't. The silence will hum with magic.

If you're alone, do the same. Just you, the tea, and the wind at the window. That, too, is powerful.

So raise our mismatched mugs and remember tea is never just tea. It is the warmth of the hearth, the whisper of the herb, the alignment of moon and breath and hope. It is the most accessible magic there is... and frankly, far more delicious than eye of newt.

Mulled Wine, Ciders & Magical Elixirs (Side Effects: Singing Carols Too Loudly)

I have a theory, and I stand by this with the same level of confidence I apply to over-salting my roast potatoes, that mulled drinks were the original witch's brew. Think about it. You take a cauldron (or a saucepan, depending on your level of drama), throw in fruits, herbs, bark, wine, sometimes honey, sometimes fire, sometimes regret, and stir until it steams like a Victorian séance. Then, in the final moments, you whisper over it and serve to guests, who invariably say, "Oh, that's lovely. What's in it?"

The answer, of course, is always "magic." Also, cloves.

Now, these potions, mulled wine, spiced ciders, enchanted cordials, are not your everyday beverages. These are winter drinks. Deep season drinks. They are the liquid equivalent of putting on a knitted jumper and muttering "I *will* get through this solstice without throttling anyone." They warm your bones, lift your spirits, and (when made properly) can function as minor rituals, tonics, and acts of social diplomacy.

So let's get to it. Pop the kettle on and light a candle, we're about to turn your drinks cabinet into a potion shelf.

The Sacred Art of Mulling

Let's start with **mulled wine**, because nothing says "I'm a deeply capable winter witch" like casually producing a steaming cup of red joy that smells like alchemy and tastes like comfort. Mulling is the process of warming wine (or cider, or juice, if you're feeling teetotal and pious) with aromatic spices and other delicious things, and possibly whispering at it until your house smells like festive seduction.

Basic Potion Principles

Here is the standard structure of any mulled drink:

- **Base**: Red wine, apple cider, pear juice, cranberry juice, or any fermented liquid that doesn't hiss at you.

- **Sweetener**: Honey, maple syrup, brown sugar, or enchanted syrup (see Elixirs section).

- **Spices**: Clove, cinnamon, nutmeg, star anise, cardamom. These are your spell components.

- **Citrus**: Orange and lemon are your bright notes. The sun returning to the dark.

- **Fruit/Herbs (optional)**: Apples, cranberries, bay leaves, sprigs of rosemary (which also serves as a magical wand if things get out of hand).

The trick is low heat. Never boil. Boiling drives off the alcohol and makes everything taste like bad choices. Gentle heat. Loving stirs. Affirming murmurs.

Bea's Midwinter Mulled Wine

For: Hearth magic, festive joy, minor acts of delicious witchcraft

Ingredients:

- 1 bottle of full-bodied red wine (EG Rioja)

- 1 orange, sliced into stars

- 5 cloves

- 2 cinnamon sticks

- 3 slices of fresh ginger

- 2 tablespoons honey

- 1 bay leaf

- 2 mint leaves

- 1 spicy pepper. Poblanos or Cubanelles. Or whatever you have to hand

- Optional: splash of brandy (for courage), handful of dried rose petals (for love), or a dash of orange liqueur (for flair)

Method:
Pour wine into a pan with all the ingredients (except the spicy pepper). Warm gently, never boiling, until the whole house smells like a Dickensian fever dream. 10 minutes before you take the pan off the heat, add the spicy pepper. Stir sunwise and whisper your intention into the steam, joy, peace, warmth, an awkward family dinner going surprisingly well.

Spell Tip:
If serving to guests, stir in a clockwise circle while saying:
"May this brew bring laughter and cheer, and blessings grow as solstice nears."

Serve in mugs or handled goblets with a twist of orange and a wink.

Apple Cider for Protection and Pep

You may be tempted to think cider is just the mulled wine's less glamorous cousin. You would be wrong. Apple cider is the potion of choice for grounding, hearth-tending witches, especially those who are trying not to pass out after two cups of wine.

Magical Correspondences:
Apples = knowledge, healing, immortality
Cinnamon = protection, energy

Clove = banishment, clarity

Ginger = fire, warmth, willpower

Basic Recipe:

- 1 litre cloudy apple cider or juice

- 1 apple, sliced

- 1 orange, halved and studded with cloves

- 2 cinnamon sticks

- 3 whole allspice berries

- 1 piece star anise

- 2 teaspoons brown sugar or maple syrup

- A splash of lemon juice

Heat low and slow. Stir with a wooden spoon (preferably charmed, or at least washed). Serve with apple slices floating like little suns.

Kitchen Charm:

Place a rowan berry or a sprig of rosemary beside the pot while mulling to ward off seasonal malaise and nosy neighbours.

Enchanted Elixirs: Cordials and Syrups for Every Spell

Now, if you want something more shelf-stable (and less likely to make your aunt dance on the table), you'll want to start making **cordials and syrups**. These are thick, sweet liquids you can mix into hot water, tea, sparkling drinks, or your latest attempt at herbal cocktails.

Cordials are, essentially, infused potions. They are what happen when a witch whispers into sugar and fruit for long enough that the molecules get nervous and agree to become medicine.

Elderberry Cordial of Immunity

For: Keeping out colds, curses, and existential dread

Ingredients:

- 2 cups dried elderberries

- 4 cups water

- 1 tablespoon dried rosehips

- 1 cinnamon stick

- 1 slice ginger

- 1 teaspoon cloves

- 1 cup honey (raw if possible)

Simmer all ingredients (except honey) until reduced by half. Strain. Stir in honey while still warm. Bottle with a label that reads something like "Witch's Winter Tonic" in your best menacing handwriting.

Usage:
One spoonful a day for general protection. Two if someone nearby sneezes. Three if Mercury is retrograde and your ex is texting.

Spiced Cherry Cordial of Comfort

For: Heartache, sadness, the cold and the cranky

- 2 cups frozen cherries

- 1 cup water

- 1 cinnamon stick

- 2 cloves

- 1 slice lemon

- ½ cup honey

Simmer, mash, strain, and sweeten. Add a whisper of rose petals if you need extra heart-healing. Best enjoyed in a bath, with candlelight and a firm boundary on your phone.

Potions for Guests (or Particularly Sentimental Ghosts)

There will come a point in the season when you'll have guests. Some may be beloved. Some may be tolerated. All of them will benefit from a warming potion disguised as a sociable beverage.

Offer drinks that enchant without overpowering. Remember, not everyone is ready to hear that the strange tingle in their throat is due to mugwort and their repressed psychic gifts.

Solstice Sangria (Yes, Really)

Who says you can't serve sangria in winter? Just give it a woolly jumper and a personality disorder.

- 1 bottle red wine (Rioja again……)

- ½ cup pomegranate juice

- Sliced apple, pear, and orange

- Clove, cinnamon, bay leaf

- Splash of brandy or ginger liqueur

Mix in advance, let sit for a few hours or overnight, and serve over ice—or gently warmed for a "mulled sangria" effect. Optional: add pomegranate seeds like little jewels.

Moonlit Mocktail

For designated drivers, expectant witches, or those who prefer their potions without a hangover.

- ½ cup elderflower cordial

- ¼ cup cranberry juice

- Splash of apple cider vinegar

- Top with sparkling water

- Garnish with frozen herb sprigs (rosemary in ice cubes = fancy magic)

Spell it silently: *"I am bright, I am calm, I am a witch who doesn't need booze to dance at the Yule party."*

Bottling and Labelling Like a Pro Witch

Let me tell you something you might already know: people love a witchy bottle. You can put nearly anything in a little swing-top flask with a parchment label and suddenly it's "Ancient Solstice Serum" or "Elixir of Shadowlight." Bonus points if you tie on a cinnamon stick or wax-seal the lid.

Tips:

- **Label Everything**: Not just name and ingredients, but the spell purpose. For example:
  "Hearthfire Cider, warmth, resilience, comfort. Brewed Full Moon, Dec. 1."

- **Add Runes or Sigils**: Sharpie on the bottom or carve into the cork.

- **Bless the Bottles**: Line them up under the full moon and whisper thanks. Bonus: neighbours will assume you're eccentric in a charmingly dangerous way.

The Magic of Sharing

Potions aren't just for the drinker, they're for the *circle*. Making mulled wine for friends is a spell of welcome. Handing someone a bottle of your home-brewed winter cordial says, "Here, I care that your throat and soul are sore." It's healing. It's connection. It's slightly sticky, yes, but entirely worthwhile.

If you're feeling particularly ceremonial, hold a *Winter Potion Toast* on Solstice night. Light a candle. Pour your chosen potion. Raise your glass and declare aloud:

"To the longest night and the growing light. May our hearths be warm, our spirits high, and our drink perfectly spiced."

You may now clink goblets with glee. Or gently thud mugs, if ceramic.

Let me remind you: these are not just drinks. These are acts of seasonal defiance. When the cold bites, the dark presses in, and the world seems frozen in place, you brew warmth. You steep intention. You stir sweetness into stillness and make a little magic in a mug.

So pour generously. Bless fiercely. Sip slowly.

The Great Pagan Bake-Off: Yule Log Cake, Biscuits & Sugar Spells

There comes a time in every witch's winter when the only possible cure for the general state of the universe is ...sugar. There I have said it out loud.... and not just any sugar, mind you, not the suspicious cube in the pub's espresso saucer or the sad sachet at the bottom of your handbag, but *real sugar*. Proper, home-blessed, hearth-fired sweetness.

This section is about *baking spells*, which are, let's be honest, perhaps the best kind of spell there is. You mix things together, mutter incantations (or sometimes just swear at your oven), and in the end, you have a tangible, fragrant offering. It's alchemy with butter…. and it smells fantastic.

I am, by nature, a savoury person. But I've come to believe that sugar, in the right hands, is sacred. Especially in winter, when the nights are long and your neighbours are beginning to feel… percussive.

So, welcome to the sweet shop of the soul. We are about to bake some magic.

The Yule Log: A Witch's Edible Spell for Light and Return

Let's start with the grand dame herself: the **Yule Log Cake**, or *Bûche de Noël*, if you're fancy or French or just someone who enjoys a bit of linguistic drama.

Now, the original Yule Log was an actual log, cut from sacred trees, brought in with ritual, sometimes anointed with wine, and burned slowly through the longest night to ensure the sun would return. These days, setting fire to logs indoors is generally discouraged by insurance companies, so we honour the tradition by eating cake. A delightful compromise.

Symbolism:

- **Log**: The enduring flame of hope in the darkness.
- **Roll**: The wheel of the year, ever turning.

- **Chocolate**: Earthy abundance and seduction (obviously).

- **Decorations**: Wishes in icing form, every mushroom, leaf, or sugared berry a charm.

A Winter Solstice spell in sponge form – rich, rolled, and ritual-ready (Gluten optional. Drama essential.)

Ingredients:

For the Sponge:

- **4 large eggs, room temperature**

- **100g caster sugar**

- **75g plain flour**

   - *or* **75g ground almonds for a gluten-free variation**

- **25g cocoa powder (the darker, the better for shadow-magic appeal)**

- **Pinch of salt (for balance and grounding)**

- **½ tsp vanilla extract (for softness and spirit connection)**

For the Filling:

- **200ml whipped double cream**

- **1 tbsp honey (optional – for harmony and sweetness of spirit)**

- **Splash of vanilla or orange blossom water (if you're feeling poetic)**

For the Chocolate Bark Buttercream:

- **100g unsalted butter (softened)**

- **200g icing sugar (sifted)**

- **40g cocoa powder**

- **1–2 tbsp milk or cream**

- **A few drops of vanilla or espresso (for intensity and depth)**

Optional Edible Decorations:

- Rosemary sprigs – for wisdom and forest vibes

- Sugared cranberries – for protection, abundance, and colour pop

- Meringue mushrooms – for whimsy, woodland charm, and conversation starters

- Icing sugar – for snow, silence, and a hint of otherworldliness

Equipment:

- Swiss roll tin (approx. 9 x 13 inches / 23 x 33 cm)

- Parchment paper (*the sacred sheet – honour it*)

- Clean tea towel for rolling (dusted generously with icing sugar)

- Electric mixer or a whisk and sheer will

- Spatula (your wand)

- A calm kitchen, a candle, and some seasonal mischief

Method (or Ritual Instructions)

1. Prepare the Realm

Preheat your oven to 180°C (350°F / Gas Mark 4).
Line your Swiss roll tin with parchment paper—neatly, respectfully, ceremonially, as this shall bear your sacred sponge. Light a candle and declare (either aloud or inwardly):

"By flour, egg, and darkest night,
I bake the spell that brings back light."

2. Summon the Air – Whip the Eggs and Sugar

In a large mixing bowl, whisk the eggs and caster sugar together for 5–8 minutes until the mixture is pale, thick, and tripled in volume. This is the air element at work: lift, breath, and magic in motion.
Test readiness by lifting the whisk, your mixture should fall in ribbons that sit briefly on the surface.

Add your vanilla extract now. Whisper something affirming like, *"May this cake be soft and kind, as dreams return and hearts unwind."*

3. Sift and Fold – The Earthly Binding

In a separate bowl, sift together the flour (or almonds), cocoa powder, and pinch of salt. These are your grounding elements, the dark soil, the stillness, the promise of spring beneath snow.

Gently fold the dry ingredients into the egg mixture, using a spatula and a patient heart. Go slowly. Overmixing will deflate the air, and you'll end up with something more like a magical manhole cover.

4. Pour and Bake – Fire Rises

Pour the mixture into your prepared tin. Tilt gently to spread it evenly to all edges. Give it a tiny shake to level it out.

Slide it into the preheated oven and bake for 8–10 minutes. Watch it like a hawk. Or better yet, like a witch with a grudge.
When done, the sponge should spring back when touched and have no raw shine.

5. The Sacred Roll – Casting the Spiral Spell

While the cake bakes, prepare your clean tea towel, dusted generously with icing sugar. This is your rolling cloth, your ritual scroll.

As soon as the sponge is out of the oven, turn it out face-down onto the tea towel, remove the parchment, and roll it up gently but firmly, towel and all, from short end to short end. This keeps the sponge flexible and instils the spiral—a symbol of continuity, return, and time.

As you roll, whisper:

"As I roll, so shall light return,
warmth and hope within me burn."

Let the rolled sponge cool completely in its swaddle, about 30–40 minutes.

6. Whip the Filling – The Heart of the Log

In a bowl, whip the double cream to soft peaks. Add honey if desired, for sweetness and the spirit of offering.
You can also add a splash of orange blossom water, rosewater, or even a hint of cinnamon—each adds a different enchantment.

Unroll the cooled sponge carefully. Spread the cream filling across the surface, leaving a slight margin at the edges to prevent joyful overflow.

Roll the cake back up, this time without the towel, with care and reverence. Place seam-side down on a serving board.

7. Bark Buttercream – The Outer Enchantment

In a clean bowl, beat the butter until soft. Gradually add in the sifted icing sugar and cocoa powder. Add vanilla or espresso, and a splash of milk or cream to achieve a smooth, spreadable consistency.

Spread the buttercream across the log with a spatula or palette knife. Texture it with a fork, dragging lines across to mimic bark. Add little knots or rough patches. Imperfection is the mark of true enchantment.

8. Decorate with Intention

Now for the fun bit—the spellwork in foliage and frost.

- Rosemary sprigs as tiny evergreen trees , for clarity, resilience, and wintergreen magic

- Sugared cranberries – for festive protection and visual delight (just roll fresh cranberries in sugar after wetting them)

- Meringue mushrooms – if you've made them, they're wonderful for woodland charm

- Icing sugar dusting – for snow, silence, and stillness; tap it gently through a tea strainer like you're blessing the log

Each decoration can be placed with a whispered wish. Example:

- *"This sprig for strength,"*

- *"This berry for laughter,"*

- *"This dusting for the quiet peace I crave."*

9. Serve and Share with Intention

Place your finished Yule log on a wooden board, a slice of bark, or anything that feels rustic and rooted. Light candles around it. Breathe deeply.

When ready to serve, slice gently. Offer to others with warmth. Each piece is a spiral of renewal, a sweet return to light.

You may wish to say:

"We eat this spell to mark the sun,
the darkest night is nearly done.
Let joy return in bite and crumb,
and peace reside in everyone."

Optional Additions for the Bold:

- Add a thin layer of cherry jam under the cream for heart magic and richness.

- Infuse the cream with a sprig of rosemary or thyme, then strain, for a subtle herbal undertone.

- Brush the sponge lightly with spiced rum or coffee before filling for a deeper, grown-up warmth.

A Yule Log Cake isn't just a dessert. It's a ritual in sponge, a solstice scroll, a spell in ganache. The spiral roll carries the turning of the year, the return of light, and the resilience we all need to face winter with a bit of humour and a chocolate-smeared grin.

Now pass the fork, will you? And maybe a second slice... for the spirits, of course.

Biscuits, Bakes & Broom-Cupboard Blessings

Biscuits are small spells disguised as snacks. They are the edible version of pocket talismans. Each one a bite-sized charm. Let's be honest, winter can be long. The days blur into each other, and you sometimes forget which solstice you're even celebrating. A biscuit with purpose is a small anchor.

Here are my favourites, all infused with intention.

1. Cinnamon Stars of Joy

Ingredients:

- **100g ground almonds**

- **100g icing sugar (plus extra for dusting)**

- **1 tsp ground cinnamon**

- **1 egg white (from a large egg)**

- **Dash of orange zest (from an unwaxed orange)**

Method:

1. Prepare Your Baking Space
Light a candle and take a moment to centre yourself. This is joyful magic, not a stress test from a baking competition. Put on music if it helps. Something gently ridiculous.

2. Mix the Dry Ingredients
In a medium mixing bowl, combine the ground almonds, icing sugar, and cinnamon. Stir them together with a wooden spoon (preferably one that's slightly scorched or mysteriously sticky - signs of a well-used witch's tool).

3. Whip the Egg White
In a separate bowl, whisk the egg white until it holds soft peaks. You can use a hand whisk or an electric one, depending on how many arm workouts you want that day. The texture should be fluffy, but not stiff.

4. Combine and Add the Zest
Gently fold the egg white into the dry ingredients using a spatula or large spoon. Add a dash of orange zest and fold until you have a slightly sticky, pliable dough. It should feel soft but not overly wet—like spell dough rather than slime.

5. Chill the Dough (Optional but Helpful)
Wrap the dough in parchment paper and chill it in the fridge for 20–30 minutes. This makes it easier to roll and cut later. As it chills, you might want to whisper a blessing into the fridge (you'd be surprised how well fridges respond to encouragement).

6. Preheat Your Oven
Preheat the oven to 150°C (300°F / Gas Mark 2). Line a baking tray with parchment paper.

7. Roll Out the Dough
Dust a clean surface (or a sheet of baking paper) with a little icing sugar. Roll out the dough to about ½ cm thickness.

8. Cut the Stars – Add the Ritual

Using a star-shaped cutter, cut out your biscuits. As you press the cutter into the dough, speak aloud:

"Light returns, joy is near,
let us laugh and bring good cheer."

This small incantation charms each biscuit with brightness and playfulness. Don't skip it—even whispering is enough.

9. Bake

Place the stars gently onto the lined tray. Bake in the preheated oven for 10–12 minutes, or until they are just beginning to firm up and lightly golden at the edges. They should be crisp on the outside and slightly chewy inside.

10. Cool and Dust

Allow the biscuits to cool on the tray for 5 minutes, then transfer to a wire rack. Once completely cooled, dust lightly with icing sugar for a snowy, sparkling effect.

Optional Enchantments:

- Thread with gold string and hang on your Yule tree for blessings.

- Tuck into gift bags with a slip of the spell written inside.

- Nibble while writing seasonal intentions, they're excellent for inspiring cheerful honesty.

2. Vanilla Moon Biscuits

A spell for peace, rest, and lunar dreaming

Ingredients:

- **200g plain flour**

- **100g unsalted butter (softened)**

- **50g caster sugar**

- **1 egg (preferably from a contented hen)**

- **1 tsp vanilla extract**

- **Pinch of ground nutmeg (for dream-deepening)**

Method:

1. Set the Intention
Before you begin, light a small white candle or place a moonstone beside your mixing bowl. Whisper your intention for calm, rest, and peaceful dreams. These are not just biscuits. These are edible lullabies.

2. Cream the Butter and Sugar
In a medium bowl, beat the softened butter and sugar together until pale and creamy. You want the mixture to look like clouds on a gentle night sky. This is your base of sweetness and softness.

3. Add Egg and Vanilla
Crack in the egg and add the vanilla extract. Beat gently until fully combined. The egg is your binder, it holds your dreams together. The vanilla adds comfort, like a whispered bedtime story.

4. Stir in the Nutmeg
Add a small pinch of nutmeg and stir slowly. Nutmeg is your dreaming spice, fragrant, sleepy, and slightly mysterious.

5. Add the Flour

Sift in the flour and mix gently until a soft, pliable dough forms. Don't overwork it, treat the dough as you would a tired child: kindly, patiently, and without shouting.

6. Shape into a Disc and Chill

Form the dough into a flat disc and wrap in parchment paper or cloth. Now, here's where the magic intensifies.

Lunar Ritual (Yes, Really)

Place the wrapped dough in a windowsill, on a balcony, or anywhere it can safely catch moonlight. Ideally during a waxing or full moon.

As the dough chills, speak quietly:

"By gentle light and starlit gleam,
let this dough become a dream.
Peace and rest in every bite,
bless the soul and bless the night."

Leave to chill for at least 30 minutes, or up to 2 hours if your moonlight is feeling particularly cooperative.

7. Preheat the Oven

Heat your oven to 170°C (340°F / Gas Mark 3). Line a baking tray with parchment.

8. Roll and Shape into Moons

Roll out the chilled dough to about 1cm thickness on a lightly floured surface. Using a crescent moon-shaped cutter (or fashion one from a round cutter by trimming with a knife), cut out your biscuits.

As you shape them, stay quiet or hum softly—these are silent spells, designed for internal work and dream worlds. If you're working at night, dim the lights. Let the atmosphere match the purpose.

9. Bake with Stillness

Place the crescent moons gently on your lined tray. Bake for 12–15 minutes, or until the edges are just beginning to turn golden. The centres should remain soft—this is not the time for crunchy boundaries.

If possible, bake in silence or gentle music. Let the calm be part of the spell.

10. Cool and Bless

Allow the biscuits to cool on a wire rack. Once cool, you may dust with a little icing sugar or edible shimmer if desired. Hold your hand over the biscuits and offer a final whisper:

"Rest be yours and trouble cease,
in every bite, a touch of peace."

Serving Suggestions

- Serve with chamomile tea, oat milk, or warm lavender milk.

- Eat just before bed or while journaling dreams.

- Place one under your pillow (wrapped!) with a note of your dream intention.

- Gift to a friend going through a stressful time, with a note: *"A biscuit for your moon."*

3. Ginger Guardians

A biscuit spell for protection, fire energy, and firm (but friendly) boundaries

Ingredients:

- **300g plain flour**

- **100g unsalted butter (softened)**

- **100g dark brown sugar**
- **2 tbsp golden syrup**
- **1 tbsp ground ginger**
- **Pinch of ground clove (for potency)**
- **1 egg (free-range or magically inclined)**

Method:

1. Prepare Your Space

Begin by cleansing your kitchen space. A quick waft of cinnamon incense or a spritz of rosemary water is enough to clear out lingering energies (or yesterday's bolognese). Light a candle, place a small protective charm (like a black tourmaline or iron key) nearby, and take a deep breath. You're baking guardians now.

2. Cream Butter and Sugar

In a large mixing bowl, cream together the butter and dark brown sugar until smooth and fluffy. The sugar brings depth and earthiness; the butter provides cohesion, just like any good ward.

As you stir, focus your intention on protection. Say aloud or silently:

"Strength and safety, warm and wise,
in dough and spice, protection rise."

3. Add Golden Syrup and Egg

Add the golden syrup, thick, sweet, binding, and crack in the egg. Mix well until fully combined. This is the heart of the guardian: golden, strong, a little sticky, and capable of holding everything together during seasonal chaos.

4. Add Spices

Sprinkle in the ground ginger and pinch of clove. These are your fire elements, sharp, assertive, ancient. Stir them in with confidence.

- Ginger fires up courage, drives away cold, and brings a bit of magical assertiveness.

- Clove seals and protects. A little goes a long way, like a warding spell in powdered form.

5. Add Flour and Form the Dough

Sift in the flour gradually, mixing with a spoon until a firm dough begins to form. Use your hands to bring it together into a smooth, slightly soft ball. If it's too sticky, add a spoonful of flour. If it crumbles, whisper to it lovingly and add a tiny splash of milk.

6. Chill with Purpose

Wrap the dough in parchment or cloth and chill in the fridge for at least 30 minutes. As it rests, it gathers strength.

Optional: place a protective rune or charm on top of the wrapped dough while it chills - Thurisaz (Þ) or Algiz (Y) are particularly good for boundary spells.

7. Preheat the Oven

Preheat to 180°C (350°F / Gas Mark 4) and line a baking tray or two with parchment paper.

8. Roll and Cut

Roll the dough on a lightly floured surface to about ½ cm thickness. Now, cut out your shapes:

- People for household protection

- Cats for independence and perimeter warding

- Houses for anchoring energy and calming nosy neighbours

Now, the most important part: the rune or sigil press.

Using a toothpick, skewer, or clean carving tool, gently inscribe a protective rune or personal sigil into centre of each biscuit. Say:

"Guard this hearth, both near and far,
bold as flame, still as star."

9. Bake with Intent

Place your guardians on the tray with a little space between them. Bake for 10–12 minutes, or until they are golden around the edges and just firm to the touch.

As they bake, stand near the oven and visualise a warm, glowing circle around your home, like these little biscuit beings are forming a shield of spicy, buttery protection.

10. Cool and Charge

Cool the biscuits on a wire rack. Once cool, you may:

- Paint the runes with a little edible gold or silver.

- Arrange them in a circle on your altar for a short time before eating or gifting.

- Place one above your doorway as a temporary ward (just remind housemates it's not a snack).

Serving Suggestions:

- Gift in bundles with handwritten tags: *"One bite for courage, one bite for boundaries."*

- Eat one before difficult conversations.

- Serve to children before large family gatherings. Warning: they may become too bold.

Sugar Spells – The Alchemy of Enchantment

You might think that spells require special ingredients, moonstone dust, phoenix tears, perhaps a raven's eyebrow, but truthfully, a teaspoon of sugar will do. Especially in winter. Especially when you charm it first.

Sigils in Icing

One of the oldest tricks in the grimoire, icing as a canvas. Draw runes of protection, love, or luck into your bakes. You don't have to be an artist. Even a wobbly heart can hold power.

Pro tip: Practice on parchment paper first. Or just call the mess "charmingly rustic."

Blessed Sprinkles

You can enchant your decorative bits. Really. Lay out your sprinkles, edible glitter, or sugar pearls and pass them through incense smoke. Sprinkle while whispering intentions.

A few suggestions:

- **Red sugar**: vitality, strength, confidence
- **Gold glitter**: abundance, solar energy, charisma
- **Silver dragees**: moon magic, intuition, glamor
- **White icing**: peace, stillness, clarity

Decorating becomes a sort of spell-weaving. You're not just making biscuits—you're making edible talismans.

4. Honey Cakes for the Spirits

Traditionally, witches have always left food for the unseen, ancestral spirits, house fae, nosy neighbours who pretend not to be interested but definitely peek in your windows at the village witch....

A small honey cake left by the hearth or threshold is a token of goodwill. Something that says, "We're all sharing this season. Please don't turn my spoons around."

A golden offering for the unseen: ancestral guests, curious fae, and the house spirits that keep your kettle from vanishing

Ingredients:

- **200g plain flour**
- **100g runny honey (local or wildflower is best; avoid supermarket blandness unless desperate)**
- **100g unsalted butter (softened)**
- **1 large egg**
- **1 tsp ground cinnamon**
- **½ tsp ground nutmeg**
- **¼ tsp ground cardamom**
- **1 tbsp finely chopped crystallised ginger (optional but delightfully zingy)**
- **1 tsp finely grated lemon zest (for brightness and invitation)**
- **1 tbsp dried edible flowers (like calendula or lavender – to impress the spirits)**
- **A splash of milk (only if the dough feels dry – spirits do not like cracked offerings)**
- **A pinch of salt (because even spirits appreciate balance)**

Equipment:

- Small cupcake tins, mini muffin tins, or a set of vintage tartlet moulds you found in your gran's attic during a thunderstorm

- Parchment paper or butter for greasing

- A small white candle (for the offering)

- Your most charming apron and an open window (just in case the spirits want to pop in)

Method:

1. Begin with an Intention

Light a candle and take a moment to acknowledge the spirits of your space, those who were here before you, those who walk unseen beside you, and those who occasionally knock things off the shelf for attention. Offer a quiet "Welcome," or, if you're on familiar terms, a "Let's bake, you lot."

Place a small token (like a stone, feather, or key) by your mixing bowl to act as a magical anchor.

2. Cream the Butter and Honey

In a medium bowl, beat together the softened butter and honey until smooth, creamy, and light golden in colour. This mixture is the heart of your cake, the offering itself. Let your thoughts drift to loved ones, ancestors, or house spirits as you stir. You are not just baking. You are remembering.

Spell Tip: Whisper gently as you stir:

"In sweetness shared and warmth bestowed,
come gather round this humble load."

3. Add the Egg and Lemon Zest

Crack in the egg and beat well to combine. Add the grated lemon zest for a little brightness. It lifts the whole cake (both energetically and flavour-wise) and keeps your spiritual guests from feeling too gloomy or Victorian.

4. Add Spices and Quirky Charm

Sprinkle in your cinnamon, nutmeg, cardamom, and a pinch of salt. Add the finely chopped crystallised ginger (for a bit of bite and wakefulness) and your dried edible flowers (for beauty and "oh hello, we're fancy now").

Give everything a good stir until it smells like a warm, spiced memory from somewhere just out of reach.

5. Stir in the Flour

Gradually add the flour and mix gently to form a thick but spoonable batter. If it's looking a bit stiff, add a splash of milk, ideally stirred three times sunwise (clockwise) while muttering something protective, like:

"No cracked cakes, no restless souls,
peace be served in sugared bowls."

6. Spoon and Shape

Grease your tins or line them with parchment squares. Spoon in the mixture so it sits just below the rim, these cakes rise modestly, like well-mannered guests.

Optional ritual: Trace a small protective sigil or rune in the top of each cake with the back of a spoon or your finger. Algiz (Y) for protection or Gebo (X) for offering are both excellent choices.

7. Bake and Breathe

Preheat your oven to 170°C (340°F / Gas Mark 3.5) and bake for 18–22 minutes, or until golden and lightly springy. Your kitchen will begin to smell like a memory, honey, spices, and something older.

Take this moment to tidy your space, hum softly, or brew a cup of tea for yourself. The spirits, after all, aren't the only ones who need tending.

8. Cool and Offer

Remove the cakes from the oven and cool on a wire rack. Once they're cool enough to touch, set one aside for your offering.

Place it on a small dish near the hearth, on the doorstep, by the back garden gate, or wherever your spirit guests tend to loiter. Add a lit white candle (always supervised), a tiny pinch of salt beside the cake (as tradition requires), and say something simple and sincere:

*"This cake I give to those unseen,
who walk the veils and dwell between.
In thanks, in peace, in sweet accord,
may joy be shared, and none ignored."*

Leave it overnight. In the morning, compost the remains (spirits rarely eat much, the polite things) and extinguish the candle with a breath of gratitude.

Optional Enchantments & Variations:

- For Ancestral Honouring: Add a few crushed walnuts or dried apple pieces—both associated with remembrance and legacy.

- For Fae Diplomacy: Drizzle with a bit of rosewater glaze or tuck a tiny flower beside the cake. Fae are terribly aesthetic.

- For House Spirit Harmony: Place your offering near a broom, hearth, or the kitchen sink—anywhere domestic guardians tend to gather.

- For Nosy Neighbours: Deliver a few cakes in a waxed paper bundle tied with red thread. Add a card that says, *"Happy Yule from the entirely harmless woman in the cottage with the crow."*

Honey cakes may be small, but they're mighty in meaning. They remind us that hospitality is at the heart of witchcraft. That the hearth is a temple, and that food, especially sweet, fragrant, golden food, is a bridge between worlds.

Plus, they're delicious. Even if the spirits don't show up, you'll have something soft and spiced to nibble with your tea while watching the snow fall.

Baking as Seasonal Ceremony

If you want to lean into it (and you should), turn your baking into a **ritual celebration**.

Host a **Baking Circle** on the weekend closest to Yule. Invite witchy friends or curious mortals. Everyone brings an ingredient and an intention. You bake together, sip herbal tea, and share stories. It becomes a spell in action—joy, creation, community.

Or, if you're solo, set up a little baking altar:

- Candle for fire

- Wooden spoon for wand

- Bowl for cauldron

- Herbs, spices, your breath, your laughter

Bless your ingredients. Thank the earth. Bake with gratitude.

Packaging Your Magic

Witchy baked goods make the best gifts. They carry energy, thought, time, and that most magical of all ingredients: butter.

Package with care:

- Brown paper, tied with twine
- A handwritten label ("Joy Biscuits – Enchanted 18th December")
- A sprig of rosemary or pine
- Maybe a tiny scroll with a blessing or poem

You'll astonish people. Not just with the taste, but with the thoughtfulness. In a world of rushed things, something slow and spiced is a marvel.

Final Spell – The Baker's Blessing

As you remove your tray from the oven, breathe in. Let the warmth of the spices, the sweetness of the sugar, the old magic of heat and transformation fill your chest.

Hold a hand over your bakes and speak aloud:

"By flour and fire, spice and spoon,
may sweetness guard each cold day's gloom.
From oven's heart and witch's hand,
may joy and magic gently land."

That's it, dear one. You've just made magic with a mixing bowl.

The Sacred Stove – Bubble, Simmer, Toil, and Trouble

(Or: how to make soup without accidentally summoning a fire sprite)

You can tell a lot about a witch from her kitchen. Some have pristine marble worktops, neatly labelled jars, and copper pans that gleam like polished moons. Others, myself included, have slightly scorched wooden spoons, a teetering pile of Tupperware lids (none of which fit anything), and herbs hanging from the ceiling like botanical batmobiles. Somewhere between these two extremes lies what I like to call *The Sacred Stove,* a place that is equal parts spell space, soup lab, and caffeine altar.

If you're going to survive winter with your wits intact and your toes warm, this stove (or oven, hob, hearth, or Aga) needs to be more than a place to burn porridge. It needs to be *blessed.* Yes. Blessed. Enchanted. Tuned, like a musical instrument or your spine before the first cup of tea.

Because cooking in winter isn't just cooking. It's *spellwork disguised as supper.* And if you're going to spend the next three months stirring things in heavy pots and muttering at turnips, you might as well do it with a bit of ceremonial flair.

Step One: Clear the Decks (and Possibly the Fridge)

Now, I realise that some people, especially the Pinterest-inclined, enjoy cleaning. They speak of "joy sparks" and have a spiritual relationship with lemon-scented spray. I am **not** one of those people. But winter cooking requires a little order, or at least a counter that's not actively sticky.

So. First, *banish the mess.* Not in the magical sense (yet), just physically remove the crusty tea rings, the expired condiments, and whatever it is that's turned into a science project in the back of the fridge. You know the one.

Then throw open a window. Even if it's freezing. Even if you're in your dressing gown and the cat looks at you like you've just declared war on comfort. Let the air move. The energy will thank you.

Once that's done, light a little bundle of herbs, rosemary, bay, or mugwort all do nicely, and give the place a bit of a spiritual polish. Think of it like a smoky reset button.

If you're inclined, mutter something like:

"Out with the crumbs and cranky vibes,
in with soup and starry tribes."

Or make up your own. The more it rhymes, the better it works. (This is not scientifically proven, but I stand by it.)

Step Two: Make Friends With Your Tools

We've all got a favourite wooden spoon. Mine has a crack running down one side and looks like it once went to war, but it stirs like a dream and never judges me, even when I burn things. If you don't have one yet, you will. Witchcraft has a way of forming attachments to wooden spoons, cast-iron pans, and ladles with personalities.

Take some time to *bless your basics.*

The Knife

The blade of truth. Also useful for carrots.

- Wash it well. Then pass it through incense smoke or flick a little saltwater on it.

- Hold it up like you're about to knight someone (but don't) and say something simple:

Sharp enough for onions, sacred enough for spells. This blade respects garlic, but fears no pumpkin.

Yes, of course I just made that up, which is exactly the point, this is personal. Recipes and potions can and sometimes must be scripted, but intentions are yours and no one elses.

The Spoon

Ah, the mighty stirrer of things. A spoon is a wand in disguise, and stirring sunwise (clockwise) is a sacred act in my house.

- Rub it with olive oil and maybe a dab of lavender oil.

- Hold it like you're conducting a magical orchestra and say:

"Spin joy, stir peace, and never fling custard on the ceiling."

Being silly and laughing at your own oddity and eccentricity is a skill - and I believe something that should be taught to children constantly. Husbands and partners too.

The Cauldron: A Witch's Best Friend

Before we even get into the chopping, let us take a moment to appreciate the **sacred vessel**. Traditionally, witches use cauldrons, which are excellent for brewing potions, burning things symbolically, and looking intimidating. But in modern kitchens, most of us rely on the Dutch oven, Le Creuset pot, the slow cooker, or, in a pinch, a really sturdy saucepan with a lid that only occasionally falls off.

The important thing isn't what your pot looks like, but how you treat it.

Bonus points if you give it a name. Something majestic, like Athena, Calliope or Obsidia or alternatively.... mine is called Maureen. She's seen some things has Maureen. Thank heavens she doesn't tell tales. But for the record, she's usually referred to as "The Heavy One." Yes, that is both a name and a lifestyle.

Important: Never use it to reheat soup while wearing a grudge. Stews absorb moods.

Step Three: Build Yourself a Tiny Kitchen Altar

Before you panic, and say *I've just built one from earlier in the book* with a frown and start rearranging furniture, no, you don't need to dedicate a whole counter or construct a mini-Stonehenge out of lentils. A kitchen altar is just a little **corner of intention**. It can sit on a shelf, a windowsill, or even the top of your tea caddy (if you promise not to knock it over when reaching for the biscuits).

What to put on it?

- A candle (white for peace, red for energy, gold for "please let me find the lid to that blasted pot")

- A small bowl of salt (for grounding)

- A sprig of rosemary or bay

- A charm or trinket, a key, a spoon, a tiny stone you found that looked like a potato but turned out to be quartz

- A photo or drawing of an ancestor. If you have one who made legendary stews, then even better.

It's not about how it looks. It's about having a space that you can see out of the corner of your eye, and it can see you. It's where you remember: this is magic. This is you, and a flame, and the power to nourish.

Step Four: Don't Just Cook, Conjure

Here's a fun little secret: ingredients have personalities. Onions are honest. Garlic is fiercely loyal. Carrots are optimists. Potatoes will do anything for you if you treat them right.

So before you start chopping, pause. Put your hands over the ingredients like you're warming them with intention and say:

"Thank you, root and leaf and seed,
for giving all the things I need."

This is not just sentimental nonsense (although I do lean heavily that way. What.... you noticed?). It's energetic exchange. You're tuning in. I swear your stew will taste better for it.

Step Five: Cook with the Season

Winter cooking is not like summer cooking. Summer cooking is full of salads and uncertainty. Winter cooking is about certainty, weight, and the subtle confidence that comes from knowing you can survive anything if there's a pot of something steaming in the corner.

Let your food reflect the **wheel of the year**:

- In **December and January**, cook slow. Stews. Roasts. Root vegetables that remind you the earth is still holding you even when it's frozen solid.

- By **February**, bring in more herbs, grains, maybe the odd egg. It's Imbolc, after all, the promise of return.

- Come **March**, let a little greenery in. Wild garlic, nettles, spinach. But still serve with soup. Because it's still cold. And because hope always goes best with bread.

Step Six: Light the Hearth (Even if It's Just the Hob)

Choose a day, any day will do, but Solstice is traditional and make it your **official sacred stove ignition day**. Light your oven or hob with a match or by pressing that uncooperative button

Then cook something simple. A soup. A stew. Porridge with butter and a bit too much nutmeg. Eat it slowly. When you're done, leave a spoonful for the **house spirits**, a bit of gratitude for all the times your oven didn't explode.

That's It

Your kitchen is now a temple. A slightly smoky, slightly chaotic, wholly magical temple of warmth, nourishment, and enchantment. You have blessed your ladle. You have thanked your onions. You have whispered into your soup.

You, dear witch, are ready for winter.

Solstice Stew – The Cauldron of Plenty

(Or: how to survive winter with lentils, carrots, and a well-placed blessing)

There's something wildly comforting about a stew. Even the word itself, **stew**, feels like a hug. It's round and soft and slightly steamy. It doesn't shout. It doesn't demand. It just sort of settles into your bones and says, *"We've got this, darling."*

If summer food is a flirtation (fresh basil, ripe strawberries, the occasional sun-drunk goat's cheese), then winter food is a marriage. It's dependable. It doesn't care if you've worn the same cardigan for three days or if your socks don't match. Winter food forgives everything. **Solstice Stew** is the high priestess of that forgiveness.

This section is about more than throwing root vegetables into a pot and hoping for the best (though, to be fair, that's a perfectly reasonable starting point). It's about turning a simple one-pot meal into **a** *seasonal spell*. A charm. A warming ritual that feeds both the stomach and the spirit.

Let's talk about cauldrons, ingredients with opinions, and the gentle power of soup to fix things.

Ingredients with Meaning: A Witch's Shopping List

Now, most people approach stew like a culinary shrug: "Whatever's in the fridge." Which is fine if you're after nourishment but not so great if you want *magic*. A friend of mine swears by taking a photo of the inside of her fridge uploading to AI and asking it to create a recipe. I just can't do it, no matter how much fun that sounds. There is wrong and wrong. I wonder if I could write a Chat GPT thingy that works with Witchcraft ingredients. If any readers think you can, let me know!

Because you see, every ingredient has a personality. A purpose. A kind of quiet opinion about what it's doing in your pot. When you bring them together intentionally, you're not just making dinner, you're casting a charm disguised as dinner.

Let's go over some of the **classic stew components** and their **magical correspondences**:

- **Onion** – Truth, purification, emotional clarity. (Also, foundational flavour. No stew without it.)

- **Carrot** – Vision, optimism, grounding. Adds sweetness and sun-coloured joy.

- **Celery** – Protection, structure, and the soothing sound it makes when chopped.

- **Garlic** – Warding, courage, and never dealing with vampires.

- **Bay Leaf** – Wisdom, spiritual insight. Must be removed before serving, or risk unearthing family secrets.

- **Lentils** – Prosperity, stability, and humble strength. They look unimpressive and taste amazing. Like magical introverts.

- **Potatoes** – Earth energy, comfort, nourishment. Can hold an entire emotional breakdown without collapsing.

- **Parsnips or Turnips** – Ancestral connection, endurance, and "I'm sorry you forgot me in the crisper drawer."

- **Rosemary** – Memory, clarity, and protection. A needle of light in your winter gloom.

- **Thyme** – Time. Obviously. Also courage and quiet confidence.

- **Salt** – Protection, preservation, truth-telling. And taste. Obviously taste.

Assemble these ingredients with care. Or at the very least, with curiosity.

Prep as Ritual: Chop, Slice, Intend

Once you've gathered your ingredients, it's time to begin the ritual of chopping.

Yes, chopping. The most underrated form of meditation known to witchkind.

Lay everything out. Put on a pot of herbal tea (or wine, depending on your level of enchantment and the time of day). Light a candle if you like. Then, chop, chop, chop with intention.

- As you slice the onion, imagine peeling away what no longer serves you.

- As you cube the potatoes, think of grounding yourself in the moment.

- As you mince the garlic, mutter something warding.

- As you toss everything into the pot, feel the energy building, a little spell growing in steam and savour.

Don't rush. If you do this right, the stew starts working on you *before* it's even hot.

The Simmering Spell

This is the part where the magic really happens. The *simmer.* That quiet bubbling, that slow dance of flavours and spells merging together like winter clouds with purpose.

Here's a very forgiving base recipe for Solstice Stew:

Bea's Cauldron of Plenty – Solstice Stew

Ingredients:

- **2 tbsp olive oil or butter**
- **1 large onion, chopped**
- **3 carrots, sliced into coins**
- **2 celery stalks, diced (you may not have tried celery sine you were 9 and decided you didn't like it. Time to try it again)**
- **3 garlic cloves, mashed.**
- **2 potatoes, cubed (skin on for grounding, skin off if you're trying to impress someone)**
- **1 parsnip or turnip, cubed**
- **1 cup dried green or brown lentils (rinsed)**
- **1 tin chopped tomatoes or 2 tbsp tomato paste**
- **1.5 litres vegetable stock - or bone broth(animal!), if that's your vibe.**
- **2 bay leaves**
- **1 tsp dried thyme**
- **1 tsp ground cumin or smoked paprika**
- **Salt and pepper to taste**

- **Optional: A handful of kale or greens near the end (for hope and vitamins)**

Method:

1. In your cauldron or pot, warm the oil. Add onion, carrot, and celery. Sauté until softened, about 10 minutes. Stir sunwise (clockwise) and breathe deeply.

2. Add garlic, potatoes, and parsnips. Stir while murmuring something like:

"From root to spoon, I nourish deep,
with warmth and spice, the cold I keep."

3. Add the lentils, tomatoes, stock, herbs, and spices. Stir and bring to a gentle boil. Then reduce to a *lazy simmer*.

4. Cover partially and let simmer for *45 minutes to an hour,* until everything is tender and the house smells like a cottage from a much kinder fairytale.

5. Adjust seasoning. Add the greens, if using, in the last 10 minutes.

6. Before serving, remove the bay leaves and whisper one last blessing over the pot. Something simple like:

"As above, so within,
let the light return again."

Serving the Spell

Now here's the part most muggles miss. Stew isn't just eaten. It's received.

Ladle it into bowls. Deep ones. Rustic ones. The ones that chip but still hold heat.

Add a chunk of bread, a knob of butter, a swirl of cream or a sprinkle of herbs if you're feeling poetic. Serve with presence.

If you're feeding others, say something, not grace exactly, but a *kitchen benediction*. Mine goes:

"Let joy rise like steam,
let peace linger like spice,
and let all who taste know they are welcome,
and they are home."

Then eat. Slowly. Let it fill the quiet. Let it feed something ancient in you.

Leftovers for the Spirits (and Your Future Self)

Don't forget to leave a *spoonful for the house spirits*, especially on Solstice Night. Put it in a bowl by the back door or hearth with a whisper of thanks. You might just make a fox's day.

If you're alone, don't think of it as leftovers. Think of it as **a** second spell, ready for tomorrow. This is the kind of food that gets better with time, like wisdom and long naps.

Solstice Stew is more than food. It's a *firelit answer to darkness.* A way to say, "I'm still here," with potatoes and bay leaves. It's a bubbling cauldron of **yes**, even when the wind howls and the sun clocks off at 4 p.m.

When you cook it, you're doing more than feeding the body. You're feeding the year. You're marking the hinge between the dark and the light... and you're doing it with lentils. Which, I think, is rather marvellous, and definitely the best use of lentils.

Root Magic – Roasted Vegetables with Purpose

(Or: how to talk to your turnips and get away with it)

Let us now discuss that most humble, earthy, often underappreciated class of magical foodstuff: **root** vegetables. Carrots, parsnips, potatoes, beetroot, swedes, turnips, and their odd but lovable cousins, all hiding underground like shy goblins with excellent nutritional profiles.

If you were raised in Britain during the 1980s, as I was, you may have grown up associating root vegetables with school dinners and feelings of mild betrayal. Overboiled carrots, anonymous mash, and parsnips that tasted like slightly angry soap. But I am here today to rescue them from the beige clutches of institutional cookery and restore them to their rightful place as kitchen royalty.

Roasted root vegetables, my dear ones, are nothing short of *culinary spellcraft.* They are simple, forgiving, and wildly flavourful if you know how to treat them right. They're also stunningly magical, both symbolically and practically. You want grounding? Roast a carrot. You want ancestral connection? Roast a beet. You want something hearty enough to anchor your chaotic emotions after a day of Christmas shopping? Roast everything and throw on some rosemary.

Let's roll up our sleeves, sharpen our knives, and dive into the root cellar of witchcraft.

Why Roots Matter (Magically and Otherwise)

Roots are, in witchcraft as in life, the *foundation.* They live underground, in the dark, out of sight, soaking up minerals and secrets. They are the deep listeners of the plant world. You can't get more grounded than a thing that spends its life literally clinging to the earth.

From a magical perspective, root vegetables represent:

- **Stability** – Potatoes, parsnips, and the like are energetically reassuring. They say, "You're fed. You're safe. Sit down."

- **Ancestry** – Beets, in particular, with their blood-coloured juice, are often used in rituals for connecting with those who came before.

- **Endurance** – Turnips, bless them, have seen things. They store energy and survive winter like pros.

- **Transformation** – Raw root veg can be hard and sharp. Roasting softens them, sweetens them, turns them into something entirely new. Alchemy, plain and simple.

Roasting root vegetables is not just cooking, it's *emotional therapy with olive oil.*

Gathering and Preparing Your Roots

Now, the first thing to remember is that root vegetables are not precious. They are not twee. They do not care if your kitchen is rustic-modern or vaguely haunted. They just want to be washed, chopped, seasoned, and roasted at a temperature high enough to blister but not burn.

Choose a few of the following (or all of them, if your chopping arm is feeling ambitious):

- **Carrots** – Use rainbow carrots for extra visual drama. Orange for joy, purple for intuition, yellow for solar clarity.

- **Parsnips** – Earthy and sweet. Excellent for grounding spells.

- **Beets (beetroot)** – Blood red. Mysterious. Slightly threatening in a good way.

- **Turnips and Swedes (rutabaga for Americans)** – Slightly cabbagey, but useful for connecting to old wisdom.

- **Potatoes** – King of the roots. Any variety will do. They are your reliable backup in both magic and life.

- **Sweet Potatoes** – Technically a tuber, but who's checking? Adds warmth, compassion, and a touch of drama.

- **Garlic** – Not a root per se, but gets honorary status. It's basically a protective spell bulb.

The Ritual of Peeling and Chopping

Begin by cleansing your veg, physically and energetically. Give them a good scrub. As you wash them, imagine rinsing away old energies, dead leaves, ancestral grumpiness, and supermarket residue.

Place them on your chopping board with purpose. Light a candle if you like, or play something ambient (or very aggressive if you're feeling feisty, I once roasted parsnips to Rage Against the Machine and it was oddly effective).

As you chop each vegetable, consider its symbolic role:

- "This carrot brings clarity."

- "This potato grounds me in my body."

- "This beet connects me to what I'm too polite to cry about."

- "This parsnip will prevent me from screaming at Susan during the family dinner."

Chop them roughly equal in size, so they cook evenly. Don't fuss. These are roots. They don't need to be primped. They just need to be respected.

The Seasoning Spell

Now comes the dressing. The enchantment. The **oily caress of purpose**.

In a large bowl (the bigger the better), combine:

- 3–4 tablespoons olive oil or melted butter

- 1 teaspoon salt (for grounding and flavour)

- A few grinds of black pepper (for protection and zing)

- 1 tsp ground cumin or smoked paprika (for fire energy)

- A few sprigs of rosemary or thyme (for clarity, courage, and fragrance)

- Optional: a dash of balsamic vinegar or maple syrup (for sweetness and balance)

Toss the vegetables in the mixture with your hands. Get right in there. Feel the weight of them. Say a little something as you work:

"As these roots roast, let burdens lift.
From earth to flame, I share this gift."

Arrange them on a large roasting tray in a single layer. Overcrowding leads to steaming, and this is **not** a steamer spell. We are invoking the **crisp gods**, thank you.

Into the Fire (or at Least the Oven)

Preheat your oven to **200°C (400°F / Gas Mark 6)**.

Place your tray in the centre of the oven and roast for **35–45 minutes**, tossing once or twice, until everything is golden and slightly blistered around the edges. You want crisp bits. *The crisp bits are where the transformation lives.*

While they roast, let the scent fill the house. Walk around like a benevolent kitchen spirit. Imagine each waft carrying comfort and enchantment into the corners of your home.

Serving with Purpose

You can serve these roasted roots in a heap (the technical term), a wreath, or a crescent moon shape around a centrepiece like your lavender lentil loaf (coming next!).

Drizzle with a little extra olive oil or scatter with toasted seeds. You can also:

- Add a spoonful to your ancestor altar
- Use a sprig of rosemary to anoint your front door with oil from the tray
- Offer one parsnip to the house fae (they will eat it, complain, and then leave you alone)

Serve them warm, preferably by candlelight, and with as few interruptions as possible. Eating roasted roots should feel like returning to your own bones. It should feel like sitting beside a long-dead relative who never interrupts and always passes the salt.

Leftovers Are Just Another Spell

Root veg are glorious the next day. Reheat in a pan with a little butter or mash into a hash. They also do marvellously well in frittatas, soups, and tarts.

Store them in a container labelled "Root Magic" or something equally daft. It'll make you smile when you're reheating them after a long day of emails, errands, and the mild horror of January.

If you're feeling particularly in a British mood, look up "Bubble and Squeak" on the internet.

A Final Root Ritual

If you want to go the extra magical mile (and why not?), here's a little ritual you can do as you roast your roots for the solstice:

1. As you preheat the oven, light a yellow or orange candle near it and say:

"I call back the sun, the light, the gold.
In every flame, let warmth unfold."

2. As you prepare the veg, reflect on your own roots, where you come from, what sustains you, what you're ready to release.

3. As the oven roars, imagine it burning away what's heavy, old griefs, old habits, old shopping lists that don't reflect who you are anymore.

4. When the tray comes out, let the steam rise like incense. Take a breath. You have made something real, something good, something witchy.

Root vegetables will not fix everything. They will not pay your bills, file your taxes, or explain why your neighbour is using a leaf blower in December. But they **will** feed you. Gently, deeply, and with utter reliability. They ask for so little, some heat, some time, a bit of olive oil, and in return, they offer everything.

Roast them with care, eat them with reverence, and remember this:
When everything feels upside down, start with what's underground.

The Lavender Lentil Loaf – A Witch's Winter Loaf for Clarity and Calm

(Or: How I Learned to Love Loafing)

Let's be honest. "Lentil loaf" doesn't exactly sing from the rafters, does it? It doesn't glide into the room wearing a feather boa and a twinkle in its eye like a Yule pudding might. It's not flashy. It doesn't sparkle. It does, however, have a quiet dignity and a sort of humble charm once you get to know it, rather like an old librarian who also happens to be a warlock.

… and my friends, that's exactly what we want in the middle of winter. Something sturdy. Something comforting. Something that sits on your plate and says, "We're not panicking. We're having dinner."

This particular loaf, my Lavender Lentil Loaf, is the result of years of fiddling, frowning, experimenting, and one particularly disastrous version that involved peanut butter. But I promise you, this final recipe is a slice of calm. Quite literally. It's a recipe I go back to whenever the world feels a bit frayed at the edges, or I do.

The Magic of Loafing

Now, I know some witches prefer cauldrons bubbling with bone broth and spells involving seventeen rare mushrooms found only under the light of a gibbous moon. But for me, this loaf is just as magical. It's spellwork baked into a tidy rectangle. Everything about it, the herbs, the way you mix it with your hands, the slow baking, feels purposeful. It grounds you. It brings clarity. If you're lucky, it also brings leftovers.

Lentils, you see, are rather special. They've been feeding us for nearly ten thousand years. They've turned up in tombs and temple kitchens and probably a few questionable vegetarian lasagnas. But magically, they represent abundance and grounding. They are the food of those who mean business. No drama. Just quiet, protein-packed support.

Then there's lavender. Now, I realise putting flowers in your dinner might raise a few eyebrows. Lavender, after all, is usually found in bath salts or eye masks, or perhaps in that dusty drawer sachet your Aunt Mabel gave you in 1994. But when used sparingly and with intention, lavender in food is something else entirely. It's like peace you can taste. Calm in crumb form. It doesn't scream "floral!", it just sits there, smoothing out your frazzled edges.

Together, lentils and lavender make a rather marvellous pair: one keeps your feet on the ground, the other lets your head drift dreamily through the clouds.

Ingredients

- **1 cup** dried green or brown lentils (rinsed and cooked until tender)
- **1 small onion**, finely chopped
- **2 cloves garlic**, minced
- **1 medium carrot**, grated
- **1 stick of celery**, finely chopped
- **1 tablespoon** tomato paste or puree
- **1 tablespoon** tamari or soy sauce (for depth and saltiness)
- **1 teaspoon** dried culinary lavender (make sure it's food grade!)
- **1 teaspoon** dried rosemary (crumbled)
- **1 teaspoon** dried thyme *or* sage
- **¾ cup** breadcrumbs (use gluten-free if needed)
- **2 eggs**, lightly beaten *(or 2 flax eggs for a vegan version)*
- **½ teaspoon** sea salt
- **¼ teaspoon** black pepper
- **Optional**: a small handful of chopped walnuts or pecans (for texture and grounding crunch)

Let's Make Magic

The making of this loaf is really half the spell. It's not a fussy process, but it is a hands-on, meditative one. You start with lentils, of course, plain old green or brown ones. Nothing fancy. You cook them gently, watching as they soften and swell, soaking in water and patience. I always feel slightly maternal watching lentils cook, as if they're hatching tiny plans of nourishment and comfort.

While the lentils simmer, you take your holy trinity of witchy aromatics, onion, garlic, and carrot, and sauté them slowly. Not quickly, mind. Slowly. Let them soften and sweeten and fill the house with that scent that says, *"Kids, dinner's on its way, and it's not just soup again."*

Then comes the celery, diced into tiny moons of crunch. It's there for texture and for the little ritual satisfaction of chopping something that doesn't roll off the counter. Celery reminds you that even in the depths of winter, something green still thrives. I know some of you will turn your nose up at celery as I mentioned earlier in the book. Yes you've hated it since childhood, but its time! Time to try again.

Once everything is soft and fragrant, you stir in a spoonful of tomato paste, not so much for tomato-ness, but for richness and heart. A splash of tamari or soy sauce deepens the flavour with its earthy saltiness, anchoring the sweetness of the veg.

Now, here's where the spellwork really begins. In a large mixing bowl, your cauldron, if you will, you combine your cooked lentils and sautéed vegetables with breadcrumbs, herbs, and eggs. This is where the loaf starts to take form. You add the dried lavender, just a pinch! More than that and it'll taste like soap, and a crumble of rosemary for memory and strength. Some thyme if you've got it, or sage if you're feeling particularly wise.

Mixing it all together with a wooden spoon is perfectly respectable, but I always end up using my hands. There's something about pressing everything together, feeling the textures combine, shaping nourishment from ingredients that, on their own, are a bit scrappy, that makes it all the more magical.

At this point, I usually say a little blessing. Not always aloud, I should have said I say a lot of the rhymes to myself. In my head, something like:

"Let this loaf hold peace. Let it feed kindness. Let it steady the stirrings of too much winter."

I press the mixture into a greased loaf tin, firmly but gently, like tucking in my daughter at bedtime, and then, if I'm feeling fancy, I glaze the top with a mixture of tomato paste and balsamic vinegar. It bakes up shiny and proud, like it's auditioning for a cookbook cover.

Into the oven it goes. I bake it at 180°C (that's 350°F for American witches, or Gas Mark 4 for those of you still valiantly using cookers from the Edwardian era) for about 45 minutes. It will firm up, brown gently at the edges, and smell, well, it will smell like home.

Serving Suggestions (Also Known as "Don't Eat it Out of the Tin Standing Up, Bea")

Once it's out of the oven, let it rest for ten minutes or so. It needs to gather itself. If you try to slice it too soon, it'll collapse like a Victorian poet in a faint. Be patient.

Then serve it up in thick slices. It's lovely with roasted vegetables (from our last chapter, of course), or a good ladle of vegetarian gravy. If you're feeling particularly aligned with the moon, add a few sprigs of fresh herbs and a drizzle of olive oil.

It's food to share, but it also makes an excellent solitary supper. I've eaten it curled up in an armchair, plate balanced precariously on my knees, dog sighing dramatically on the rug, while snow drifted down like someone had shaken the sky.

The best bit? The leftovers. A cold slice of lentil loaf makes an unexpectedly perfect breakfast, especially if you pan-fry it until crisp and serve it with an egg or a spoonful of chutney. Or you can crumble it into soup. Or mash it into a kind of herby hash. Or just nibble it like a guilty snack straight from the fridge while whispering, "It's protein, it's practically medicine."

One Last Spell

If you have a little slice left, and the house is quiet, consider offering a crumb or two on your hearth or doorstep. Not just to the ancestors (although they do love a good lentil), but to the spirits of calm, the unseen guardians who keep us from throwing things during December.

A plate of roasted roots, a slice of lavender lentil loaf, a warm fire and a quiet heart, this, I think, is winter magic at its very best.

Sacred Sides and Magical Gravy: Companion Spells on the Plate

(Or: the secret to family harmony is gravy, obviously)

Let's begin with a universal truth: no one has ever written poetry about plain boiled potatoes.

Ok here's my best shot:

Boil, boil, little spud,
bobbing in your starchy sud.
Soft inside and skin so thin,
let the butter seep right in.

Mash you, fry you, roast or bake,
still it's boiling makes you great.
Golden treasure, humble prize,
king of dinners in disguise

Yet, every winter feast I've ever been to has had at least one table where the sides, those humble little dishes meant to support the main act, arrived with all the enthusiasm of a tired ghost. You know the ones. Vegetables boiled into submission. Gravy that whispers of brown, but tastes of despair. A stuffing so dry it might legally qualify as a building material.

This, my dear witchlings, will not do.

Winter suppers, especially those tied to solstice, Yule and Christmas and the long nights of December, are rituals. Every ritual deserves its sacred circle. Your loaf, your stew, your roast roots, they are the fire. But the sides? They are the stones around it. They hold the space. They offer contrast, warmth, brightness, and the very important illusion that you've made *a balanced plate* when really, you're just looking for excuses to eat more crispy things.

So here we are: an ode to sides and sauces. Let's talk buttery mash with protective herbs. Let's explore greens that still have opinions. And let's conjure a gravy so good it might just solve your sibling rivalry in a single ladle.

Bea's Silky Mash with Grounding Spells

We'll start, of course, with mashed potatoes. There are fancier things, yes, pommes purée, duchess swirls, that thing where someone uses a piping bag and too much time, but none quite so emotionally satisfying as a bowl of hot, buttery mash.

The key, I find, is not to overthink it. This is food for grounding, not for showing off.

Take about 1.5kg of floury potatoes, Maris Piper or King Edward if you're in the UK, or Yukon Gold if you're Stateside. Peel them if you like things smooth, leave the skins on if you like a bit of texture and extra nutrients. Boil them in salted water until they sigh when poked.

Then comes the transformation.

Drain them well, mash with commitment, and stir in about 100g of butter (or olive oil, if dairy isn't your familiar), a good glug of warm milk or oat milk, and a sprinkle of sea salt. For the witchy touch, stir in a tiny pinch of nutmeg (for comfort and calm) and a sprig's worth of finely chopped rosemary or thyme (for clarity and protection). Now the important bit. Add mustard. 1 teaspoon. It has to be strong mustard, preferably English mustard. French/Dijon=No, Whole Grain=No, Honey Mustard=No, American Hot Dog yellow=No, No, No. English=Yes. If you really can't find English then add 4 teaspoons of Dijon or 1 teaspoon of horseradish sauce.

Mash is a spell. You stir it with intention. You serve it in a heavy bowl. When people eat it, they close their eyes and remember they are loved.

Greens That Still Know They're Alive

I have a deep, often controversial belief that green vegetables should be *respected, not punished*. That means no more boiling them until they plead for mercy. No more hiding them under cheese to disguise the fact they taste of nothing. Let's allow our greens to be who they are: bright, bitter, strong, and occasionally a little fierce.

Two options I adore for a solstice table:

1. Buttered Kale with Lemon and Garlic

Take a great heap of kale (curly or cavolo nero, both have lovely personalities) and sauté it in butter or oil with slivers of garlic. When it wilts but still holds shape, squeeze over half a lemon and add a pinch of chilli flakes. Serve it in a wooden bowl with a wish for bravery and sharp wit.

Kale, magically speaking, is full of protection and strength. It's also one of the few vegetables that looks like it's dressed for Yule.

2. Cabbage with Chestnuts and Juniper

Now hear me out. Cabbage gets a bad reputation, mostly because people cook it like they're hoping it will go away. But cabbage is loyal. It just needs friends.

Shred a small red or savoy cabbage and sauté it gently in a splash of oil. Add a handful of cooked chestnuts (for grounding and generosity), a few dried juniper berries (for clarity and seasonal mystery), and a spoon of apple cider vinegar to brighten everything up. Cook until tender, not soggy.

It's oddly lovely. Festive. Slightly woodland.

Stuffing That Doesn't Make You Sad

Stuffing is often the side dish that suffers most. It gets boxed, dried out, or, worst of all, forgotten entirely.

But real stuffing is bread alchemy. It's leftover ends reborn. It's herbs and onions and a bit of stock turning into something far greater than the sum of its crumbs.

Start with stale bread. Tear it. Don't cube it. Tearing creates crags that soak up flavour. Add sautéed onions, celery, garlic, a bit of apple or pear for sweetness, sage and thyme for tradition, and a good splash of stock (vegetable or your favourite potion). Press it gently into a baking dish and bake until the top is crisp and golden, the middle soft and fragrant.

Stuffing is also brilliant for making wishes. As you press it into the dish, whisper your hopes for the season. Health. Healing. A working boiler.

The Gravy of Eternal Peace

Drumroll…. and now, the main event.

Gravy.

You may think this excessive. You may say, "Bea, it's just a sauce." But I've seen entire family arguments quelled by good gravy. It's the spell that binds everything together. It's the cauldron poured on the plate.

Let's make it magical.

Bea's Enchanted Gravy (Vegetarian)

Start with a generous knob of butter in a saucepan. Add finely chopped onion or shallot, a few mushrooms (finely minced), and a garlic clove. Sauté until caramelised and golden. Add a spoon of flour, rye, spelt, gluten-free, what have you, and stir into a roux. Slowly whisk in about 500ml of good vegetable stock, infused with herbs.

Here's the trick: add a splash of soy sauce or tamari (depth), a glug of red wine (cheer), and a pinch of dried thyme or rosemary. Simmer until it thickens, then strain if you want smooth, or leave it chunky and rustic.

Right before serving, whisper a naughty thought over the saucepan:

Or just taste it and nod solemnly. Both work. If you have any left in the jug at dinner, throw in a single shot of tequila, stir and re-heat. Tell me what you think? Trust me.

Little Extras, Big Magic

If you're looking to pad your table further (or if Aunt Minerva has decided to turn up with her new vegan drum circle boyfriend), here are a few easy additions that feel like spells:

Roast Garlic Cloves

Just slice the top off a whole garlic bulb, drizzle with oil, wrap in foil, and roast until soft and golden. Serve with a little knife and let people squeeze the cloves out like butter. Protection and warmth in every smear.

Herbed Oil Drizzle

In a jar, mix olive oil with crushed rosemary, thyme, and sage. Let sit overnight. Drizzle over potatoes, veg, or bread with a murmured thanks to the herbs for staying green when everything else went grey.

Spiced Cranberry Chutney

Simmer fresh cranberries with orange zest, a pinch of cinnamon, and a splash of port. Stir in a little sugar and a handful of chopped dates or raisins. This tart-sweet concoction is excellent for balancing out richness, and for sweetening slightly sour family dynamics.

The Assembly of the Sacred Plate

This, dear ones, is when everything comes together. The loaf, the mash, the greens, the gravy, it's not just food, it's a map. A winter altar. You place everything with care. The round things for continuity. The crisp things for contrast. The greens to remind you that life still stirs.

You sit down. You breathe. You pass the gravy to someone without being asked.

You eat. Slowly. Gratefully. Wondering how, despite the world, you've managed to create something so warm and good and real on a plate.

Sides and sauces may seem small. But in the witch's kitchen, nothing is small. Every herb holds a purpose. Every stir is a spell. Every bite, if taken with intention, is an offering to your own endurance.

"May your mash be silky, your stuffing soft, and your gravy well-seasoned."

CHAPTER FIVE

Christmas Dinner - Midwinter Magic

Why We Always Serve Yorkshire Puddings

It starts, as these things often do, with a question from a child. Possibly one of your own, or possibly one that wandered in from next door clutching a glitter-streaked drawing of something that might be a donkey but is definitely wearing fairy wings.

"Mum," they ask, eyes wide and earnest, "is it Yule or Christmas?"

There it is, the modern witch's seasonal riddle. Because if you're anything like me, your fireplace holds both holly and LED fairy lights. Your kitchen smells of cinnamon and rosemary. There's a sprig of mistletoe above the door and a pine-scented candle flickering beside a bowl of Quality Street. You've been muttering about solstice blessings since mid-November, but also yelling, "Who took the scissors?" while wrapping presents at 10:43pm. You are living in the joyous, chaotic, sparkly-tinselled overlap between two great winter traditions: *Yule and Christmas.*

Let me tell you now: that overlap is not only okay, it's beautiful.

Why We Blend

The idea that you must pick a side in the great December Divide, Team Pagan or Team Tinsel, is, frankly, nonsense. The truth is that midwinter has always been a **time of layering**: of old customs threaded through new ones, of torchlit solstice vigils leading into Christmas Eve storytelling, of kitchen smells that tell a thousand stories from different places, hearts, and belief systems.

Yule is ancient. It's the fire festival that marked the longest night and the turning of the wheel, when people gathered to feast, to sing, and to light the dark with hope. The return of the sun, that golden god-child of the sky, was something worth celebrating when your hearth was low on wood and the turnips were looking tired.

Christmas, in its joyful abundance, borrowed from these old traditions with admirable enthusiasm. Candles, evergreens, feasting, songs, there's not a part of modern Christmas that doesn't carry echoes of something older, earthy, and wise.

Then of course, **we added children**.

The Magic of Messy Plays and Glitter Glue

Let's talk about the children, shall we?

Because no matter how refined your altar, no matter how ancient your solstice chant, your December is not truly complete until you've sat through a school Christmas play involving **a jellyfish, three donkeys, a**

pineapple, and at least one child loudly announcing they need the loo mid-recital.

...and that's the point.

Children don't care if it's Yule or Christmas. They care that it's **magical**. They care that they get to be part of something, whether they're dressed as a star, an angel, or a rogue sheep with glitter on their elbows. They care that you clap when they forget their line but beam anyway. They care that there's a tree and lights and a sense that something is **happening**.

So we make it happen, for them and for ourselves.

We blend. We wrap cinnamon sticks in ribbon and hang stockings over rune-marked hearths. We read them the story of the sun's return and also, somehow, squeeze in The Snowman and a sing-along to "Last Christmas."

Because magic isn't about being pure and perfect. It's about being **present**. It's about saying: *yes, my love, it's both*. It's everything. It's ours.

Now, in case it hasn't become clear already, I don't mind what you believe, or don't believe, at this time of year. I've celebrated Yule with druids in snowy fields and danced around solstice bonfires with people who weren't entirely sure why they were there, other than someone mentioned cider and a chance to wear a cloak.

I've also attended Christmas carol services with friends whose idea of spirituality mostly involves crying during *Love Actually* and buying bath salts for people they barely know.

In every single case, **the point was the same**: to **gather**, to **laugh**, to remember that we belong to each other, even if we have different ways of saying it.

The important thing isn't the name of the holiday. It's that we celebrate the turning of the wheel, because it turns whether we notice or not, and it turns *better* when we mark it with love, food, and sometimes, yes, even a little chaos.

So if your neighbour has fairy lights blinking to the rhythm of Wham! and you have a Yule log burning beside a pile of hand-foraged pinecones blessed at the full moon, invite them over anyway. Share the cider. Share the stories. Share the fact that you both once set fire to something accidentally while trying to be festive. That is the real spirit of the season.

The Great Midwinter Feast (or... "We're Eating *What* This Year?")

Let's talk food.

Oh, food.

If you ask five people what their essential Christmas/Yule dish is, you'll get seven different answers and at least one impassioned monologue about stuffing. You know what? That's marvellous.

In this house alone we've had:

- **Turkey**, naturally, centre-stage and basted like it's going to win a beauty contest.

- **Nut roast**, for our more herbivorous guests—rich with mushrooms and walnuts and smugness.

- **Salmon en-croute**, from the year I tried to be "elegant and continental" and ended up using a witch's rune to summon the courage to roll puff pastry while weeping.

- And one year, **a giant cauliflower**, because a visiting cousin had gone vegan and possibly joined a cult that thought cheese was a tool of the patriarchy.

The point is, the **centrepiece is negotiable**.

But what is *not* negotiable, what must never, ever be forgotten, is the **Yorkshire pudding**.

The Gospel According to Yorkshire

I don't care if you're eating turkey, tofu, or tinned beans while wearing a holly crown and humming "Greensleeves"... **there must be Yorkshires**.

Yorkshire puddings are more than just a vessel for gravy. They are **the edible embodiment of hope**. They begin as almost nothing, milk, flour, eggs, and then, with heat and love and probably a little shouting, they rise.

What could be more magical than that?

I've seen them served with roast beef, nut roast, and even, once, as a dessert (filled with brandy cream and orange zest... questionable yes, but strangely effective). The only rule is: **make more than you think you'll need**. Because if you run out of Yorkshire puddings during Christmas dinner, you may as well pack it all in and move to a cave.

Also, and this is important, Yorkshire puddings are the great equaliser. You can serve goose, gammon, or a lentil terrine in the shape of Stonehenge. If there are Yorkshires on the plate, *everyone* feels seen. Even the picky cousin who's only come because they heard you were doing homemade cranberry sauce.

So yes. You can be a Green Witch or a glitter-loving reindeer wrangler or someone who just enjoys a good stuffing ball. You can celebrate Yule, Christmas, Saturnalia, or "That time of year I panic-buy socks." But **if**

you want a table where everyone feels welcome, make sure there's laughter, something warm in the oven, and a Yorkshire pudding with their name on it. I'll explain how to make them later.

The Ritual of Gathering (with Optional Crackers)

Now, let's not underestimate the power of **ritual**. Ritual, as I often explain to the dog, is just a repeated act done with purpose. It doesn't need incense or Latin, though if that's your thing, light it up and chant away. A ritual can be as simple as setting the table with intention.

I lay the table with candles, pinecones, a little bowl of dried orange slices, and a stack of questionable jokes hidden inside crackers. I do this not because it looks good on Instagram (it doesn't, my cat eats the pinecones), but because it marks the day. It says: *something is happening*. This meal is a spell, and you, dear witchlings, are part of it.

Whether your guests are children in paper crowns, friends still in pyjamas, elderly neighbours who miss the noise of their old kitchen, or a lone auntie who just wants to talk about The Queen (may she rest in peace), the ritual works. You're saying: you belong. You're welcome. You're fed.

So, What Are We Celebrating?

Everything.

We're celebrating **the return of the sun**, even if we're doing it under a plastic star from a supermarket.

We're celebrating **family**, chosen or born or picked up along the way like interesting pebbles.

We're celebrating **food**, and the miracle that we made it to the end of another year still laughing (or at least snorting into our wine).

We're celebrating **magic**, the everyday kind. The "how did I survive that week in November" kind. The "I grew this rosemary myself and now it's in my stuffing" kind.

We're celebrating **us**, together, in the mess and wonder of it all.

So here we are, plates cleared (or in some cases still being battled with), cheeks flushed, and the children now mysteriously sticky despite being nowhere near dessert. There may be wrapping paper in your hair. Someone may have mistaken the cat's bed for a footstool. You might be sitting quietly by the fire, glass of something mulled in hand, wondering how on earth you managed to cook a full feast with only two working roasting tins and a packet of emergency parsnips. But you did it. It matters.

Because what we're really doing here, amid the roasties and ribbon, the carols and candle wax, is **weaving the old ways into the new world**.

That, my loves, is what modern witchcraft really is: it's not about rejecting the now, it's about recognising where the ancient still whispers through the present. It's there in the lighting of a candle on the darkest night. It's there in the laughter around the table. It's there in the way we make something from what we've got and call it holy.

… and it's very much there in Yorkshire puddings. (Sorry, I'm not letting that go.)

You don't have to pick a side. You don't have to explain your beliefs to every relative who wants to know or why someone left a sprig of rosemary under their napkin. You don't have to correct people when they say "Merry Christmas" while you were halfway through saying "Blessed Yule." Just smile. They mean the same thing in the end: **I wish you joy. I wish you warmth. I'm glad you're here.**

So whether you're a cauldron-stirring crone, a festive chaos goblin with a glitter glue problem, or just someone who likes candles and carbs, this is your season. Midwinter is **for all of us.**

It's for the little ones in cardboard crowns and tea-towel headdresses. It's for the parents trying to look excited about yet another Lego set. It's for those of us who miss someone at the table this year, and light a candle in their name. It's for the loud, the quiet, the believers and the curious.

… and if you're doing it "wrong," darlings, I promise you… you're probably doing it perfectly.

The Night Before – The Calm Before the Cauldron

There comes a moment, usually sometime around 8:42 p.m. on Christmas Eve, when the kitchen is quiet, the dog is asleep under the table, and you realise, with a mixture of dread and glee—that tomorrow, you are responsible for orchestrating the biggest meal of the year.

But here's the secret, my darlings: **tomorrow only goes well if tonight gets a bit organised**. That doesn't mean panic. It doesn't mean spreadsheets (unless you're into that sort of thing). It means lighting a candle, pouring a small something festive, and gently preparing your kitchen like a spellcaster laying out her charms before a ritual.

Let's start with the **turkey**—or whatever beast or blessed bean loaf you're roasting. If you're brining your bird, now's the time. Submerge that plump poultry in a bath of salt, herbs, citrus slices, and intent. Whisper a few kind words to it. ("Thank you for your service. Please don't dry out.") If you're not brining, just take it out of its packaging and pop it on a tray in the fridge, uncovered, to dry the skin slightly. This helps achieve that golden, crispy exterior that makes people gasp approvingly.

Next, the **vegetables**. Peel your potatoes, parsnips, and carrots. Honestly, future you will thank you for this. No one wants to be elbow-deep in peelings on Christmas morning. Store the peeled veg in cold water in the fridge—labelled, if your household includes tricksy family members who think raw carrots are a midnight snack.

Brussels sprouts, those much-maligned little cabbages, can also be trimmed and halved now. Toss them in a bit of olive oil, salt, and pepper, and keep them in a container ready to go. If you're feeling extra, chop the chestnuts too. They don't mind the cold.

Then comes the **cranberry sauce**. This is an overachiever of a condiment and gets better with a bit of time. Simmer your cranberries with sugar, orange zest, and a whisper of cinnamon tonight, and by tomorrow they'll be practically glowing with smug flavour. Store it in a pretty bowl with a lid, ready for its moment.

Stuffing mix can be sautéed and assembled—onions, garlic, breadcrumbs, sage—and shaped into balls if you like. I like mine rustic and slightly asymmetrical, like edible moons. Chill them overnight on a tray. Don't worry, they won't wander.

Now's also a good time to **lay out your tools and trays**. Find the roasting pans. Check the gravy jug hasn't mysteriously vanished (again). Set the table if you're a Virgo. Fold the napkins if you're a Capricorn. Light another candle if you're me.

Yorkshire Pudding batter.

Needs to be made the night before to avoid the panic of *"Holy S#*t I forgot the Yorkshires"*

Ingredients (makes 12 medium puddings):

- **140g (1 cup) plain flour**

- **4 large eggs**

- **200ml (scant 1 cup) whole milk**

- **Big pinch of salt**

- **Sunflower oil, goose fat, or dripping**

In a large bowl or jug, whisk the eggs and milk together first (it creates more air). Add the flour and salt gradually, whisking until smooth. It should be the consistency of single cream. Cover and **let it rest**, this is crucial. A rested batter puffs better and tastes richer, like it's been dreaming of gravy all day. After 10 minutes cover jug with cling film or foil and put in fridge – but don't forget it!

Most importantly: breathe. The feast begins not tomorrow, but tonight, with calm hands, a stirring spoon, and the quiet knowledge that you're already halfway to a magical meal.

8:00 AM – Rousing the Bird and the Witch

The alarm rings. Or the cat sits on your face. Or a child bursts through the bedroom door wielding a plastic wand and shouting that Santa's been and you simply *must* come see. Either way, it's Christmas morning. You are awake, and there's no going back. While the rest of the household is dreaming of pudding, presents, or possibly plotting their attack on the Quality Street chocolate tin, you, dear witch, are about to tiptoe, somewhat bleary-eyed, into the kitchen to begin the day's most sacred rite: feeding the people you love **without completely losing your mind**.

Let's be honest. If you've got **young children**, you've not *just* woken up. Oh no. You were likely pulled from your solstice dreams at some ungodly hour, say 5:47am, by the unmistakable sound of a stocking being violently dismantled in the hallway, followed by shrieks of joy, a demand for batteries, and the beginning of a 14-hour campaign to eat chocolate coins for every meal. Your day has already included locating a missing shoe, refereeing a Lego-related dispute, and pretending to be amazed by a toy you purchased yourself three weeks ago... and it's not even light outside.

In the spirit of seasonal honesty, I must admit that I occasionally begin Christmas morning **a little slower** than usual. One mulled wine becomes three you see the night before. You sit by the fire with your feet up, whispering to your mince pie, and the next thing you know, it's midnight and you're explaining the symbolism of holly to a confused-looking cousin. You tell yourself it's fine. It's Christmas. You're a witch. You're made of fire and honey and willpower.

But come 8:00 AM, that festive magic can feel more like festive fog.

Yet, *this is the moment.* This slightly hazy, slightly chaotic, slightly-too-warm moment is when the magic truly begins. You make your way to the kitchen. You pass the pine-scented living room strewn with wrapping paper and dreams. You dodge a rogue bauble. You whisper good morning to the kettle.

Because even though you may be a little tired (or mildly hungover), and even though you're sharing your kitchen with toy packaging, charging cables, and Grandma loudly demanding to know where the children have hidden the toilet paper, you know what must be done.

You take a breath. You claim your wooden spoon like a wand. You light a candle on the windowsill. The house hasn't quite noticed you're up yet. This is your chance to centre yourself, to greet the day with a little intention before the onions need chopping and the gravy needs conjuring.

So no matter how your morning began, with chaos or cuddles or clove-scented regret, know this: you are exactly where you need to be. The cauldron awaits. The feast will follow... and you, slightly dishevelled but full of love, are absolutely the right witch for the job.

The very first act? **Liberate the turkey.**

That majestic, mildly terrifying bird has been sleeping in your fridge like a frosty ghost, and now it needs to rise, quite literally, to room temperature. Take it out of its wrapping and place it gently in its roasting tin, breast-side up. (If you're unsure which side is which, the breast is the smooth, plump bit, not the bit that looks like it might chase you through a forest.)

Now, some people will tell you this resting period is optional. It is not. It's essential for even cooking. A cold bird straight from the fridge will roast unevenly, drying out the outside while the inside remains ominously raw. We're not here for that kind of drama.

Cover it loosely with foil and place it somewhere calm, out of direct sunlight, away from curious pets, and ideally not somewhere in the presence of Lego. Let it come up to temperature for at least **an hour and a half**, depending on size. (We're assuming a 5kg turkey here, which means about 3 hours in the oven at 180°C later.)

While the turkey adjusts to its new reality, you, too, must **ready yourself**.

Put on the kettle. Make tea. Or coffee. Or a restorative potion involving orange peel, cinnamon and just the tiniest shot of whisky. Light a candle near the stove. Take out your favourite spoon. Open the back door for a moment and breathe in the crisp morning air. If you're lucky, you'll hear birdsong. If you're really lucky, you won't hear anyone asking what time presents are.

This is your grounding moment, the calm before the stuffing storm. The turkey is your centrepiece, yes, but **you** are the true magic behind the feast. So wrap yourself in something cosy, put on your playlist (mine starts with Enya and ends with Elton John—don't judge), and spend a few quiet minutes reconnecting with your kitchen.

Now's also a good time to **double-check your prep list**. Open the fridge and greet your vegetables like old friends. "Hello, my sweet parsnips. Good morning, smug little cranberry sauce." Run through your timeline. Make sure the butter is out. (Room temperature butter is a Christmas miracle in itself.)

And then? Take a moment to cast this small spell, just to start the day on the right foot:

"May pots not boil over, may tempers stay cool,
May all those who gather remember the Yule.."

9:00 AM – Preheat the Portal, Butter the Beast

Right then. You've had your tea (or something stronger), you've lit a candle, and the turkey is now reclining on the counter like a Victorian aunt waiting for someone to bring her a sherry. You, dear witch, are ready for the next step in the Midwinter miracle.

It's oven time.

At 9:00 AM sharp, you must do something that shall summon a whole day of good fortune: **preheat your oven**. Yes, it seems simple. Yes, it's a button press. But may I gently remind you—especially if you're still wearing your dressing gown and talking to the dog like it's your sous-chef—that this is no ordinary oven today. This is the **portal to the sacred hearth**. This is where alchemy happens. This is the stage upon which poultry becomes legend.

So preheat it you must, and at precisely **180°C** (or 160°C if your oven runs hot, or fan-assisted, or inhabited by temperamental fire elementals).

While that's warming up, it's time to **prepare the turkey**. This is the moment many fear. But fear not—we are witches. We roast with intent.

First, remove any giblets. If you've bought a bird with the surprise packet of inner organs still tucked inside like a particularly grim Christmas cracker prize, now's the time to deal with it. You can use the giblets for stock, or offer them to a grateful pet, or—as I do—stare at them thoughtfully and then quietly bin them.

Place your turkey on a rack in a sturdy roasting tin. This raises it up, lets the hot air swirl like a cauldron current, and stops the bottom going soggy. If you don't have a rack, scrunch up some foil or use halved onions underneath. Very rustic. Very earthy. Very "I meant to do this."

Now, **seasoning**. Be generous. Salt and pepper, obviously, but also herbs—**sage, thyme, rosemary**—and citrus if you like it. I often pop half an orange inside the cavity, along with a bay leaf and a few garlic cloves. Not because it does anything too dramatic flavour-wise, but because it makes me feel competent and smells like I know what I'm doing. Which is most of cooking, really.

Next, **butter the beast**. Softened butter, maybe mixed with herbs or lemon zest, goes over the skin. Gently rub it in like you're apologising for what's about to happen. If you want to be very fancy, you can slip it under the skin on the breast—but only if you've had enough sleep and emotional resilience to manage the eerie texture.

Once buttered and seasoned, cover the turkey **loosely with foil**, shiny side in. This keeps it moist while roasting and stops the skin from catching fire before it's time to shine.

And finally, before it goes in—**speak your spell**. You can say it aloud or just murmur into the roasting tin:

"By rosemary's strength and lemon's cheer,
Let this feast bring warmth and cheer.
As this bird roasts golden and true,
May love and peace fill all we do."

9:30 AM – Into the Oven and Into the Fray

Right. The turkey is buttered, blessed, and bewildered, but ready. The oven is hot, your spoon is sacred, and hopefully by now someone else has taken over the task of managing the sugar-high children who are recreating the Nativity with Lego.

It is time.

The turkey goes in.

Yes, this is the moment, the moment when all other moments pivot around one large, uncooked bird entering a hot portal of transformation. Open the oven door, slide her in (carefully! Arms are not fireproof, even at Yule), and say a little something. Some people prefer kitchen timers. I prefer a spell:

"May this bird cook true and golden,
Not too dry, not too cold'n.
Juicy leg and crispy skin,
Let the feast of love begin."

The oven door shuts with a gentle whoomph, and just like that, we've begun the long, slow march toward dinner. Your home will soon smell like hope. Hope, sage, butter, and slight panic.

Now, you may think the next few hours are free time. You may think you can sit down, sip some tea, and read a book.

Ha. Adorable.

Here's what really happens: this is the window for serious prep. Because while your bird begins her transformation, *everything else* needs to get ready for its big moment. So let's talk potatoes.

You've already peeled them the night before, haven't you? Clever you. So now: parboiling.

Put a big pot of salted water on the hob. Once it's boiling like a witch's brew (fitting), add the potatoes. Let them bubble for 10 minutes, or until they're just soft enough that a knife enters with a bit of resistance but doesn't split them like a party guest on their third snowball.

Drain them well and, this is crucial, *rough them up.* Shake them in the colander until the edges look scruffy. That scruffiness is the key to crunchy golden roasties later. It's science. Or magic. Or both.

Lay them on a tray to cool and dry out a little. You can even sprinkle a bit of flour over them and pretend you're doing something very technical.

Next, while the potatoes are relaxing, turn your attention to the *stuffing balls*. These you prepared last night, so really you're just rearranging them on a tray and congratulating yourself. They can go into the oven later, but give them a quick check for shape and seasoning. If one looks like it's trying to escape the tray, gently nudge it back into line. This is not the time for rebellion.

If you're feeling especially efficient, now is a good moment to make a *second cup of tea (or cheeky sherry).* Why not? It's Christmas. The turkey is roasting, the potatoes are fluffed, and you, dear witch, are halfway to greatness.

10:00 AM – Root Magic and Seditious Sprouts

So here we are at **10:00 AM**, and the kitchen is starting to hum like a cauldron full of anticipation (and maybe a bit of BBC Radio 2). The turkeys in the oven, sending out warm, buttery prayers through the house, and you've successfully parboiled your potatoes without crying or summoning anything unholy. You're doing *brilliantly*.

Now, we turn our attention to that ancient art form known as: *prepping everything else.*

We begin with the *root vegetables*, those loyal companions of winter: carrots, parsnips, and perhaps the occasional sweet potato if you're feeling modern and controversial. These are your earthy, grounded staples. The soul food of the soil. Just like witches, they do best when lightly oiled and occasionally roasted. (Ha!)

You may have peeled them last night, good for you, or you may be doing it now, muttering about how carrots are oddly shaped and shouldn't be allowed to be this smug about it. Either way, once peeled and chopped (carrots into friendly little batons, parsnips into those flamboyant spears they love to be), toss them into a big bowl.

Add a *glug of olive oil, a sprinkle of salt, a crack of black pepper,* and here's where the magic happens: *a drizzle of honey or maple syrup.* Trust me. It caramelises in the oven and makes the parsnips sing. Add a pinch of dried thyme or rosemary if you're feeling herbal and toss it all together like you're blessing them with joy.

Next, lay them on a roasting tray, one layer only! Overcrowded veg are cranky and steam instead of roast, and nobody likes a soggy parsnip. You can cover these with foil and leave them on standby to go in the oven later. Or, if oven space is at a premium (and it *will* be), assign them a roasting slot while the turkey rests later on.

Now, brace yourself. Because it's time to face... *the sprouts.*

Yes. The Brussels sprout, that tiny cabbage that people love to hate. I, personally, think they get a bad rap. Sprouts, when treated kindly, are delightful. But if you boil them to grey mush, they *will* haunt your dinner like a farting ghost.

So: trim the ends, halve them, and toss them with oil, salt, and—if you're feeling frisky—a bit of crushed garlic or chopped chestnut. Some people like a touch of pancetta or even pomegranate molasses (which is delicious and also a fantastic sentence to say aloud in a country accent). Roast them, don't boil them. They deserve it. *You* deserve it.

By now, you'll be looking at your trays of prepped vegetables, your rising turkey aroma, and your still-reasonably-clean apron, and thinking: "I'm actually doing this."

Yes, you are... and you're doing it *brilliantly*.

10:30 AM – Setting the Table (Intentionally, Magically, and Without Crying Over the Napkins)

Right, we've reached **10:30 AM**, and now that your vegetables are prepped and the turkey is steaming its buttery prayers through the kitchen air, it's time for what some might consider the *calm* part of the process. Ha.

Setting the table.

Now, I know some people rush this bit. "Just chuck the cutlery out, Bea," they say, waving a fork like a wand with no direction. "No one cares." And to those people I say, kindly, and with a smile, **are you mad?**

Because this isn't just setting a table. It's laying a scene. It's building a portal. This table will witness joy, laughter, eye-rolls, overeating, over-sharing, and at least one person knocking over a gravy boat in slow motion. It deserves to be special.

Let's begin.

First, clear it. I mean really clear it. Remove the junk mail, the half-finished craft projects, the Lego shepherd from last night's living room rehearsal. Wipe it down with something fragrant, lemon balm or rosemary water is nice, or just a damp cloth and a hopeful attitude.

Then, choose your tablecloth (or not, bare wood is rustic and deeply respectable). I like to layer a deep midnight-blue runner over the centre of mine. It looks like the night sky. You can scatter it with pinecones, dried orange slices, bay leaves, or if you're living dangerously, a little glitter to look like stars. (You'll still be finding it in July, but it's festive, so we forgive.)

Now for the place settings. I'm a big fan of mismatched plates and vintage cutlery, like a coven tea party from another century. Napkins don't need to match either, but do **fold them with intent**. A simple triangle. A loving tuck. Whisper a wish into each one. (Even if it's just, "May you not end up covered in cranberry.")

Add name cards if you like, especially helpful for large gatherings or families who argue over who sits where. Do look in my book The Witch's Botanical Apothecary about the Herb Dittany of Crete, as there is fun to be had.

Candles. Always candles. Tall ones if you've got them, tea lights if you don't. Pop them in jam jars, crystal glasses, hollowed-out apples, anything that feels beautiful and vaguely fire-safe. I usually anoint mine with a drop of cinnamon.

Music? Optional. I suggest something instrumental until the sherry kicks in.

Just like that, your table is ready, not just for eating, but for gathering, feasting, storytelling, and the odd overenthusiastic cracker duel.

11:00 AM – Puddings, Parboiling, and Possibly Prosecco

Now, by **11:00 AM**, the house should be smelling like **the best kind of spell**, buttery, herby, with undertones of ambition and lightly frayed nerves. If you've timed it well, you've already prepped the roots, tamed the sprouts, and whispered into your napkins. The turkey is cheerfully roasting. The children are briefly distracted by new toys. You, dear witch, are doing marvellously.

But now it's time to tackle two of the more misunderstood yet magical parts of the festive feast: the puddings and the parboiling. Depending on your audience and level of stress, possibly a small bottle of prosecco with a straw in it.

Let's begin with the puddings.

The Pudding Ritual

If you've made a **traditional Christmas pudding**, it's probably been maturing in a cupboard for weeks like a Victorian ghost with brandy breath. Good for you. All you need to do now is steam it gently for **two hours** to warm it through. If you haven't then see the section on Christmas Pudding.

Take a deep, calming breath and locate your pudding basin. Place it in a saucepan with a few inches of gently simmering water (don't let it boil dry or it will sulk). Lid on. Simmer. Do not panic. You have time. It knows what to do.

If, like me, you sometimes forget the traditional pudding or prefer a Chocolate Yule Log or witchy honey cake, now's the time to finish that off. Ganache the log. Glaze the toffee. Whisper "please set properly" to your cheesecake.

Remember: not everyone loves Christmas pud. That's why you also make something chocolatey, something creamy, and possibly something cold with fruit in it that everyone says they'll eat but don't. This is not failure, it is hospitality.

Parboiling, Part Deux

Next, we return to the sacred art of potato parboiling, if you didn't do it earlier (or if you've just realised you forgot the second tray of spuds). The principle is the same: peel, chop, boil for ten minutes, then rough them up like they owe you rent.

Lay them out to dry. Give them a moment. You don't want to rush a potato, it's the quiet type, the dependable introvert of the root world.

Also at this point, take a glance at your oven timetable. The turkey has probably been in for around 90 minutes (if it's a 5kg bird), which means you're about halfway. Baste it, lovingly. Say something encouraging. "You're doing so well, darling." Yes, to the bird.

Optional Prosecco Break

Now, if everything is under control, and even if it isn't, this is the moment for a **small glass of something sparkly**. A reward. A breather. A toast to your own culinary prowess. Somehow it's even better if someone else pours it for you. Hint hint!

Sip gently, stretch your back, and light a fresh candle on the windowsill.

You've earned it, witch.

11:30 AM – The Sacred Symphony of Gravy and Giblets

Now listen, I don't want to alarm anyone, but we have officially reached **the Gravy Hour**.

This is not a drill.

Because no matter how perfectly your turkey roasts, no matter how crisp your parsnips or how lovingly your sprouts have caramelised, *without proper gravy*, you may as well have served a warm salad and left the room.

Gravy is more than just a sauce. It's *the elixir, the binding spell, the liquid bridge between dry and divine.* Today, dear witch, *you* are the conduit through which this brown magic flows.

Let's begin with the giblets.

Yes, *those*. The unloved collection of turkey innards that have been sitting quietly in a bag in your fridge, waiting to fulfil their noble purpose. If you've made stock with them overnight, brava! You are a high priestess of preparation. If not, we're still in business.

Place the giblets (except the liver, which can go back in the fridge or quietly into the bin, too bitter for gravy) in a saucepan. Add:

- Half an onion

- A carrot (snapped in half, no need for fuss)

- A celery stick if you're fancy

- A bay leaf

- A few peppercorns

- A sprig of thyme or rosemary (if you've got one lying about, looking mystical)

Cover with water, bring to a simmer, and let it bubble quietly while you work on other things. This is your gravy base stock. Let it hum in the background like a low chant.

Now, turn your attention to the roasting tin. Peek in on your turkey, it should be browning beautifully now. Baste it again like it's a sacred ritual (because it is), and then, using a spoon or small ladle, *scoop some of the lovely fat and juices* into a clean pan.

You are now entering the **gravy zone**. Deep breaths. You've got this.

To that pan of glorious fat and juice, add a spoonful of flour (plain, not self-raising, gravy is not cake). Stir. Keep stirring. Cook the flour out for a minute or two until it smells less like raw panic and more like roasted possibility.

Now slowly, **slowly**, ladle in your giblet stock. Stir after each addition, muttering gentle encouragements. The gravy will thicken, darken, and begin to **smell like everything good about December**.

Taste it. Adjust the seasoning. Some witches add a splash of red wine or sherry. Others, a dab of cranberry jelly or a teaspoon of marmite (I do!). I once knew a woman who swore by Worcestershire sauce and swore like a sailor if you questioned it. The point is, *make it yours.*

At this point, you may wish to strain it, or not. Rustic is charming. Let it bubble gently on the hob. You'll reheat it later, just before serving, but now it's ready… and so are you.

12:00 PM – Pigs, Blankets, and the Oven Tetris Begins

Right then. It's midday, and you've made it to the point where the turkey is halfway bronzed like a holidaying pensioner, the gravy is humming peacefully on the back burner, and you've consumed just enough prosecco to feel brave but not reckless. Excellent.

Now we face one of the great logistical challenges of the modern kitchen: *the oven is full, the fridge is full, your brain is full, and yet somehow… nothing's finished.*

Welcome to *Oven Tetris*, that sacred moment in the cooking ritual where everything needs to be hot at the same time, but your oven has the real estate capacity of a shoebox. Not to worry. You are a witch. We *thrive* under creative constraints.

Let's start with one of the most beloved components of the entire feast: **pigs in blankets**.

Even those who don't eat meat get a twinkle in their eye when you say the name. They're not just sausages. They're an *event*. A golden snuggle of salt and joy. If you've made them fresh, wrapping chipolatas in streaky bacon with the tenderness of a lover tucking someone into bed, well done. If they're pre-packed, we say nothing and honour your wisdom.

Lay them out on a baking tray with a sprig of rosemary and a whisper of honey or mustard if you're feeling adventurous. Then place them in the oven, but where? Aha. This is where the rotation method comes into play. (no it's not a form of contraception)

Here's what you do:

1. **Check your turkey.** If it's looking golden and the internal temperature is approaching 65°C (149°F), you're getting close. Keep it in until it hits 74°C (165°F) at the thickest part of the thigh. If it's already there, congratulations, you now enter *Resting Turkey Mode* (more on that at 1:00 PM).

2. Make space for sides. Start sliding in the trays of roast potatoes, carrots, parsnips, and our dear pigs in blankets. Stack smart. Use the bottom shelf for things that want to crisp, like roasties. Keep stuffing balls and pigs higher up, where they'll colour and sizzle.

3. If you have a second oven or even a countertop plug-in thing (what I call the "Goblin Oven"), now is the time to use it.

This is also the moment when things get hot, literally and emotionally. You will sweat. You will mutter. You will look at your kitchen timer like it has personally betrayed you. But you will triumph.

Also, bonus tip from an old hedge witch I once met in Norfolk: "When the pigs go in, the prosecco comes out." Wise woman. Refresh your glass. Hydration is vital.

Soon, your kitchen will smell of bacon and sage and that impossible-to-name aroma that only arrives when all the foods of home are cooking at once. It's memory, comfort, and low-level panic in scent form.

Important witchy tip:
Take out your Yorkshire Pudding batter from the fridge about **30–45 minutes before you plan to use it** so it can return to room temperature. Cold batter poured into hot fat can *still work*, but room temperature batter hits hot oil like a potion meeting the cauldron, **poof! Instant rise.**

12:30 PM – Basting, Brussels, and the Brief Existential Crisis

At this stage of the day, the *aroma* in your house has reached such celestial heights that even the most cynical teenager has wandered into the kitchen and mumbled, "When's lunch?" You will not answer this question. You will instead hand them a carrot stick and gently redirect them to another room. You are busy performing a midwinter miracle.

Let's take it from the top, literally.

The Final Baste

By now, the turkey is likely on its last stretch. If your bird is nearing perfection, it may already be resting quietly in a foil tent somewhere, glowing with internal smugness. But if it's still in the oven, this is your **last official baste** before carving.

Use a ladle or spoon and give it a final luxurious wash in its own delicious juices. Speak kindly to it. You've been through a lot together.

Check its temperature one last time, if it's hit 74°C (165°F), take it out and let it rest for at least an hour, wrapped in foil and a clean towel. That rest is not optional. It's where all the juice magic happens. Carving too early is a crime against poultry.

Now we move on to the Brussels sprouts.

Brussels Sprouts: The Comeback Kids

Here's the thing. Sprouts were the shame of Christmas dinners past, boiled to oblivion, served with a threat. But we have learned. We have grown. We now **roast** them.

Hopefully you've prepped them earlier, halved, tossed with olive oil, a crack of sea salt, maybe some crushed garlic or diced pancetta or chestnuts if you're feeling fancy. You can even drizzle them with a splash of balsamic vinegar and maple syrup if you want them to flirt with your tastebuds.

Slide them into the oven on the top shelf. You want that **caramelised kiss of heat** on every flat little face. Stir halfway through so they roast evenly.

Let them crisp. Let them shine. Let your aunt who "hates sprouts" try one and suddenly realise she's been wrong for decades. It's a powerful moment. We light a candle when it happens.

The Inevitable Wobble

Now, somewhere around this time, *you will have a wobble*. Possibly small. Possibly large. You'll glance at the clock, notice the slightly charred edge of a parsnip, realise someone forgot to lay out the cranberry sauce, and wonder aloud whether this whole seasonal cooking thing is worth the trouble.

Let me tell you now: **it is**.

This little spiral? It's part of the ritual. Like forgetting to buy foil or realising you need five more pans than you own. The wobble means you care. It means you want this to be special. It is.

So take a breath. Light a candle. Stir the gravy. Glance at your well-laid table, your resting turkey, and the pigs in blankets crackling away. You are doing beautifully.

If all else fails, have a nibble of stuffing. That's what it's for.

1:00 PM – Turkey Resting, Tray Juggling, and Strategic Mince Pie Deployment

You've made it to the halfway mark between lunch and madness. Take a breath. Sip your lukewarm tea or revive your fizz, and look upon your kingdom: roasting trays lined up like soldiers, gravy bubbling like a philosopher in a heated debate, and your turkey, oh glorious bird, *resting like royalty under a foil duvet.*

Let's talk turkey first.

Turkey in Recovery

That bird has done her part. After several hours bathing in herb butter and positive intentions, she now lies peacefully in the corner like a sun-dazed queen bee. Let her rest. I mean it.

This is the moment her juices redistribute, her texture settles, and she becomes the succulent centrepiece you swore she'd be when you woke up this morning dreaming about burnt wings. Don't peek. Don't prod. Just whisper thank you and let her snooze.

The resting time also means, thank heavens, you now have *oven space.* Which brings us to...

The Great Tray Migration

Now begins the sacred and slightly swear-filled game of Tray Juggling.

Let's assess:

- Roast potatoes? These go in now if they aren't already.

- Carrots and parsnips? Check. Slide them onto the middle shelf, uncovered.

- Stuffing balls and pigs in blankets? They want golden crispness. Top shelf, where the heat licks like dragon's breath.

Keep a note of timings. Potatoes and pigs need around 40–50 minutes. Roots, about 30–40 minutes. Sprouts need only 25–30, depending on how charred you like your redemption arcs.

Pro tip: Rotate the trays. Shift top to middle and middle to top every 15 minutes or so. It helps with even browning and makes you look extremely competent to nosy kitchen visitors. Bonus: It gives you a reason to banish said visitors again.

Mince Pie Mischief

Now listen carefully, this is where the real witchcraft begins.

If small hands or idle adults are starting to circle like seagulls, deploy the mince pies. Yes. It's early. No, you're not supposed to serve dessert yet. But this is a tactical offering, not a pudding, but a *diversion spell*.

Warm a few in the oven (bottom shelf, keep them discreet) and hand them out with stern warnings not to spoil their appetites. They will. That's fine. It's Yule. Everything is permitted.

This is also a great moment to press someone into *table-checking duty*. Cutlery aligned? Crackers in place? Enough wine glasses for unexpected uncles? Let them feel useful. It will distract them from asking when dinner is ready.

Because you, dear witch, **are not finished yet.**

1:30 PM – Sauce Sorcery, Sprout Alchemy, and One Final Deep Breath

We've entered the **golden hour** of Christmas dinner: everything smells done, but *nothing is actually done yet.* It's a liminal space. A moment between roasting and feasting. You, dear witch, are its guardian.

This is where *sauce magic* comes into full force, and when we bless the Brussels with their final char.

Let's begin with the sauces. Yes, plural.

The Sauce Trifecta

You will now create, or artfully reheat, what I refer to as the *Holy Trinity of Festive Condiments.*

1. Cranberry Sauce

If you made your own: gold star, you overachiever. If it came from a jar, you still win, just decant it into a rustic bowl and add **a grating of orange zest**. That's called *alchemical transformation*. Stir it and whisper:

"Berry red, both sweet and tart,
May you warm each winter heart."

2. Bread Sauce

This is an ancient delight, invented to confuse guests and comfort introverts. If you've prepped it earlier, now's the time to warm it gently on the stove. Add a splash of cream, a grind of pepper, and possibly a clove if you're feeling bold. Stir lovingly. Ignore anyone who asks what it actually is, but if they do...

Ah, **bread sauce**, that gloriously odd, deeply comforting, thoroughly British Witchy concoction that no one quite understands until they try it. To make it, start by gently heating about 300ml of milk in a saucepan with a halved onion, a couple of cloves poked into it like tiny magical studs, a bay leaf, and a pinch of nutmeg. Let it infuse slowly, don't rush it, until the kitchen starts to smell like Christmas Eve in a Dickens novel. After about 15–20 minutes, fish out the flavourings and stir in a large handful of white breadcrumbs (stale bread is best—like most good spells, this one honours leftovers). Add a knob of butter, salt and pepper to taste, and if you're feeling luxurious, a splash of cream. Stir gently until it thickens to a cosy, porridge-like consistency. It should be soft, savoury, and inexplicably perfect with roast poultry. Serve warm, and ignore the cousin who asks if it's "just soggy bread." You know better.

3. Horseradish sauce

This fiery little sibling at the festive table who turns up late, steals the spotlight, and makes your nose tingle in the best possible way. It's not just a condiment; it's a *reckoning*. Made from freshly grated horseradish root (or the reliable jarred stuff if you value your knuckles), stirred into a mix of thick cream, a dab of mustard, a whisper of vinegar, and a pinch of salt, it delivers a bright, bold punch that cuts through the richness of any roast like a truth spell through polite conversation. It's the sauce that wakes people up. That makes quiet uncles suddenly comment on the weather with urgency. That sends a little firework straight to your sinuses and makes you feel *triumphantly alive.* Serve it cold, in a pretty dish, and watch it transform meat, potatoes, and even reluctant vegetables into something with purpose.

Line them up. Lay tiny spoons beside each like ceremonial tools. You are anointing the meal with flavour and meaning. You are, in this moment, the Sauce Priestess.

Sprout Alchemy

Your Brussels should now be nearing peak transformation, crisped and caramelised, their bitter past banished. Lift the tray. Gaze upon them. Perhaps you're tempted to nibble one.

Do it.

Go on.

Hot sprout, crisp garlic, tiny crunch of sea salt. You're welcome.

Toss in some toasted walnuts or pomegranate seeds if you're feeling extra radiant. Or don't. You've already won.

Transfer them to a warmed dish, cover loosely, and place somewhere visible, because these, my friend, are no longer a side dish. They are a statement.

One Final Deep Breath

Now pause.

Yes, just for a moment. Step back. Glance at your table. Smell the air. Notice the glow on the turkey's foil, the candles flickering with barely restrained excitement, the fact that a roast potato tray has left a perfect rectangle of oil on the worktop. It's all part of it. The magic. The muddle. The miracle.

You've done so much. You're nearly there. Take a breath. Stretch your shoulders. Top up your glass. Light that last candle on the sill.

2:00 PM – Carving the Bird and Summoning the Masses

The hour of reckoning is upon us. You've stirred, basted, chopped, steamed, whispered incantations at your stuffing balls, and even survived the sprout mutiny. You are, quite frankly, **a marvel**.

Now: the **carving of the bird**.

Let's be honest, this part can strike fear into even the most confident kitchen witch. You've lovingly roasted this creature for hours. It's crisped to golden perfection, resting patiently under foil and tea towels. Now you're expected to *dismember it with elegance* while five relatives hover like vultures asking if the gravy is done.

Here's the secret: *confidence and a very sharp knife.*

Unveil your turkey with reverence. The skin should sigh a little when the foil peels back. The juices will shimmer, the meat tender and fragrant. Place the bird on a large wooden board or platter (preferably one that makes you feel like a medieval banqueter or village matriarch).

Now channel your inner ceremonial carver:

1. **Remove the legs first**, cutting through the joint where thigh meets the body. Place them on a serving dish, whole or sliced depending on your flair and your guests' general chewing enthusiasm.

2. Then, **the breast**, slice thick or thin, always against the grain, and let the juices run across the cutting board like a sacred offering to the roast gods.

3. Don't forget the **oysters**, those two magical little morsels tucked near the back of the bird, sweet and tender. These are the cook's reward. You may share, but you are not *obliged* to.

If this all sounds too much? Ask someone else to carve. There's always a cousin with a carving set they got for Christmas three years ago and have been dying to use.

Once carved, cover the platter loosely with foil and place in a **just-warm oven** to keep until serving time.

The Summoning

With your centrepiece ready, it's time to summon the household, like a magical roll call of hungry souls. But this is not a rushed shout up the stairs. No. This is **an event**.

Put on the kettle for the gravy. Light (or relight) the candles on the table. Turn on some soft music, instrumental carols or a bit of folk, if you're feeling enchantingly traditional. Then, with ladle in one hand and a touch of theatre in your voice, declare:

"The table is set,
the feast is hot,
Come forth, my darlings—
and eat the lot."

… and they will come.

From bedrooms, sheds, back gardens, and mysterious pre-dinner walks.

Even hurriedly back from the local pub clutching the phone with text on it. Children appear with glitter on their foreheads from the nativity. Grandparents in paper crowns. The dog, obviously.

They will come because **the feast has been conjured**, and it is time.

2:30 PM – Yorkshires & Plating Up with Purpose:

Now is the time to put the Yorkshires in the oven. Do it quickly and with purpose. Batter into smoking tins, oven closed immediately. Do **not** open the door. Yorkshire puddings have trust issues, and if you let the heat out too soon, they'll sulk and sit flat. Give them 20–25 minutes.

Bea's Method (or: How to Charm a Batter)

1. **Preheat your oven to 220°C (fan 200°C) / 425°F / Gas Mark 7.**
    Yes, it has to be **blazing hot**. Yorkshire puddings don't rise out of politeness, they need drama.

2. **Get your tin ready.**
    Use a 12-hole muffin tin. Add about a teaspoon of oil/fat to each well. Put the tin into the oven to **heat up until the oil is smoking**. Not just warm. **Smoking.** This is not a drill.

3. **Act quickly, with purpose.**
    When your oil is ready (this usually takes 10–15 minutes in a hot oven), pull out the tin carefully (it's basically a tray of tiny volcanoes now) and pour in your batter, filling each cup **just under halfway**.

4. **Back into the oven immediately.**
    Shut the door and do not open it. Not to peek. Not to poke. Not even if a child says they've dropped a toy in there. Leave them for **20–25 minutes** until gloriously risen and golden brown.

3:00 PM – Crackers, Crowns, and the Slow Descent into Pudding

This is the moment between **culinary climax and collective consumption**. The food is hot, the drinks are flowing, and the relatives are beginning to hover with expressions of practised anticipation, like hungry ghosts circling a Victorian buffet.

You have two main jobs at 3PM:

1. **Final plate assembly and warmth maintenance.**

2. **Getting everyone to sit down.** (Yes, including that one cousin who's just "checking WhatsApp.")

Let's take this step by magical steps.

- **Check your vegetables.** Are they caramelised? Glorious? Shiny with promise? Good.

- **Keep everything else warm**—stuffing, pigs in blankets, mash, sauces—either in a just-warm oven, covered in foil, or with lids on the hob. Now is the time to turn *every available radiator into a warming tray.*

- Pour **your second gravy boat**. One will not be enough. Trust me.

Gathering the Clan

Now begins the truly arcane task of **getting everyone to the table**.

Start by gently herding. A few cheerful yells:

"Dinner in fifteen!"
"Get your crackers ready!"

Lay the final things:

- Crackers, placed diagonally for dramatic flair.

- Candles lit.

- Jugs of water and wine topped up.

- A little **greenery or rosemary sprig** on each napkin, if you're feeling Pinteresty.

If you have **children**, give them jobs. Let them take the bread basket, the sauces, the napkins. This makes them feel very important, which they are, and also distracts them from trying to sneak a roastie.

As guests arrive and sit, this is the perfect time to **pause and admire**.

Look around. You've built something from scratch. You've summoned a feast from flour, fire, and a slight panic about the carrots. The table is glowing. The air is thick with warmth, laughter, and the perfume of roast poultry and potential.

Pulling the Crackers

Now then. **Crackers.**

One of the more peculiar British rituals, involving:

- Loud pops

- Paper hats

- Jokes so bad they circle back to being good

Pull them now, before food hits plates. The bang sets the mood. The hats soften it. The jokes ("What's a snowman's favourite snack? Ice Krispies") fill the air with groans and glee.

Everyone wears a crown. No exceptions. Even Grandma. Especially Grandma.

Let the photos be taken. Let the wine be topped. Let the children giggle and the uncles argue over the tape measure that came in their cracker.

Because **this**, dear witch, is the feast before the feast. It is **magic wrapped in paper**, and it is yours.

This is it. The *moment before the moment*. The kitchen is a cathedral. The air is thick with the scent of rosemary, roasted root, and righteous anticipation. You, dear witch, stand at the pass like a Michelin-starred matriarch, ladle in hand, smile just slightly unhinged, ready to serve *the meal you have manifested from flour, fire, and sheer determination.*

Now, depending on the style of your coven, I mean, *family,* you will either be:

A) **Plating up everything in the kitchen** and delivering curated, symmetrical plates of joy to each guest, OR

B) **Laying it all out on the table** buffet-style and letting people help themselves while pretending not to judge how much gravy Uncle Terry has taken.

Either is acceptable. Both are beautiful. I do a mix: carve and plate the turkey, gravy in a jug, roasties in a bowl big enough to bathe a toddler in, and let everyone serve themselves as if they're passing around ancient treasures. Because they are.

Let's break it down.

1. The Plate: Canvas of Plenty

Start with a warm plate if you can. No one wants their roast art served on cold porcelain.

Then, build your base: usually the slices of turkey (or nut roast or herby mushroom Wellington), fanned out in a gesture of hospitality and mild perfectionism.

Next, add:

- **A scoop of stuffing** (or two, you're not made of stone),

- **Three roasties** if you're polite, five if you're honest,

- **One honeyed parsnip**, but maybe two because you don't want to appear biased,

- **A tangle of sprouts** kissed by balsamic and fate.

Now you have the structure. But we're not done yet.

2. The Crown Jewels: Yorkshire Puddings

Let's pause here and address a truth: **Yorkshire puddings are essential**, regardless of your protein. Turkey? Yes. Beef? Obviously. Nut roast? Also yes. Yorkshires are edible joy-baskets. They do not ask permission. They arrive, triumphant and golden, declaring, *"Fill me with gravy or perish."*

Place one, no, **two**, on the plate. Give them space. They are proud creatures.

3. The River of Gravy

Gravy is not a drizzle. It is not a dot on the side. Gravy is the unifying force of Christmas dinner, the elixir that binds, the liquid that whispers, *"You did it. You really did it."*

Pour it generously. Let it pool in the Yorkshire. Let it dance across the plate. If you spill a little down the side, don't wipe it. That's **art**.

4. The Final Touches

A spoonful of **cranberry sauce**, glowing like a ruby beside the meat. A dollop of **bread sauce**, creamy and confusing to guests who've never had it before. A dab of **horseradish**, if that's your custom (just keep it away from the toddlers, ask me how I know).

Step back. Admire your work. You've created something that transcends mere nutrition.

The Blessing of the Feast

Before anyone takes a bite, take a moment. A toast. A wish. A quiet moment of gratitude or a loud clinking of glasses.

This, my darlings, is **The Moment**.

The **Yorkshire puddings** have emerged from the oven like golden phoenixes rising from a lightly oiled tin. Your **roast potatoes** are bronzed and crisp, having spent just enough time plotting their revolution against soggy traditions. Your turkey, or nut roast, or lentil-stuffed squash, is carved, glistening, and ready for adoration.

Now... you **release the feast** to the table like a benevolent enchantress unlocking the pantry of plenty.

The Centrepiece: Turkey (or Your Chosen Star)

With a flourish, you place the turkey at the centre, sliced, confident, proud. Don't worry if it's a bit rustic. This isn't the cover of a food magazine, it's **real food**, for real people, created with love, herbs, and minor incantations muttered over a pot of parsnips.

Vegetarians and flexitarians have their own glorious dishes. Maybe a mushroom Wellington cloaked in puff pastry. Or a lentil and chestnut loaf with a gleam of tomato glaze. **No one goes hungry on your watch.**

The Gravy Flood

Pour it. Drench the plate. Let it find every hill and valley. If Yorkshire puddings are goblets, gravy is their wine. Let it flow.

If you made two types (because you're that kind of witch), place both jugs on the table and *watch the power struggle unfold*.

The First Bite

And then... finally... the first bite.

It might go quiet. A sort of reverent hush descends as everyone samples the work of your hands and your very frazzled soul. The clink of cutlery. The murmured *"Mmm."* The occasional *"What's in this?"* and *"Pass the horseradish."*

This is **why**.

Why you got up early. Why you juggled roasting trays and gravy boats. Why you whispered to vegetables like a root-witch at moonrise. This moment is the reward, not just the food, but the **togetherness**.

Around your table sit the people you love, perhaps not all, perhaps not perfect, but here. That is its own kind of magic.

CHAPTER SIX

The Flaming Heart of Yule

The Familiar's Guide to Setting Your Dessert on Fire

Stirring Up Spirits – The Pagan Roots of Christmas Pudding

Let us begin with a truth: no other Christmas or Yule dessert is as utterly *bonkers* as Christmas pudding. I say this with affection, naturally. After all, what other dish requires you to mix fruit, suet, ale, fire, and hope together in a bowl, make a wish while stirring, then steam it for seven hours and feed it brandy like a Victorian invalid for weeks on end, just to eventually **set it on fire** in front of your startled family? It's theatre. It's time travel. It's a pudding, yes, but it's also a ritual.

Like all good rituals, its roots go far, far deeper than the Victorian parlour or the pages of Dickens. Christmas pudding, or "plum pudding" as it was once known (despite the complete absence of plums, more on that in a moment), has origins that reach back into the pagan soil of the British Isles, long before Christmas was even a thing on the calendar.

The Ancestral Bowl: From Frumenty to Feast

Our tale begins not with cake but with gruel. Yes, really. The pudding's ancestor was a thing called frumenty, a sort of wheat-berry porridge mixed with dried fruits, spices, and a dash of ale or mead. It was eaten during the midwinter festivals, think Solstice, Saturnalia, and assorted celebrations of surviving another year of darkness without freezing to death.

Frumenty was nutritious, sustaining, and, if you were lucky, just the right side of edible. But more than that, it was symbolic. You weren't just cooking. You were honouring the harvest, calling on the spirit of the grain, preserving what you had, and quietly praying the root cellar wouldn't run out before spring.

The ingredients were chosen not just for taste (though dried fruits were a treat back then) but for meaning:

- **Grain**: A symbol of life, fertility, and the spirit of the earth.

- **Dried fruits**: Sweetness in the dark; a reminder of the sun's return.

- **Spices**: Once rare and exotic, representing warmth, wealth, and the spark of the divine.

- **Ale or mead**: Libation and laughter, bonding the living with the spirits of ancestors.

You didn't *make* frumenty, you *summoned* it. You stirred sun and soil into a bowl and offered it to the long nights.

Over the centuries, it began to evolve. More fruit. Less wheat. More spice. Eventually suet was added (because no British dish is safe from it). The porridge thickened into a paste. The paste, in time, became pudding.

The Great Turning of the Spoon

One of the most delicious remnants of its pagan past is the tradition of the "Stir-Up" Sunday, still honoured in many households today. On the last Sunday before Advent (usually the end of November), families gather to make their Christmas pudding and stir the mixture east to west, in honour of the journey of the Magi, they say. But witches know better.

Stirring from east to west mirrors the sun's path, especially significant at this time of year when we are about to reach the solstice and the sun begins its slow return. This motion is known as deosil (sunwise), a movement associated with growth, luck, and harmony in many magical traditions.

Everyone in the household is supposed to stir and make a wish. Not just children. Everyone. Aunt Eileen. Grandpa Malcolm. Even the cat, if it consents. It's not just a cute family moment. It's a shared spell, spun with spoons and spice.

You are, quite literally, stirring up spirits, calling on warmth, hope, prosperity, and protection for the cold months ahead.

Fire in the Darkness

What do you do after lovingly steaming a pudding for half a day? You set it alight, of course.

The flaming of the pudding is probably the most overtly magical part of the whole affair. Pour brandy (or rum, if you're wild) over the warmed pudding, dim the lights, and set it ablaze. The flames leap blue and gold. People gasp. The dog hides.

To most modern guests, this is theatre. But to witches of old, it was ritual fire, a symbol of the returning sun, the sacred blaze that drives away shadow, spirits, and stagnant energy. Fire is cleansing. It's celebratory. It's how we mark endings and beginnings.

The pudding, served flaming, becomes the hearth incarnate, a ball of spice and flame passed from cauldron to table. You're not just ending the meal. You're inviting light back into the world.

Don't forget, the pudding is round, like the sun, and often decorated with holly, one of the sacred plants of the season. Holly protects. Holly sharpens the air. If you don't pick the berries off, holly also mildly poisons your in-laws. (Don't worry, just a nibble. They'll be fine.)

Echoes of the Wheel

All in all, Christmas pudding is a ritual compressed into a dessert. Its ingredients mirror the cycles of the year:

- **Dried fruits** – The memory of summer.

- **Spices** – The heat of high sun, imported into the dark months.

- **Alcohol** – A reminder that joy survives.

- **Slow cooking** – The passage of time.

- **Flame** – Rebirth.

It embodies the Wheel of the Year, turned into something sticky, spicy, and slightly overcooked if you forget to top up the steamer.

Christmas pudding isn't just a dessert. It's a pagan relic, hidden in plain sight. It survived Puritans, war rationing, and microwaves. It evolved, adapted, and nestled itself into the heart of a Christian holiday while never losing the essence of its earthy, ancestral magic.

So next time you lift your spoon to a flaming mound of pudding, think not only of sugar and spice, but of the hands who stirred it before you.

The women in wool skirts grinding cinnamon. The children whispering wishes. The fires lit in cottages on the cusp of winter. Think of the old gods, still smiling somewhere in the steam.

Stir sunwise, always.

Plum Pudding and Ghosts – A Literary Legacy

If you want to understand the soul of a culture, look at how it writes about its puddings. Nowhere is this more true than in British literature, where the **Christmas pudding** is not just dessert, it's character, plot device, metaphor, and mischief-maker, all rolled into one dense, brandy-soaked cannonball.

Let's begin with the obvious: **Charles Dickens**, who effectively gave the pudding its PR glow-up.

Dickens and the Pudding That Defined a Nation

In *A Christmas Carol* (1843), Dickens delivers a scene so glorious, so mouthwateringly jubilant, that you can practically smell the treacle through the page:

"In came Mrs Cratchit, flushed but smiling proudly, with the pudding, like a speckled cannon-ball, so hard and firm, blazing in half of half-a-quartern of ignited brandy..."

There it is. The iconic Christmas/Yule pudding, ablaze and triumphant. The Cratchits may have little, but the pudding, steamed in secret, carried in ceremony, is their feast of hope. It is both humble and heroic, comical and reverent. It's the underdog of puddings, rising (well, steaming) to become the blazing symbol of resilience and joy in the face of adversity.

Dickens was no fool. He knew that pudding, for Victorian Britain, wasn't just food. It was memory, nostalgia, family, and theatre. He was selling a vision of old-fashioned Christmas, with holly, roast goose, ghostly redemption, and a pudding that practically needed a health warning.

And readers *ate it up*, literally and figuratively.

Pudding as Haunting and Hearth

Beyond Dickens, the Christmas pudding lurks in many a tale, often as an object of memory or a haunting presence. It's the thing Aunt Muriel used to burn. It's what the cook dropped in the scullery in 1897, never to recover. It's the food you eat, even if you don't like it, because your grandmother made it, and her grandmother made it before her.

It becomes ancestral.

In ghost stories, puddings often appear as leftover relics of festive cheer. Half-eaten, wrapped in cloth, still potent with scent. In supernatural fiction, it's often the *ordinary object* charged with memory, emotion, or even regret, the leftover figgy slice that reminds a widow of a lost husband, or the scorched edges of one made in haste on the eve of war.

In fact, pudding might be the only dessert you can describe as "poignant" without sounding daft.

The Plum That Wasn't

Let's clear something up for the record: there are **no actual plums** in traditional plum pudding.

Not now, not really ever.

The "plum" refers to dried fruits in general, particularly raisins and currants. In the days before our grocers sparkled with imported blueberries and fresh figs in December, "plums" were any sweet thing that didn't rot by Michaelmas.

But the name stuck. Plum pudding sounded luxurious, vaguely exotic, and just archaic enough to feel seasonal.

This linguistic quirk pops up throughout literature. In *Pride and Prejudice*, Mrs Bennet dreams of a Christmas ball with "a good dinner and a plum pudding." In Victorian poetry, children were often rewarded (or bribed into obedience) with the promise of one.

... and in nursery rhymes?

"Little Jack Horner sat in a corner
Eating his Christmas pie;
He put in his thumb and pulled out a plum
And said, 'What a good boy am I!'"

Not a pudding, but still plum-adjacent. (And mildly threatening, if you ask me.)

The Pudding as Spellbook

As a witch, I can't help but notice that the pudding behaves a lot like a grimoire, a book of spells passed through generations, dog-eared, splattered, and deeply personal.

In many households, recipes are handwritten on lined notepaper, annotated with things like "add more brandy than last year" or "don't let Tony stir it, he overdoes the cloves."

That's storytelling. That's lineage.

You can trace family lines through these recipes. You can chart a nation's shifting fortunes by what ingredients appear: more suet in wartime, more fruit in peace, a sudden outbreak of glacé cherries in the

1970s (we don't talk about that). Literature simply catches up to what the pudding has always known: it tells a story. Not just your story, but everyone's.

Pudding and the Passage of Time

The pudding's presence in fiction often signals **a turning point**. A Christmas pudding means we've hit the heart of the season. It means someone's coming home or coming clean. It's the edible punctuation mark of reunion and revelation.

You'll find it, quietly present, in:

- E.M. Forster (*Howards End*, briefly, gloriously)
- Evelyn Waugh (*Brideshead Revisited*) as part of Christmas melancholy
- The *Paddington* books, where the bear ends up wearing a fair amount of it

Even in murder mysteries, the pudding often appears, steaming, unsuspecting, never quite the culprit but always in the room.

So much literature is obsessed with what people eat, and rightly so. But the Christmas pudding isn't just about flavour. It's about feeling.

In every story where it appears, it signals a coming together, a clumsy attempt at peace, or the yearning for connection. Whether it's in a Dickensian hovel or a BBC period drama, it represents ritual, a warm, sticky thread binding character to past, table to tale.

Because whether we're reading about the Cratchits, the Bennets, or your Aunt Joan's slightly scorched attempt in 1974, the pudding always returns us to the same place:

The table. The fire. The people who matter... and just enough brandy to make it glow.

The Witch's Pudding Bowl – How to Make a Traditional Christmas Pudding (with Enchantments & Herbal Mischief)

Let's be perfectly honest. Most traditional Christmas puddings are already magical by nature. However, if you're a witch, a proper green-fingered, moon-whispering, cat-negotiating sort of witch, then you know better than to stop at raisins and brandy.

This isn't just pudding. It's a spell, slow-cooked.

It is ancestral food alchemy. When you stir this enchanted bowl, you're not merely making dessert. You're weaving wishes, banishing winter shadows, and stuffing a year's worth of hope into something the shape and weight of a cannonball.

Put the kettle on, light the candle, and let's get started.

Bea's Bewitched Christmas Pudding Recipe

(Yields one large pudding for eight mortals, or several small enchanted ones for gifting)

Mundane Ingredients (you'll find these in any respectable pantry):

- **150g plain flour**
- **150g breadcrumbs, preferably from bread baked under a waxing moon**
- **150g suet, vegetarian or traditional, both are excellent magical binders**
- **150g dark brown sugar, to ground the sweetness with depth**
- **200g raisins, for remembrance**

- 200g sultanas, for joy

- 100g chopped dates or figs, to encourage abundance

- 75g chopped glacé cherries, for light and frivolity

- 75g mixed peel, to sharpen wit

- 1 small apple, grated, offering grounding and balance

- Zest of 1 lemon, for clarity and truth

- Zest of 1 orange, for warmth and solar strength

- 1 teaspoon cinnamon, bringing love

- 1 teaspoon mixed spice, to harmonise the flavours and energy

- A good grating of nutmeg, for protection

- 2 large eggs

- 150ml dark ale or strong black tea

- 2 tablespoons brandy or spiced rum

Secret Witch Ingredients:

- 1 tablespoon dried mugwort, for prophetic insight

- 1 teaspoon dried elderflower, to invite ancestral wisdom

- ½ teaspoon ground rose petals, for sweetened emotion and peace

- A few dried juniper berries, lightly crushed, to ward off mischief

- 1 tablespoon honey harvested on the summer solstice

- A pinch of sea salt, to seal the spell and balance flavours

Add one calendula petal per family member to represent their health and joy. Speak their name softly as you stir each one in.

Charm Inclusion:

- One silver sixpence or charm, well cleaned and wrapped

- A dried bay leaf, included with care

- One whole star anise for clarity

- A small protective bell tied to a string and nestled into the pudding after cooking if needed

Ritual Instructions: Stirring Up Spirits (and Batter)

Combine the Dry Ingredients

It is a really simple recipe. Use a ceramic or wooden bowl for the best magical results. Combine the flour, breadcrumbs, sugar, suet, dried fruits, apple, zest, and spices.

Now is the moment to add your herbal mischief. Sprinkle mugwort, rose, and elderflower as though you are casting a spell over your ingredients. Let them rest in the bowl like old friends gathering near the fire.

The Stirring Spell

Invite every member of the household to stir the pudding clockwise. This movement follows the sun's path and encourages growth, joy, and clarity.

Should someone stir in the wrong direction, gently correct them and pour another cup of tea. There is no such thing as a ruined spell, only a lesson.

Add the Wet Ingredients

Whisk together the eggs, ale or tea, and brandy. Pour this mixture into the bowl and stir thoroughly. Your batter should be thick and luxurious, falling slowly from the spoon.

If it seems too stiff, add more liquid. If it flows too freely, toss in another handful of breadcrumbs. This pudding has opinions and will let you know.

Now is the time to fold in your charms and tokens, if using.

Fill the Pudding Basin

Butter a ceramic pudding basin and spoon the mixture into it, gently pressing it down. Leave a small gap at the top to allow for swelling during steaming.

Cover the top with a layer of greased parchment and foil. Tie securely with string and create a handle with the string across the top for easy lifting.

Steam with Witch Patience

Place the pudding in a large lidded pot with water reaching halfway up the basin. Bring it to a gentle simmer and steam for six hours.

Keep a watchful eye and top up the water every hour. Settle nearby with a book, sip something warming, or tend to your herbs. This is an excellent time for quiet spellwork or reflective journaling.

Avoid lifting the lid unless truly necessary. The pudding steams best when undisturbed.

Cool and Store

Once steamed, allow the pudding to cool completely before unwrapping. Rewrap in fresh parchment and foil. Store it in a cool, dry cupboard.

If your cupboard is dark and drafty, that's even better. Feed the pudding weekly with a spoonful of brandy or honeyed tea and whisper:

"This I give to bless and bind,
A golden crumb of peace to find."

On the Day of Celebration

Reheat the pudding by steaming for another two to three hours. Turn it out with flair and drizzle warm brandy over the top.

Strike a match, light the flame, and dim the lights. Watch the blue fire dance across the glossy top like a spell leaping into the world.

Serve with clotted cream, or brandy butter.

The Silver Sixpence – Rituals, Charms & Superstitions

To those unfamiliar with old ways and family lore, a coin inside a pudding may sound like a dental emergency waiting to happen. For witches and traditionalists alike, however, it is nothing less than a spell tucked inside a dessert. The silver sixpence is not merely decorative, nor is it just a Victorian quirk. It is a token of fate, prosperity, and the quiet magic of sharing something made with intent.

Every proper Christmas pudding ought to hide at least one charm. This little treasure carries with it a whisper of prophecy and possibility, a flicker of fate disguised in brandy and breadcrumbs.

In folk tradition, the sixpence brings wealth in the year ahead to the one lucky enough to find it. This belief is older than the coin itself. Ancient Romans baked similar tokens into festival cakes during Saturnalia. They believed whoever found the object would hold fortune's favour for the coming year. In many households today, that tradition carries on with coins, rings, thimbles, and even tiny charms baked inside, each with its own meaning and energy.

While the silver sixpence is the most common, it is far from the only symbolic choice. A thimble foretells industriousness or perhaps warns that someone is about to take up an inconvenient hobby involving felt. A miniature horseshoe offers luck, while a button is said to signal a year of steadying influence or, in some cases, that you'll finally get around to fixing that coat with the missing fastener.

Some witches, myself included, tuck in a pressed bay leaf to signify victory in whatever challenge the new year might bring. Others add a dried bean or lentil, symbolising new growth or unexpected fortune. The charm does not need to be valuable. Its power lies in intention.

Before placing any charm in your pudding, give it a proper cleansing. Rinse it with cool water, then pass it through incense smoke or hold it in a bowl of salt for an hour. Whisper your intent into it. Tell it what it is meant to represent and ask that it bring joy, not cracked molars.

Once clean, the charm should be wrapped in parchment or baking paper, especially if it is metallic. This step ensures nobody bites into something too sharp or finds themselves explaining pudding-based mishaps to a dentist. Tuck the charm gently into the mixture before it is spooned into the basin, or wait until after steaming and press it in then, noting its location in case any small children are involved.

When served at the table, the pudding becomes a miniature oracle. Guests prod gently with their spoons, giggling and pretending they are not secretly hoping to be the chosen one this year. The person who finds the charm must lift it out carefully, wipe it clean, and raise it high with the solemn pride usually reserved for sports trophies and unusually large roast potatoes.

Once revealed, the charm's meaning is read aloud. This can be done with a formal rhyme, or simply explained by a helpful kitchen witch who keeps a charm glossary at the ready. Some families read the fortune aloud with mock ceremony. Others invent entire tales based on what was found, declaring that Uncle Gerald will become fabulously wealthy or that Cousin Jean is doomed to start a quilting club.

The beauty of this ritual lies not in accuracy, but in imagination. For one brief moment, magic becomes visible, resting on a dessert spoon.

In magical households, charms may be chosen each year based on what energies are most needed. A house recovering from grief might include charms of love and healing. A family embarking on new paths could stir in keys for unlocking potential or feathers for lightness. The pudding becomes more than food. It becomes a snapshot of hopes and dreams hidden in plain sight.

There are, of course, certain taboos. Never put a broken charm in a pudding. Never ignore the charm if it falls out during mixing. That is a message. At the very least, it is an invitation to pay attention.

If more than one charm is found in a single slice, take note. That guest is having an important year, or they may simply have sliced with more enthusiasm than grace. Either way, pour them more cream and ask if they have made any big decisions recently.

Finally, it is worth remembering that the act of hiding charms is a kind of quiet rebellion. In a world that often forgets its old stories, placing a sixpence in a pudding is a declaration that some things still matter. Hope. Connection. A little mystery served with custard.

Next time you find yourself holding a pudding spoon over a steaming bowl of tradition, take a breath. Feel the weight of that small coin. Know that you are taking part in a ritual older than Christmas, older than pudding, older perhaps than even the idea of dessert as celebration.

A silver sixpence, hidden in fruit and spice, is not just a charm. It is a promise.

CHAPTER SEVEN

Rituals of Light & Fire

Solstice to Sizzle: The Sun's Dramatic Comeback Tour

"Even a single candle, on the darkest night, dares to be the sun." – an ancient witchy proverb

Let us begin with fire. Not the kind that requires a fire extinguisher (though you might want to have one handy just in case. I speak from charred experience), but the kind that lives in matchsticks and memories. The kind that flickers quietly, courageously, in the corner of a room where the sun has forgotten to rise.

This is the magic of the Winter Solstice.

The sun, in its great celestial drama, has slunk as far away from us as it can get without needing a passport. The nights are long, the mornings reluctant, and the hedgerows look like they've given up and joined a nunnery. It is the still point of the year. The hush. The pause. The sacred exhale.

Yet, within this moment of shadow, something stirs.

A spark. A flicker. The turning begins.

For witches, the solstice is not a time to bemoan the dark but to welcome the light. Not because it arrives in some grand Hollywood sunrise (although wouldn't that be lovely), but because it returns in whispers. A fraction more sunlight. A bird dares to sing a note. A snowdrop starts planning its debut. The earth, ever the introvert, starts to come back to life.

So, we honour it the way witches always have, by lighting a flame.

A Candle, A Spell, A Sacred Spark

Now, don't get me wrong, I love a dramatic bonfire as much as the next cloak-wearing enchantress. But this is not that ritual. This is not about spectacle. This is not about summoning the sun back with twelve flaming torches and a goat called Kevin. (Though, for the record, Kevin was a very cooperative goat.)

No, this ritual is simpler. Quieter. Intimately powerful.

All you need is one candle.

At sunset on Solstice Eve, usually around the time you're wondering whether it's socially acceptable to open a second bottle, find a quiet space in your home. It doesn't need to be fancy. A cleared windowsill. The top of the radiator. That one shelf that hasn't yet collapsed under your rock collection. Anywhere will do, as long as it feels like a place you can breathe.

Take a moment. Breathe in. Breathe out.

Feel the weight of the year behind you. All its joys, its sorrows, its endless Zoom and Teams calls and occasionally mysterious smells coming from the back of the fridge. Let it all hang out there and let it all be OK.

Now light your candle.

Watch the flame catch and tremble. That's it. That's the magic.

You have just created a sun. A small one yes, but a sun never the less.

The Symbolism of the Flame

This single flame, tiny and fragile though it may seem, is more than wax and wick. It is a sun-spell. A miniature bonfire. A declaration of hope that dares to burn in the face of darkness.

For thousands of years, our ancestors lit fires on this night to coax the sun back into the sky. They may not have had Instagram or central heating, but they understood something elemental: that fire was life. Warmth. Illumination. Transformation.

To light a candle at the solstice is to say, "I remember."
I remember the wheel turns.
I remember that light returns.
I remember that I, too, am capable of warmth in cold seasons.

(Perhaps say that last line to yourself more than once.)

In a world obsessed with immediate results and next-day delivery, this candle asks for patience. It doesn't flood the room. It doesn't burn the shadows away. It simply glows. Quietly. Steadily. As if to say: I'm here and I'm not going out.

Whispering Hopes into the Flame

Once your candle is lit and the room has settled into its new sunlit silence, it's time for the whispering.

Yes, whispering. No chanting required (unless you want to), and no need to scare the neighbours by yelling incantations through the open window.

Lean in… safely… and speak your hopes into the flame.

These can be wishes, intentions, prayers, or just beautifully half-formed thoughts that feel right. My advice and some may agree or disagree, but keep the mood light, and add a bit of humour. There is something good about laughing at yourself or raising a smile for the words you have just spoken.

Things like:

- *"May I be more gentle with myself this year."*

- *"Let love return to my doorstep, with biscuits."*

- *" … and PLEASE help me find my other glove."*

Say them aloud. Say them softly. The flame hears.

If you'd like something a bit more poetic (and you're the kind of person who enjoys words that rhyme with 'ignite'), here's a *Sun-Blessing Incantation* you can use:

Solstice Candle Blessing
"On this night of longest dark,
I light a flame, I strike a spark.
Return, O sun, with golden might,
Bring warmth, bring hope, bring growing light.
By candle's glow and heart's desire,
I welcome back the sacred fire."

You can recite this once or as many times as you like. Sing it if the mood strikes you. (Bonus points if you're wearing slippers shaped like dragons.)

Safety, Socks & Sacred Fire

A brief word from the Bureau of Witchy Practicality (a division of me):

Please, for the love of all that's holly, do not set yourself or your kitchen on fire.

Candle flames are magical. So are smoke alarms.
Use a proper holder. Keep it away from curtains, tea towels, trailing scarves, and particularly inquisitive cats.

If you're lighting candles with children, pets, or guests with a fondness for overenthusiastic gesturing, consider LED candles or tea lights in jam jars. The magic is not in the danger. It's in the intention.

Also, there's no rule that says you can't do this ritual in fuzzy socks with a mug of mulled wine. If anything, that might only enhance it.

A Ritual of Joy, Not Urgency

The beauty of this ritual is that it asks nothing of you except presence. You don't need to fix anything. You don't need to manifest a five-year plan. You don't need to "make the most" of the solstice.

All you need to do is light a flame and remember what it means.

Remember that slow returns are *still* returns.

Remember that *you* are allowed to begin again. Gently.

Remember that you, too, carry a *sacred* fire.

Perhaps most importantly: remember that hope doesn't always arrive as a thunderclap. Sometimes, it sneaks in like a candle on a windowsill, flickering, faint, but utterly determined to burn.

Optional Additions for Extra Magic

If you'd like to expand the ritual or add a few more witchy flourishes, here are some gentle suggestions:

- **Anoint your candle** with a drop of cinnamon or clove oil for warmth and courage.

- **Place herbs/crystals** nearby (sunstone, citrine, rosemary, bay).

- **Use a fire-safe bowl** to burn slips of paper with old habits, worries, or 'stuff you're emotionally done with'. Say goodbye with gratitude as the paper curls into smoke.

- **Share the moment** with others. A group candle-lighting via phone call or video chat can be surprisingly moving. Just avoid synchronised fire-dancing unless you've done a risk assessment.

During Covid lock down, we had a video call with friends and family, everyone turned their lights out and the cameras focussed on a single candle each. It brought something new, something we hadn't done before, a candle lit, shared with people we cared about all around the world, all at the same time. It was very emotional, not just because of what was going on around us at the time, but it made us all real. All together.

The Morning After

Leave your candle to burn out safely, or extinguish it with reverence, blowing it out as if sending a final breath of thanks to the sun.

In the morning, when you wake up and realise the days are ever-so-slightly longer, even by a minute, take a moment to stand in that new light. Stretch. Smile. Make a cup of something delicious. Whisper, "Welcome back," to the rising sun.

Then go about your day knowing you've done something ancient and brave:
You lit a flame in the darkness……. You welcomed the sun home.

Candle Magic for the Longest Night

Let me say something heretical: you can tell a lot about a witch by the way they handle a candle. Some of us are "strike-a-match, light-it-quick, shove-it-on-the-table" sorts. Others, me included, approach it with the kind of reverence usually reserved for ancient manuscripts, sleeping cats, and really good jam. There's a ceremony to it. A sacredness. A sense that what you're doing might just alter the course of the universe (or at least your Tuesday).

At Yule, candles are not just decorative. They are the ritual.

They remind us that even when the sun is playing hard to get and your garden looks like a despondent salad, the light *still* lives here, in flame, in you, in the small, steady glow that says, "We're not done yet."

In witchcraft, the candle isn't just a light source. It's a spell. A symbol. A vessel for your intentions, hopes, muttered prayers, and occasionally a small bit of cookie crumbs from waving your hand about too excitedly. Let's dive in.

The Anatomy of an Intention Candle

An *Intention Candle* is a candle that doesn't just burn. It *speaks*. It speaks your wishes into the world, crackles with meaning, and (if you've done your herb-dressing properly) smells of cinnamon and mystery.

To create your own, you'll need:

- **A candle** – any size or shape, though taper or pillar candles work beautifully.

- **A sharp tool** – a toothpick, nail, or ritual knife (I use a blunt knitting needle I call *Pointy Thing*).

- **Herbs, oils, or glitter** – optional but glorious.

- **A sense of humour** – essential.

205

Step 1: Choose Your Candle Like You're Hiring It for a Job

Colour matters in candle magic. Yes, you *could* use a tealight leftover from Halloween, but Yule is a festival of *intention*, so let's be deliberate.

Here's a cheat sheet of colour correspondences:

Colour	Magical Correspondence
Gold	Return of the sun, abundance, renewal
White	Peace, purity, clarity, new beginnings
Red	Courage, love, strength, festive oomph
Green	Growth, healing, earth connection
Blue	Wisdom, introspection, emotional calm
Orange	Joy, creativity, spark (great for low winter moods)
Black	Release, protection, transformation (best when used with others—not as your solo candle unless you're *very* ready to let go of something, like an ex or a lifelong grudge)

Pick the colour that speaks to what you're calling in. Or mix and match. I've done a trio of red-gold-white before, which looked like a patriotic cake but worked like a charm.

Carve Your Intentions

Take your pointy tool (*Pointy Thing,* in my case), and carve words, symbols, or runes into the candle.

What to carve?

- A single word: *Hope, Courage, Health, Cheese* (if relevant).

- A rune or sigil that holds meaning for you.

- A sentence, if your candle is large enough and your handwriting isn't terrible.

Remember: it's not about legibility. It's about energy. You could scrawl "sun please" in crooked runes and it would still mean more than any glitter-drenched Pinterest ritual done without heart.

This is your spell. Say it aloud as you carve, if you like. Or hum a tune. I once carved a candle to the theme of *The Great British Bake Off*. Oddly enough, it did help me feel more stable, more buttery inside. (No comments about a soggy bottom please)

Dress the Candle

No, not in tiny trousers. (Although now I write that I could do that...hmmm)

To *dress* a candle means to anoint it with oil and sprinkle herbs along its surface. It's like seasoning a roast, but magical, flammable, and less edible.

Here's how:

1. Choose an oil that aligns with your intention.

   o **Olive oil** is fine (especially if it's already in your cupboard).

   o **Cinnamon oil** for warmth and love.

   o **Frankincense** for spiritual connection.

   o **Clove** for protection and insight.

2. Rub a little on your fingers and stroke the candle, either from bottom to top (if calling something in) or top to bottom (if banishing something). Yes, this direction matters. Think of it like energetic hairbrushing.

3. Sprinkle your chosen herbs:

   o **Rosemary** for remembrance and protection.

   o **Bay** for vision and wisdom.

   o **Orange zest** for joy.

   o **Lavender** for peace.

   o **Nutmeg** for abundance.

   o **Dried apple peel** if you're feeling witchy and wholesome.

Warning: Do not turn your candle into a spice rack. A gentle dusting will do. If your candle starts looking like a heavily seasoned roast chicken, start again. Safety first.

The Circle of Light: A Yule Ritual for Families & Covens

Now let's talk about a group ritual that warms the soul and produces gorgeous Instagram photos (should you be inclined). I call it **The Circle of Light**, and it's one of my favourite Yule traditions.

Here's how to do it:

1. **Gather your circle**, family, friends, coven members, your book club (as long as they're flame-tolerant).

2. **Prepare a large spiral** of tealights or small candles on the floor or table, tracing the shape of a spiral sun, or the Wheel of the Year.

3. **Each person takes a turn** entering the spiral from the outside, lighting one candle as they go, and speaking a wish or blessing aloud.

4. **At the centre**, they light a special candle, the "Sun Flame", and pause for a moment of gratitude, silence, or song.

5. Then they walk the spiral back out, lighting another trail if desired.

The effect is magical. Slowly, the whole spiral glows. Each flame is someone's dream, someone's voice added to the turning of the year.

Children love this ritual. Adults get misty-eyed. Pets try to eat the un-lit candles. (Secure them appropriately.)

For the Solo Witch: Flame-Gazing for Vision and Clarity

What if it's just you this Yule? No spiral. No crowd. No Kevin the goat.

Perfect. Because solo magic can be the most powerful kind of all.

Flame-gazing is an old technique. Sometimes called *pyromancy*, which makes it sound like you're about to launch a dragon, but really it's just you, a candle, and the ability to stare without blinking for an unreasonable amount of time.

How to do it:

1. Sit comfortably with your candle in front of you, preferably dressed and carved with intention.

2. Darken the room, light the candle, and breathe slowly.

3. Fix your gaze gently on the flame. Not in a creepy way. Just... attentively.

4. Let your thoughts float. Don't force them. Just watch. The flicker, the shifts in colour, the way the light dances and wobbles.

As you gaze, you may notice:

- Images forming in your mind.

- Forgotten memories surfacing.

- An idea rising up, uninvited but brilliant.

- A sudden realisation that the thing you've been clinging to is ready to be released.

The flame becomes a mirror. A companion. A doorway.

Some witches write down what they saw or felt after. Others sketch, journal, or make tea and talk to their houseplants about it (hi Geraldine, you wise old fern).

If nothing happens, that's fine too. Magic isn't a vending machine. You don't put in a spell and get an answer in 30 seconds. Sometimes the insight comes three days later while you're peeling potatoes. It's all part of the process.

A Few Final Tips from the Candle Drawer of Life

- **Trim your wick.** A too-long wick leads to wild flames. A short wick struggles. Aim for about ¼ inch. Yes, there is such a thing as candle maintenance.

- **Watch for signs.** A candle that crackles, gutters, or leans dramatically to the left might be trying to tell you something. Or it might be a breeze. Use discernment.

- **Snuff, don't blow, if possible.** Especially if you're doing this ritually. Use a candle snuffer, your fingers, or a respectful whisper. Blowing out a spell-candle can scatter its energy like a sneeze in a library.

- **Keep the wax.** Leftover wax can be saved and melted into new spell candles. That's right, witchcraft is sustainable.

The Fire You Carry

Candle magic, like all good witchery, is about *presence*. It's not about how elaborate your altar is or how many Latin words you can mispronounce. It's about whether you mean it.

When you light a candle this Yule, you are doing what thousands of witches, wise folk, forest-dwellers, and hearth-keepers have done for centuries: naming your hope. Calling back the light. Saying, "I still believe in warmth, even now."

That's brave. That's sacred... and if your candle happens to smell like gingerbread and be shaped like a hedgehog, that's valid too.

The Bonfire Blessing – Outdoor Ceremonies for the Brave

There is something satisfying about setting things on fire at the winter solstice. I'm not talking about your neighbour's garish plastic reindeer (though believe me I understand the temptation), but standing in front of a crackling fire in the middle of winter makes you feel like a proper witch. It's primeval, dramatic, and ever so slightly dangerous, three things' witches excel at. The Winter Solstice is the perfect time to indulge this fiery urge. After all, our ancestors were practically pyromaniacs when it came to midwinter. Bonfires on hilltops, torches carried in procession, fire wheels rolled down hills (health and safety would *never* approve), all of it was part of a single shared prayer:

"Please, sun, for the love of all that is holy, come back."

These days, we tend to settle for central heating and fairy lights. But if you have even the faintest opportunity, I highly recommend embracing the solstice bonfire tradition, even if it's scaled down to a few logs in a brazier or, for the brave, a stubborn barbecue that refuses to die despite three winters of neglect.

The Origins of Solstice Bonfires

The midwinter fire ritual is as old as storytelling itself. Celts, Norsefolk, and Romans all shared this fiery practice in one form or another. Fire was a symbol of life when the world felt perilously close to freezing. It was a physical manifestation of the sun, glowing defiantly in the darkness. Witches and wise folk lit flames not just to keep warm, but to declare to the universe, "We will *not* let the dark have the last word."

Imagine a hilltop centuries ago: a group of villagers huddled in cloaks, clutching mugs of something that could probably remove paint, watching as a pile of logs bursts into glorious flame. They would chant, sing, and throw offerings, herbs, bread, wishes, into the fire, watching sparks fly like messages to the stars.

You can recreate that spirit today, even if your "hilltop" is a patch of patio and your cloak is a suspiciously fluffy dressing gown. Bonfires also have a certain defiance about them. "Oh, it's dark and cold? Fine. We'll just make our *own* sun," says the witch, striking a match with the flair of a stage magician. There's power in that defiance. It tells the soul: *"We have the tools. We have the magic. We have a bag of marshmallows. We can handle this."*

Let's be honest, nothing brings a group of people together faster than a roaring fire and a slightly chaotic singalong of "Here Comes the Sun" after two mugs of mulled cider.

Finding Your Fire

You don't need a Viking funeral pyre, convenient pagan stone circles, or a ceremonial oak tree (though if you have one, I applaud you). A **bonfire** can be as humble or as grand as your circumstances allow:

- **Hilltop Beacon:** Perfect for those with adventurous spirits, sensible boots, and no fear of frostbite. There's something incredibly magical about lighting a fire on high ground and watching the flames flicker against the sky like a signal to the gods.

- **Backyard Blaze:** A garden fire pit, chiminea, or brazier works beautifully. Decorate the surrounding space with lanterns or strings of fairy lights. Place a few sprigs of pine or rosemary in the fire for a fragrant boost.

- **The Stubborn Barbecue:** For urban witches with no fire pit, a barbecue grill can work surprisingly well. Bonus: you can toast things while you chant.

- **The Indoor Cauldron:** If outdoor fires are a no-go, a cast-iron cauldron (or fire-safe bowl) filled with charcoal disks or small logs will do. Safety tip: open a window unless you enjoy explaining smoke damage to your landlord.

Remember: fire is less about size than sincerity. Even a single candle flame, tended with intention, carries the essence of the solstice bonfire. So don't fret if your "bonfire" is more "tealight in a jam jar." Magic doesn't judge.

Writing What You'll Release

Before lighting the fire, take a moment to reflect on what you're leaving behind in the old year. This is where magic meets a little therapeutic witchcraft.

The Ritual of Bay Leaves

Bay leaves are not just for stews. They're also for spells, wishes, and the satisfying crackle they make when tossed into flames. Take a handful of dried bay leaves and write, using a pen or sharpie, the things you want to release. Old habits. Worries. That tendency to say "yes" when you mean "absolutely not." Scribble them down. Be honest. Be specific.

When you're ready, hold the bay leaf to your heart, whisper "Thank you for what you taught me. I release you now," and then toss it into the fire. Watch as it flares and disappears, leaving only a curl of smoke and a sense of lightness.

Now comes the joyful bit: calling in the light. This is where off-key chanting is *not just encouraged but required.* Fire rituals should never feel too serious. (Unless you're a Druid in full ceremonial robes, in which case I bow respectfully to your gravitas.)

Here's a simple sun-inviting chant you can use. Sing it, hum it, shout it into the night sky:

"Golden sun, returning light,
Break the darkness of the night.
Rise again, our spirits sing,
Bring the warmth of every spring."

Repeat it as you circle the fire (or the barbecue) a few times. If you have companions, create a call-and-response, one side chants, the other echoes. Add clapping or drumming. Or just stomp your boots in rhythm until your toes warm up.

A Mini Fire Festival

If you're the kind of witch who looks at a bonfire and thinks, *"This could use more drama... and possibly snacks,"* then I invite you to host your very own **mini fire festival**. It doesn't have to be grand. Just a few little touches can turn an ordinary solstice evening into something unforgettable, and slightly sticky.

First things first: **marshmallows**. Yes, the humble marshmallow. Turns out, they make excellent offerings to the spirits of joy. (... and to small children who are pretending to be fire demons.) The ritual is delightfully simple: toast your marshmallow over the flames, and as it begins to puff and sizzle, lean in and whisper a blessing. Something like, *"May sweetness return with the sun,"* or *"Please don't let me drop this into the fire again."* Then eat it reverently. Preferably with chocolate. Possibly in sandwich form. Because, let's be honest, magic always tastes better with a bit of melted chocolate.

Once the flames are dancing merrily, pass around mugs of something hot and lovely. Mulled cider, spiced wine, or hot chocolate with a suspicious number of toppings will do nicely (or a splash of rum...). As you hand someone a cup, bless it with a tiny wish: *"May we be warm. May we be kind. May we always have biscuits."* It's not just hospitality; it's enchantment by the ladleful.

Then, if the spirit moves you (or if someone puts on music), there's always the **fire dance**. Now, before you panic, this doesn't require interpretive choreography or a background in flamenco. A gentle sway with a scarf will do. Or a slow shuffle in a woolly hat. Even a spirited jig that looks like a cross between Morris dancing and dodging sparks counts. The point is to move, to warm the body, and to stir the energy. Fire loves movement. So does joy.

Finally, one of my favourite little solstice traditions: **Sparks of Gratitude**. As the fire crackles away, take a moment to toss in a twig, a pinecone, or a pinch of dried herbs. As you do, speak aloud something you're grateful for. *"I'm grateful for my weirdly psychic dog." "I'm grateful for this year's tomato harvest, even though it was mostly snails."* Each offering feeds the fire, turning it into a living gratitude journal, smoky, sacred, and thoroughly witch-approved.

Songs, Shouts & Slightly Off-Key Solstice Joy

Now, let's talk about what happens once the fire is going, the marshmallows are half-eaten, and everyone's cheeks are glowing like enchanted apples. That's right, it's time for singing. Or shouting. Or something in between that involves enthusiasm, questionable harmonies, and at least one person insisting they don't *really* know the words.

Solstice fire rituals have always made space for sound, not just solemn chants and carefully curated invocations (though those have their place), but *joyful noise*. Think of it as a magical release valve for the year's tension. A good song around the fire is part spell, part celebration, and part hilarious chaos.

You could start with something traditional, of course, like *"Here Comes the Sun"*. I know, it's on-the-nose, but that's sort of the point. As soon as someone launches into the opening notes... "doo, dun, doo, doo"... the whole group is humming along before the second line. If the sun happens to peek out the next morning, you'll all feel wildly powerful and slightly smug.

If you're in the mood to get creative, try twisting a carol into something witchier. A version of *"Deck the Halls"* with lines about bay leaves, evergreen spirits, and dancing hedgerow faeries is always a winner. Bonus points if someone brings a tambourine, though it's not mandatory. The solstice is forgiving that way.

If you're blessed with one of those brilliantly odd friends who makes up songs on the spot, cherish them. One year, a dear witchling I know serenaded our Yule log with an improvised ballad about rebirth, fire spirits, and red wine. It was deeply moving. ... and weirdly catchy.

Remember, it's not about sounding good. It's about *sounding*. Whether you sing, hum, chant, or bellow into the wind like a Norse god on karaoke night, what matters is the energy behind it. Make some noise.

Invite the sun back with laughter in your throat and smoke in your hair.

Cold Weather Advice from a Witch Who's Froze Her Toes Off

Of course, while you're making all this merry, your body might gently remind you that you are, in fact, outdoors... in December. Possibly in a garden. Possibly at night. Possibly regretting your aesthetic decision to wear floaty skirts in minus-two temperatures.

So allow me to pass on some wisdom, bought with shivering and stubbornness.

First: layers, darling. Layers. There's nothing noble about hypothermia, even if you're wearing a handmade rune cloak. Underneath the robes and glamour, I recommend thermals. Several. Pile them on like you're dressing for a fashion show themed "Victorian onion."

Socks matter. Thick ones. Woolly. Possibly enchanted. Boots, sturdy ones that will withstand mud, frost, and that one cousin who always steps on your toes during circle dances.

Gloves? Choose wisely. Yes, mittens are charming. Yes, they make you look like a Dickensian ghost child. But they are completely useless if you're trying to toss bay leaves into the fire or hold a marshmallow stick. Fingerless gloves are the unsung heroes of solstice rituals. You'll thank me later.

Don't forget the shawl. Preferably tartan. Preferably large enough to wrap around yourself and the person next to you, like a Victorian widow making dramatic declarations to the wind. Nothing says midwinter witch like flapping your shawl open as you invoke the returning light.

Lastly, safety. I know it's not glamorous, but fire spirits appreciate it when we don't burn down the herb shed. Keep water or sand nearby. Don't leave the fire unattended. And if someone gets *too* inspired and starts dancing with a sparkler and no trousers, intervene gently but firmly.

We may be witches, but we're also responsible adults. Mostly.

Bonfires are messy, smoky, and often a little unpredictable. Which is exactly why I love them. They remind us that magic isn't always neat and tidy. Sometimes it's sparks in your hair, ash on your cheeks, and a sudden laugh at how wonderful it is to be alive, even on the longest night.

Whether you're on a hilltop with a blazing pyre or in your tiny garden coaxing a reluctant barbecue to life, remember this: fire doesn't care about scale. It cares about sincerity.

If you can toast a marshmallow while whispering a spell? Well, you've basically achieved witchcraft's highest form.

Family Fire Magic

Let's be honest: not everyone in your life has memorised the Wheel of the Year or has a working knowledge of where to source ethically harvested frankincense resin. Some of your solstice guests may be curious newcomers. Some may be small humans with sticky fingers and limited patience. Some may be mildly bewildered in-laws who think Beltane is a type of cheese.

Which is why I love crafting **joyful, accessible rituals**, the kind that welcome everyone in, regardless of age, experience, or magical credentials. These aren't solemn ceremonies locked behind Latin incantations and 900-page grimoires. These are simple, meaningful acts of midwinter magic you can do in wellies, dressing gowns, or even novelty reindeer pyjamas. (... and yes, all three are deeply witchy if worn with intention.)

So let's begin with the outdoor version of a bedtime story...

The Solstice Lantern Walk

There's something unspeakably magical about walking through the dark with your own light in hand.

For the **Solstice Lantern Walk**, all you need is a garden, a patch of nearby woodland, or even just a slow saunter down the street. Give each person, young, old, sceptical, or enthusiastically pagan, a lantern, a jam jar with a tealight, or a battery-operated fairy light crammed into an old pickle jar. (We're very into repurposing. It's witchy *and* eco-conscious.)

As twilight deepens, gather your little group, light your lanterns, and begin a slow, gentle walk. It doesn't have to be long, just long enough to feel the hush of winter settle around you.

Encourage everyone to walk in silence for a moment or two, listening to the sounds of night: the rustle of leaves, the breath of wind, the crunch of frost underfoot. It's not just a walk; it's a moving meditation. A procession of light through the longest night.

You can end the walk by placing your lanterns in a spiral on the ground or lining them up along the path to "guide the sun home." Or return indoors for cocoa and stories by candlelight. Which brings me to...

Making Citrus Pomanders – Sunny Spheres of Scent and Spell

There are few things more gloriously satisfying than sticking cloves into an orange. Honestly, if you haven't tried it, please do. It's therapy, art, spellcraft, and aromatherapy all in one.

Pomanders are clove-studded citrus fruits that have been made for centuries as symbols of protection and light. Their shape and colour mirror the returning sun. Their scent lifts the spirits. Making them can be surprisingly meditative.

Gather your supplies: fresh oranges (or clementines for smaller hands), whole cloves, ribbon or twine, and a sharp cocktail stick to pre-poke holes for little fingers. As you work, hum happy tunes… any…

Arrange the pomanders in a bowl as a centrepiece or hang them near doorways to bless the threshold. Children love them. Grown-ups become quietly obsessed… and your house ends up smelling like a festive apothecary….. win, win, win.

Cinnamon Wishes on the Fire

This one is deliciously simple and surprisingly touching.

Each person takes a cinnamon stick, those sweet, spicy scrolls of bark, and whispers a wish into it. It might be a single word. It might be a whole sentence. Doesn't matter. Cinnamon, being one of the warmest and most generous of herbs, carries messages beautifully.

Then, toss your cinnamon stick onto the bonfire, the brazier, or even your fireplace. If you're indoors with no flame, lay them in a dish on the radiator and let the scent rise like smoke signals.

You'll find the room slowly fills with the aroma of sun-baked spices, and your wishes seem to rise with it. The children will giggle, the adults will sigh, and someone will inevitably say, *"Can we make spiced buns after this?"*

The answer, of course, is yes. Always yes to buns.

The Gratitude Circle (with Cocoa, Obviously)

Sometimes the most powerful rituals are the quietest.

At the end of your solstice gathering, once the songs are sung, the marshmallows toasted, and the fire is flickering low, invite everyone to gather in a circle, cocoa in hand. One at a time, each person shares one thing they're grateful for from the year just passed.

This isn't about being profound. It's about being present.

"I'm grateful for my cat not bringing in live mice this week."
"I'm grateful Bessie's operation was success."
"I'm grateful ITom came back from his gap-year safe"

The act of speaking gratitude aloud, wrapped in warmth, surrounded by loved ones (and possibly cinnamon buns) is as sacred as any high ritual. It roots us. It connects us. It reminds us that even in the dark, there is sweetness.

Stillness and Spark – The Witch's Personal Solstice Rite

Now, once everyone has toddled off to bed, sugar-high children, slightly bewildered neighbours, cinnamon-scented partners, you may find yourself with a quiet moment alone.

This is where the magic sharpens.

Because while Yule is a time of communal joy, it is also a moment of deep, personal turning. It's a hinge in the wheel. A still point in a season of sleep. That, my darling witch, is when your **personal solstice rite** begins.

Let's keep it simple. And sacred.

Begin by preparing a small space just for you. It doesn't have to be an altar, though if you have one, dress it in something golden or evergreen. Just clear a space where you can sit comfortably without interruption.

Light a single candle. One flame is enough.

Take a few slow, deep breaths. Feel your body where it rests. Feel the ground beneath you. Feel the quiet settling over the house like snowfall.

Think of something you're ready to release. Maybe it's a fear. Maybe it's a pattern. Maybe it's the strange urge to reply to emails at 2am. Whatever it is, say it quietly, whisper it, out loud followed by

" I release you now."

Now think of something you're calling in. A quality. A dream. A guiding word. Again say it quietly so only you can hear. You've planted the seed.

"I welcome you"

Then you might

Place a **sunstone** or **clear quartz** on your windowsill to soak up the solstice light and charge it for the coming year, or, leave an **offering of seeds and honey** outside, a gift to the spirits of light, the animals, or simply the Earth itself. Think of it as paying your respects to the returning sun. Or simply wrap yourself in a soft shawl, drink something warm, and allow the stillness to sink in. listen to the creaks of the house. This, too, is ritual. This, too, is holy.

Whether you've spent the solstice with lanterns and laughter or in candlelit silence with only the cat for company (and honestly, cats *are* sacred beings), know this:

You kept the light.
You lit the flame.
You turned with the wheel.
You remembered how to hope.

If all you managed was to light a candle, breathe deeply, and not set your tea towel on fire, well, that's a win in my book.

Because this night, the longest of the year, is not about perfection. It's about presence. It's about finding the spark that lives in you and tending it gently, like a hearth you can carry through the winter.

So wherever you are, whoever you're with, however you celebrate, know that you are enough.

The light is returning.   You, dear witch, are still glowing.

CHAPTER EIGHT

The Yule Altar

Sacred Stuff, Shiny Things and Magical Bling

Now, let's have a quiet word about Christmas.

If you're a witch with children, or know children, or have even glimpsed a child once from a safe distance, you'll know that **Christmas is not going anywhere**. You can craft the most exquisitely pagan, perfectly aligned, herb-scented, moon-blessed Yule ritual, and your small human will still be galloping about, asking if Santa will bring a LEGO Death Star.

… and that's as it should be.

The truth is, Christmas and Yule have been dancing together for centuries. The Christians, in their infinite wisdom, looked at all the wonderful pagan festivities, the greenery, the feasting, the candlelight, the midwinter bonfires, and said, *"You know what, we'll have some of that."* So, it's only right and fair that we, modern witches, return the favour and entwine both traditions into one beautiful, chaotic, tinsel-draped, evergreen-hung celebration of light.

Because the magic is in the layers

The Family Altar is the Christmas Tree

You may have a formal witch's altar in your home, an elegantly arranged slab of oak adorned with crystals, a cauldron, and a carefully positioned athame. That's lovely. Treasure it.

But if you have a Christmas tree in the living room festooned with paper snowflakes, glittery baubles, and an angel that looks vaguely traumatised, then **congratulations**, you already have a Yule altar. It just doesn't know it yet.

The Christmas tree is a direct descendant of ancient evergreen rituals. Long before it was crowned with plastic stars and fibre-optic lighting, it was brought indoors by Norsefolk and Druids as a living spell of resilience, a promise that life persists even through the frost. Every branch is a symbol of hope. Every bauble a charm. Every garland a ribbon of magic.

So, let's make it conscious.

- The **star** or **sunburst** on top? That's the returning sun, my dear. Whether it's gold plastic or hand-crafted by a 5-year-old with a questionable understanding of symmetry, it holds the same symbolism.

- The **baubles**? Solar charms. Or protective orbs. Or tiny moons reflecting the light. Take your pick.

- Those **paper garlands** your children made at school, with all the sticky-tape enthusiasm in the world? They're unity spells, links of connection, joy, and slightly lopsided friendship.

- The **tree itself**? A green pillar of life, standing defiantly alive through winter's sleep.

You don't need to throw out the tinsel and replace it with foraged ivy (though you absolutely can if it sparks joy). You just need to look at it differently. Whisper a blessing as you hang each ornament. Hide a sigil in the ribbon bow. Turn decorating the tree into a spell in motion. This is your **family altar**, loud, glittery, joyful, and absolutely sacred.

The tree is not a dignified altar, at least not in our house. Not a solemn altar. But an altar that glows with life, glitter, paper chains held together by sheer willpower, and an angel on top who looks like she's seen things.

It's an altar built by sticky fingers, bursts of song from Alexa, and the sheer, determined enthusiasm of three children, two girls and a boy, who approach tree-decorating like it's an Olympic sport, judged on volume, glitter fallout, and number of biscuits consumed during the event.

The Tree-Dressing Ritual: Music, Mayhem & Magic

It starts with the music. Because no tree can be dressed in silence. That would be sacrilege.

We call upon **Alexa**, our slightly sassy household deity, and summon the *"Family Christmas Playlist"* through Amazon Prime Music. It's an eclectic mix, which is a polite way of saying it's a chaotic collision of classic carols, 80s pop, Disney singalongs, and that one song about a donkey that my son insists is "the best Christmas song ever." (It's not. But we let him believe.)

You'll hear *"Fairytale of New York"* giving way to *"Frosty the Snowman"*, followed by a rousing rendition of *"Let It Go"*, because apparently, it's not Christmas until Elsa's had her moment... and then, because the universe has a sense of humour, Alexa will mishear a request and we'll suddenly be decorating to "hey you , the rock steady crew". Magic comes in many forms.

While the music plays, we open the "Christmas Boxes", ancient, slightly battle-worn cardboard boxes that smells faintly of cinnamon, tinsel, and loft dust. The children dive in with gleeful abandon, emerging with baubles in their hair and a dangerous number of fragile ornaments clutched in tiny hands.

Little Hands, Big Magic

This is where the spell begins.

My youngest daughter, the artiste, immediately claims the job of hanging "the special ones", the delicate glass baubles, the snowflakes with the twiddly bits, the ornaments that came from Granny's house. She hangs them all on the same branch, of course. Because in her eyes, that's the most important branch, and it deserves all the good stuff. Balance is a mortal concern. She's here for beauty.

My son, meanwhile, is on *garland duty*. Which, in his world, involves wrapping the garland around the tree like a boa constrictor and seeing how many laps it can make before someone intervenes. He's also the designated "bauble tester," which means he taps each one to ensure it makes the proper tinkling sound and doesn't fall off immediately. Quality control is vital. Especially when there is a cat in the house.

My eldest daughter, ever the organiser, takes charge of the "breakables" and supervises with the seriousness of a High Priestess overseeing a sacred rite. She's the one who gently moves baubles when no one's looking to ensure there's some semblance of balance. She also insists we have a "theme" every year, which lasts approximately three minutes before the younger two start sneaking Peppa Pig ornaments onto the branches.

Me and The Gardener (husband)? We are weaving between them all, hanging baubles in the high-up places, pretending to referee but really just soaking it all in, the giggles, the arguments over who gets to hang the angel, the songs, the sheer, beautiful mess of it.

The Dog & The Cat (Supporting Cast of Mischief)

The dog, bless him, is utterly convinced that the tree is done just for him, an amazing festive chew toy delivered by the gods. He circles it like a knight preparing for a joust, eyes gleaming with the thrill of the challenge. We distract him with treats, but there's always that moment when his nose is dangerously close to a dangling star, and we all hold our breath.

The cat, of course, is far too dignified for such nonsense. She sits aloof on the arm of the sofa, tail twitching, casting disdainful glances as if to say, *"Fools. All of you."* But we all know that when the lights go out, and the house settles into its quiet nighttime hum, she will be the first to investigate. I've caught her more than once, batting at the lowest bauble with a level of concentration that borders on reverence.

In truth they remember and are incredibly excited. They remember when they were kitten and puppy and have the same excitement now. Which bounces right off the kids.

The Tree as Living Spell

So the tree takes shape, slowly, chaotically, beautifully.

Every ornament holds a memory. The star just below the top? It's not a fancy one, just a glittery cardboard cut-out made by my eldest when she was five, slightly wonky, gloriously imperfect. But that's our sun symbol. That's the promise of return, the crown of light that turns the tree into a pillar of life standing in our living room.

The baubles, despite their variety (glass, felt, plastic dinosaurs wearing Santa hats), are solar charms, protective orbs, reflections of hope. I whisper a blessing into each one as I hang it: *"For joy." "For peace." "For strength." "for each of the children".*

The paper chains and garlands, many of which come from school, crafted by small fingers and a heroic amount of glitter glue are our spells of connection. Every link a wish, a promise, a bit of tangled joy.

Even the tinsel, often dismissed as tacky, becomes a river of light winding through the green. In our house, it represents the silver threads that bind us to each other, to the season, to the magic we're weaving without even noticing.

Decorating as Spellcraft (With Biscuits, Naturally)

We don't rush the decorating. This is an afternoon-long event, fuelled by **hot chocolate and a questionable number of biscuits**. Gingerbread men are decorated (and beheaded) in quick succession. The dog, despite our best efforts, manages to steal at least one. There is always an argument about whether mince pies are "nice or gross." (I am firmly on Team Nice. The children remain divided.)

As each decoration goes on, I sneak in small moments of witchery, whispering a wish as I tie a bow, tucking a sprig of rosemary into the garland for protection. The children don't need to know the specifics. They're already spellcasting, in their way. Every laugh, every song, every hand placing a bauble with intent is an act of magic.

When the tree is finally dressed, when the fairy lights are switched on, the main light off, and the living room is bathed in that soft, enchanted glow, there's a hush. A moment of awe.

Even the dog sits quietly (for a minute). The cat, of course, remains unimpressed. On the surface, at least.

The Moment of Light: A Family Altar Blessed

When the tree is lit, we gather around for what I secretly consider our Tree Blessing. It's not formal. No Latin chants. No incantations. Just a moment where we all stand, slightly breathless, and take it in.

I remind the children, softly, that this tree isn't just decoration. It's a symbol. A sun-standing, life-holding, hope-giving symbol. It's the green breath of the earth inside our home, holding the light steady through the longest nights. Every ornament we hung, every song we sang, every giggle, every carefully placed bauble, it's all part of the spell... and they get it. They may not have the words yet, but they understand.

The magic of the tree isn't in its perfection. It's in its story. In the way it holds our family's joy, our history, our hopes for the year ahead.

It's loud. It's a bit mismatched. It has a paper chain held together by sheer tape and goodwill. But it's alive. It's ours. It's our *family altar*, dressed in baubles, tangled in lights, shimmering with magic.

So no, you don't need to dismantle Christmas to celebrate Yule. You don't need to swap the tinsel for ivy unless you want to. The tree doesn't care. It's been a pagan symbol, a Christian symbol, a family symbol, and it wears each identity with grace.

What matters is the *intention...* and if that intention is joy, connection, and keeping the light alive in the dark of winter, then my dear, you are already crafting one of the most beautiful Yule altars the world has ever seen.

The Mantelpiece: Hearth Altar of Dreams

There's something about a fireplace that makes a house feel like a home. Even if it's one of those electric ones with glowing plastic logs and a button for "extra crackle," the symbolism is the same. A hearth, real or imagined, is the heart of the home, the place where warmth lives, stories are told, and, if you're like me, no fewer than seventeen mugs of half-drunk tea gather over the course of December.

But for witches, the hearth is more than just a practical feature. It's the original altar, the sacred fire that once kept our ancestors alive through frostbitten nights and kept the spirits of home and hearth content. It's where magic happens, where spells are woven between stirring the stew and drying the laundry. Above it, there, on that lovely ledge of pure possibility, is altar real estate at its finest.

In my house, the mantelpiece becomes a swirling, ever-evolving tapestry of Yule magic and family tradition. It's where the old world meets the new. It's where I get to sneak in little witchy touches while the children pile on their Christmas crafts, and The Gardener grumbles good-naturedly about tinsel shedding onto the kindling.... and it all starts with the evergreens.

Dressing the Mantel: More Than Just Greenery

Every December, there's a ritual trek into the wood, and even sometimes, yes I admit, the garden centre, where we gather armfuls of pine, holly, and bay. The kids love this part. They're armed with their own tiny baskets (which, let's be honest, mostly get filled with pinecones and mud) and are on a mission to find "the most magical leaves." My son usually comes back with a twig that "looks like a wizard's wand." My eldest daughter, ever the serious decorator, selects sprigs of rosemary and sniffs them approvingly, claiming she's checking for "good vibes."

Back home, the greenery is woven into a garland. Not with Pinterest perfection, but with the kind of enthusiastic craftsmanship that involves a lot of floral wire and the occasional squabble over whose turn it is to hold the cinnamon sticks. We thread in dried orange slices, not just because they look beautiful, but because they're little suns, tiny orbs of warmth and brightness to honour the returning light.

Bells get tucked in here and there, partly for protection, partly because I'm a firm believer that everything is improved with the occasional festive jingle. They're meant to ward off mischief, but in our house, they mostly signal that the cat has launched a surprise assault on the garland while pretending to be completely disinterested.

The result is a garland that spills and swoops across the mantelpiece, lush and alive, smelling of pine, citrus, and just a hint of chaos. It feels... right. Like the house itself takes a deeper breath once it's in place.

Candles: The Four Elements with Extra Wobble

Once the greenery is in place (and the cat has been gently removed for the third time), we begin the Great Candle Arranging. This is an event.

The mantelpiece becomes a miniature landscape of flames, each candle chosen with care, by which I mean the children pick the ones with glitter, and I sneak in the elemental colours when they're not looking.

A tall green pillar for Earth, a squat white votive for Air, a bold red taper for Fire, and a calm blue glass candle for Water. They might not always be perfectly spaced (the youngest likes to create "candle towers," which is as precarious as it sounds), but the intent is there.

Every time I light these candles, whether for a formal Yule rite or just because the kettle's on, I'm calling in the elements. A little grounding from Earth when the to-do list is overwhelming. A breath of clarity from Air when the house is full of pre-Christmas frenzy. Fire's courage for when the mince pies are burned, and Water's calm for when bedtime is... optimistic.

Yes, sometimes the flames flicker wildly when no window is open. No, I'm not saying it's definitely a sign, but I'm also not saying it's not.

The Yule Log That Never Burns (But Always Works)

Nestled amidst the garland and candles sits our ornamental Yule log. Not the big, ceremonial one that gets dragged into the hearth for burning (though we have that too, waiting in the wings), but a small, decorated log that holds court on the mantelpiece for the whole season.

It's an old piece of birch, about the size of a loaf of bread, lovingly dressed each year with ribbons, herbs, and whatever bits the kids decide are essential. One year it sported googly eyes. Another year, my son added a LEGO wizard riding it like a sleigh. Witchcraft evolves.

The Gardener (BTW if you don't know why my husband is called The Gardener, do read my other book.... Sorry a bit of product placement there....) carves a new rune into it every Yule Eve, sometimes a sun symbol, sometimes a bind rune we create together. The children take this very seriously, whispering wishes into the wood as if the log itself were listening. Perhaps it is.

This Yule log isn't for burning. It's a guardian of the season, absorbing our hopes and holding the hearth's magic like a battery of joy.

Stockings Hung with Intent (and Slight Panic)

Ah, the humble Christmas stocking. So often dismissed as a Victorian add-on to the festivities, a quaint tradition of hanging up a sock and hoping for an orange, lump of coal and a handful of walnuts. But in our house? The stocking is an altar of abundance, mischief, and a yearly test of parental logistics that would make a NASA launch sequence look casual.

For me, the act of hanging stockings is as ceremonial as any high ritual. It's a moment of intention, a spell of joyful expectation, wrapped, of course, in a healthy dose of slight panic. Because no matter how early I start planning, there will come a night, somewhere in mid-December, when I find myself rooting through drawers and muttering, "Where on earth did I put the stocking hooks?" as if the hooks themselves have sprouted little legs and scurried off to cause mayhem. Which, considering the general magical chaos of this season, is entirely possible.

The Great Stocking Debate (Also Known as Tuesday)

In theory, each child has their own designated stocking. In practice, this becomes a diplomatic negotiation every single year. Yes, we could sow names, but where is the fun in that!

My eldest daughter is very clear on the importance of aesthetics. She insists on having "the fancy one," a velvet number with gold embroidery that makes her look like she's about to host the Yule Ball at Hogwarts. My youngest, in contrast, always gravitates toward the most garish option, last year's choice being a bright pink stocking with a cartoon unicorn and inexplicably attached fairy wings. My son, naturally, changes his mind three times in the space of ten minutes, often settling on the biggest stocking available, because he's a realist.

This leads to a level of stocking diplomacy that would impress the UN.

In the end, they all choose something that feels like theirs. It doesn't have to match. The point is, these stockings become more than decorations. They become personal altars of anticipation, hanging expectantly above the hearth, swaying gently every time someone walks past, like festive pendulums ticking down the hours to Christmas morning.

The Dog, The Cat, and Their (Unspoken) Expectations

Then there's the dog's stocking. Officially, he pretends not to care. He sits there, all dignified, casting a long-suffering glance at the proceedings. But we all know he's watching. Oh, he's watching. Because every year, like clockwork, when the stockings are finally hung and everyone's back is turned, he casually saunters over, nose twitching, as if to double-check that his stocking is where it should be. Filled with treats? Not yet. But it will be.

The cat, of course, does not do stockings. She's far too superior for that nonsense. Stockings are for dogs and small humans. She prefers direct offerings, preferably presented on her armchair-throne with much grovelling... and yet, despite her disdain, she's always the first to "inspect" the stockings once the lights are out.

The Hunt for Stocking Fillers: A Magical Quest

Now, if the stockings are altars, then the filling of them is a spellcraft all its own. Not just any spellcraft, a particularly tricky one, requiring both creativity and stealth.

You see, these aren't the "main presents." The big gifts wait under the tree for later, when we've had coffee, found the camera, and are at least 60% awake. No, the stocking presents are for that sacred, unearthly hour of the morning, when the children wake up at dawn, slightly feral with excitement, and are allowed to open their stockings on their own while we, the parents, lie in bed trying to pretend we're not slightly hungover from the night before. It's a beautiful system. The children get their first burst of festive joy; we get an extra hour of semi-consciousness. Everybody wins.

But this means that the stocking fillers have to be special, weird and distracting.

So begins the Annual Hunt for the Perfect Stocking Fillers, which is part treasure hunt, part chaotic dash through every quirky gift shop and online rabbit hole available. I'm not looking for generic plastic tat that will be forgotten by lunchtime. No. I'm looking for things that will ignite curiosity, spark giggles, and, most importantly, buy me time for a cup of tea in bed on Christmas morning.

There's a particular joy in finding the unexpected. The tiny snow globe that plays "Jingle Bells" at a pitch only the dog can hear. The bath bomb shaped like a dragon's egg that my son will inevitably try to hatch. The unicorn-shaped notepad that my youngest daughter will immediately start filling with "secret spells." The pocket magnifying glass that my eldest will use to inspect every bauble on the tree for manufacturing flaws.

One year, I found a set of tiny wind-up toys, penguins, reindeer, a very confused-looking elf. They spent a solid hour racing them across the living room floor while I sipped my tea and congratulated myself on my own genius.

Then there are the magic snacks. Not the main chocolate haul (that comes later), but little quirky treats, candy canes shaped like wands, tiny bags of "Reindeer Nibbles" (really just trail mix, but with a label that makes it exciting), and those peculiar novelty jelly beans that come in both "nice" and "nasty" flavours, which the children treat as a game of edible Russian roulette.

The Sacred Early Morning Ritual (Otherwise Known as Parental Survival Strategy)

Here's how it plays out, year after year.

At some unspeakable hour, somewhere between "still technically night" and "possibly justifiable to get up for a wee but not for presents", the children start calling out to each other to see if they are all awake as they know they can't go down unless they go together. Then they thunder down the stairs. Sometimes two steps at a time. The dog will join them, tail wagging, ready to supervise. The cat will pretend to stay asleep but will mysteriously appear in the living room within minutes, perfectly poised for any unguarded wrapping paper.

They know the rule. Stockings first. Tree later.

This is a sacred agreement, forged in the fires of parental necessity. They may open their stockings, unwrap every tiny, weird, wonderful gift, eat the permitted amount of chocolate coins, and play with their wind-up penguins to their hearts' content, but the big presents wait until we're all up.

So, the early morning unfolds in a flurry of excited whispers, rustling paper, and bursts of gleeful exclamations from downstairs, while we, the grown-ups, lie in bed, willing our hangovers into submission, grateful for the magic of well-chosen stocking fillers.

I call it "witchy delegation", a spell cast in advance that allows the house to be filled with joy while I negotiate with my own head to allow coffee to happen before parenting resumes.

The Stockings Are Altars of Anticipation

As much as the stockings serve a practical purpose (i.e., letting the adults stay horizontal for an extra hour), they're also steeped in something deeper. Each one is a little altar, not just of giving, but of possibility.

When the children hang them up on Christmas Eve, they're not just decorating. They're making a promise to the universe: *"I believe in magic."*

We, the weary, glitter-covered adults, answer that belief by filling those stockings with gifts that say, *"We remember the wonder too."*

Every tiny toy, every odd little gadget, every lovingly wrapped chocolate is a spell of connection. It's not about value. It's about joy. About showing that magic doesn't always come in big boxes, it can come in something that fits in the palm of a hand but sparks the imagination wide open.

The Aftermath: A Tangle of Joy and Wrapping Paper

By the time we emerge from the bedroom, somewhat restored, caffeinated, and blinking at the mayhem, the stockings have done their job. The children are delighted, engaged, and eager to show us every tiny treasure they've unearthed.

The dog has found his way into his own stocking, proudly parading his chew toy as if he hunted it himself. The cat, in true form, has claimed a patch of crinkled wrapping paper as her royal domain and is glaring at anyone who dares to approach.

As we gather around the tree for the main event *"the big presents"*, the shared oohs and aahs, I take a moment to look at the now-empty stockings, still swaying gently from the mantelpiece.

They're not just empty fabric tubes. They're vessels that have just poured out a morning's worth of wonder. They've held space for excitement, for patience, for the kind of giddy anticipation that adults often forget to feel.

That, to me, is the heart of the Yule season.

Stockings: The Witch's First Spell of Christmas Morning

Stockings may seem simple. Small. A side dish to the main feast of presents under the tree. But in truth, they're the first spell of Christmas morning, a soft, joyful opening to a day steeped in tradition, family, and light.

They represent abundance, not in size, but in intention.
They're spells of giving, not in grandeur, but in joy.
They hold magic, not in price, but in the memories they create.

As I hang them up, hooks finally located (usually), I know that I'm not just preparing for a practical early-morning buffer. I'm crafting a sacred moment. A pause between the frenzy. A space where magic sneaks in quietly, wrapped in paper and tied with ribbon.

Even if it's at six o'clock in the morning.

The Mantelpiece as Daily Magic

Once the mantelpiece is dressed, it transforms the room. The fire below it crackles (or hums, if we're on electric mode), and the garland above breathes life into the walls. The candles flicker. The stockings sway. It becomes impossible to walk past without straightening a bauble, lighting a candle, or whispering a thank-you to the house for holding us through another year.

It's not a grand, sweeping ritual. It's daily magic in motion.

The children start leaving little "gifts" on the mantelpiece, pinecones they found on the way home, drawings of the sun, scraps of paper with secret wishes folded up tight. I sneak in herbs for protection, a crystal or two, perhaps a quietly placed charm bag tucked into the greenery where small hands can't reach.

When friends and family visit, they're drawn to it. They might not know why, but their eyes linger. They'll reach out to touch an orange slice, comment on the cinnamon scent, and smile in that quiet, knowing way. The hearth draws people in. It always has.

A Place of Stillness Amidst the Storm

In the whirlwind of December, school plays, shopping lists, last-minute dashes to the post office, the mantelpiece becomes a still point. It's where I can pause, even for a breath, and remember what this season is really about.

It's not the perfect roast potatoes (though we do try). It's not the presents (though I do keep a spreadsheet). It's the light we keep for each other. The way we hold space for joy, even when the world outside feels dark and overwhelming.

It's in the simple act of lighting a candle in the morning, while the house is still, and whispering, *"Thank you, thank you, thank you."* It's in adjusting a stocking and feeling, in that small gesture, the thread of connection to my ancestors who did the same in hearths long gone. It's in the way the children's laughter mixes with the scent of pine and orange, turning the living room into a temple of everyday magic.

The Mantelpiece Knows

Perhaps that's the greatest magic of all.

The mantelpiece doesn't mind whether it's adorned with ceremonial candles or a string of battery-powered fairy lights. It holds our traditions, old and new, in equal reverence. It watches the seasons turn, the family grow, the chaos swirl, and it remains, quietly sacred, quietly proud.

It knows it's an altar.

It knows it's the heart.

And so, every December, as we weave greenery, light candles, hang stockings, and argue about whose turn it is to light the fire, we're not just decorating.

We're blessing.

We're spellcasting.

We're holding space for the light.

That, my darling friend, is witchcraft in its purest, most joyful form.

The Traditional Witch's Altar (Now with Bonus Reindeer)

Yes, of course, you can still have your classic altar. The one in the corner of your room, or on a shelf, or even on a discreet windowsill (ideal for those who are *witchy but with plausible deniability*).

At Yule, this altar becomes a microcosm of the season.

Here's how you can dress it:

- **Sun symbols**: A golden dish, a sunstone, or even a child's drawing of a big yellow sun.

- **Evergreens**: Ivy for protection, holly for resilience, pinecones for abundance.

- **Candles**: Gold for the sun, white for peace, red for courage.

- **Offerings**: A small dish of dried fruits, nuts, or winter spices.

- **A little silliness**: A handmade ornament, a tiny reindeer, or a scrap of wrapping paper with a wish scrawled on it. Magic doesn't have to be serious to be sincere.

Invite the children (or willing grown-ups) to add to the altar. They can place a pinecone, whisper a wish into a cinnamon stick, or make a "Yule wish stone" by painting a pebble with their hopes for the new year.

The altar isn't a museum exhibit. It's alive. It's a place of connection.

Entwining Christmas and Yule (Because the Kids Already Have)

Here's the thing: children are natural spellcasters. They make wishes, they believe in magic, they create rituals instinctively, whether it's writing letters to Santa, hanging stockings, or sneakily eating advent calendar chocolates ahead of schedule.

At school, they're busy crafting paper chains, sticking glitter on everything, and singing carols with such wild abandon that half the lyrics turn into gleeful mumbles. They are **already practising rituals of light, giving, and community**.

So rather than trying to "replace" Christmas with Yule, the real magic happens when you **blend them together**.

When they make Christmas cards, suggest drawing the sun alongside the snowman. When they write to Santa, encourage them to whisper their wish into the fire (or a candle flame) as well, as an extra bit of magic. When they perform in the school nativity, yes, even if they're cast as Sheep #3, remind them that stories have power, and we tell them every year to keep the light alive.

Yule isn't a rival to Christmas. It's the roots beneath it. And when we show children that, they get it, instantly. They're quite happy to have two festivals rolled into one, thank you very much.

The Everyday Altar: Kitchen Tables & Windowsills

Not every altar needs to be formal. Some of the best ones are quietly tucked into everyday spaces.

- The **kitchen table**, where you stir intention into your tea.

- The **windowsill**, where a single candle glows against the night.

- The **bedside table**, with a jar of herbs and a notebook for dreams.

These small, living altars are just as potent. They remind us that magic is in the daily gestures: the way you sprinkle cinnamon on your porridge, the way you arrange the fruit bowl, the way you pause to breathe before rushing out into the frost.

Bea's Yule Altar Blessing

So, whether you're standing in front of a glitter-drenched Christmas tree, a mantelpiece dripping in garlands, or a modest corner shelf with a single candle and a hopeful pinecone, know this:

You're standing at an altar.

You're weaving together centuries of traditions, pagan, Christian, familial, personal, into a celebration that is wholly, beautifully yours.

The light doesn't mind whether it comes from a handmade beeswax taper or a battery-powered reindeer with a flashing nose. The light is in the intention. The altar is wherever you choose to recognise the sacred. In a house filled with love, laughter, and possibly an alarming amount of glitter, you'll find it everywhere.

This Yule, don't worry about doing it "right." Blend. Combine. Honour the tangled, wonderful, festive knot that is your family's way of celebrating.

Let the children hang their paper chains. Let the tree wear its plastic baubles. Let the fire mantle hold cinnamon sticks and stockings alike. Let the altar be the whole home, singing with life and light.

Because when the sun returns, it's not going to stop and inspect whether your garland was for Yule or for Christmas.

It's just going to shine.

CHAPTER NINE

Forage, Craft, and Conjure

Witchy Winter Projects That (Mostly) Work

Crafting Herbal Bundles & Intention Ornaments

There's a particular magic in the moment you arrive home after a family foraging trip. You stand in the kitchen, boots caked in mud, the kitchen table vanishing beneath a chaotic heap of pine branches, holly sprigs, dried orange slices, and an alarming quantity of twigs that your son swears are "light sabres." The dog is circling, tail wagging and the cat has assumed a lofty position on the windowsill, disdainfully observing the whole affair with the look of one who was never required to forage for anything in her life.

This is when the real witchcraft begins.

Because foraging is only half the spell. The other half happens here, in the weaving, tying, bundling, and blessing of those humble, slightly soggy treasures. It's in the crafting of **herbal bundles and intention ornaments**, small acts of magic that somehow gather all the laughter, mud, and joy of the adventure and tie them up with a bit of string and a lot of love.

The Foraging (Or: Muddy Boots & "Treasure Hunts")

Every year, we set out on a grand family foraging expedition, which sounds far more serene than it is. Picture this: three children, two with baskets, one wielding a stick that is most definitely too large to be safe, stomping through the woods in what can only be described as "enthusiastic disarray." The dog is delighted, bounding from puddle to puddle, while the cat, no fool, is at home on her throne, no doubt drafting a letter of complaint.

We're out hunting for **pinecones, holly with the glossiest leaves, sprigs of rosemary**, and the odd bit of "enchanted moss" (which, to my youngest, is any moss she can reach). My eldest, being the self-appointed crafting director, insists on examining every piece of pine for "aesthetics." My son, meanwhile, is on a noble quest for sticks shaped like wands. He found one last year that looked suspiciously like a garden rake, but we applauded his dedication.

Foraging with children isn't quick. Nor is it neat. But it is wildly joyful. Every find becomes a treasure. Every trip a story. Somehow, by the time we trudge back home, there's a kind of spell already woven between us, a spell of shared adventure, fresh air, and muddy socks.

The Crafting Table of Mayhem

Once home, we tip the foraging spoils onto the kitchen table, transforming it into what I fondly call the *Crafting Table of Mayhem*. The dog hovers, hoping to steal an orange slice (he never succeeds), while the cat does her best to look entirely disinterested, despite the occasional twitch of her tail every time a sprig of holly falls to the floor.

This is where the **herbal bundles** come to life.

The bundles themselves are simple, pine for cleansing, rosemary for protection, a cinnamon stick for warmth, and a slice of dried orange for a touch of sun magic. But oh, the making of them is anything but.

The Art of the Herbal Bundle (With Glue-Gun Duels)

We start by laying out the ingredients. This sounds orderly, doesn't it? It's not. There's always a heated debate over who gets the "best cinnamon stick" (spoiler: they all look the same), and someone inevitably decides to wave a rosemary sprig like a wand, knocking over the jar of cloves.

But eventually, we get there. Each child gathers their bundle, three or four sprigs of pine, a few stalks of rosemary, a cinnamon stick, and an orange slice, and brings it over to me like a proud offering.

The binding process is where the magic (and chaos) happens.

We use **natural twine**, I've learned not to bring out the fancy ribbon until the final stage, otherwise it turns into a competition of who can wrap the most knots in the least helpful way. The children help wrap the bundles, and as they do, I guide them to whisper a blessing or an intention into each twist of the twine.

"For a happy home."
"For good dreams."

"For biscuits whenever you want them." (That one's from my son. Wise beyond his years.)

Then comes the glue gun.

Ah, the glue gun. A noble tool of crafting, responsible for equal parts creativity and mild panic. My eldest, being the responsible one, takes charge, carefully adding a dab of glue to fix the orange slices into place. My youngest insists on "helping," which usually means I'm gently redirecting her from gluing her fingers together while maintaining an encouraging smile.

At some point, the glue gun will rebel. It always does. It drips, it strings, it leaves mysterious cobwebs of glue across the table. But by the end of it, we have a collection of beautifully imperfect **herbal bundles**, each one humming with intention, laughter, and a few fingerprints of glue.

These bundles find their places tucked into garlands, perched on the mantelpiece, or given as gifts to friends. They're not polished. They're not symmetrical. But they are alive with the magic of the moment we made them.

Intention Ornaments: Wishes Wrapped in Twine

With the table still strewn with foraged bits and bobs, we move on to the *intention ornaments*.

These are, in essence, tiny spell bundles designed to hang on the Yule tree or altar. They're simple enough for small hands to make, yet potent with personal magic.

The children each select a small square of muslin or scrap fabric, though last year, my son insisted on using an old sock "because it's lucky. Obviously. " We filled the fabric with a small pinch of herbs, rosemary, lavender, a clove or two. Then, with absolute reverence, the children wrote their wishes on slips of paper.

My eldest wished for peace and happiness. My youngest wished for a unicorn. My son... well, his wish was for "a light saber and also world peace." Balance.

We folded the wishes into the herb bundles and tied them up with twine, whispering a blessing with every knot. The dog, by this point, had resigned himself to lying under the table, watching us with the solemn patience of a creature who knows the humans are up to something odd.

The ornaments were decorated with whatever the children fancied, tiny pinecones, bits of cinnamon stick, a dab of glitter (which, naturally, ended up on everything else). Each ornament was entirely unique. Some were neat little pouches, others looked like herb-filled tumbleweeds, but every single one was perfect.

Hanging them on the tree is a ceremony in itself. Each child carefully chooses a branch, holds their ornament up, and we all pause as they speak their wish aloud. There's always a hush in that moment. A stillness, even amid the glitter chaos. It's the kind of moment you can feel in your chest, the moment where crafting tips into spellwork, where the ordinary becomes sacred.

Beauty in Imperfection

I won't lie to you. These aren't Pinterest-perfect crafts. There are lopsided bundles, ornaments that look like they've survived a small hurricane, and at least one that gets mysteriously repurposed as a cat toy.

But that's not the point.

The point is that every bundle, every ornament, carries with it a piece of us, a laugh shared over a glue-gun mishap, a whispered wish, the scent of pine still clinging to fingers. They are spells in the truest sense: *intentions wrapped in joy, tied with a ribbon of family magic...* and every time I pass the tree and see those slightly wonky ornaments swaying gently in the light, I'm reminded that magic isn't in the flawless finish. It's in the making. In the moments of shared creation. In the imperfection of life, beautifully embraced.

Grannies Wreath

I remember a wreath my grandmother used to make. Not the sort you see in glossy magazines or YouTube tutorials, but a beautiful, wild-hearted circle that for her pulsed with memories. Every year, as the frost crept along the windowpanes and the garden sighed into its winter slumber, she would fetch her old wicker basket, the one with the frayed handle and the broken clasp that never quite stayed shut, and announce with quiet determination, "Time to make the wreath, ma chérie."

We would pull on our wellies, scarves wrapped around our noses, and step into the December garden, which looked, to anyone else, like a place that had long since given up. But not to Grandmother. She had a way of seeing life where at the time I saw only bare branches and stubborn mud.

The rosemary bushes, evergreen and tenacious, were her first stop. She would clip a few sprigs, the scent bursting bright and sharp in the cold air. "For remembrance," she'd say to the crisp air, and more to herself than to me. Then came the bay tree in the corner, its dark, waxy leaves gleaming against the grey sky. "Wisdom for the doorway," she'd say, carefully snipping only what the tree could spare.

Holly, of course, was essential. Not the manicured kind from garden centres, but the wild holly from the thicket near the shed, glossy leaves bristling with attitude, berries like drops of ruby that the birds had not yet stolen. Grandmother would always whisper an apology to the plant before she took a few sprigs. "She's a prickly lady," she'd say.

The ground would often yield a few surprises, too. Mossy tufts, clinging to the stone edges of the path, were gently teased free and tucked into the basket. "A soft bed for the old year to sleep on." I wouldn't understand the poetry of it until much later.

Once the garden had shared its winter offerings, we would retreat to the garden shed, a humble sanctuary that smelled of soil, lavender sachets, my dad's pipe tobacco and old wood. Hanging from beams, in faded bundles, were the treasures of earlier seasons: dried lavender from summer's bloom, brittle but still fragrant; thyme sprigs, wrapped in red cotton thread; seed heads from poppies, their fragile pods rattling like nature's maracas; and her favourite.... blue cornflowers, pressed and preserved, little scraps of sky caught in a circle of petals.

"These," she would say, holding the cornflowers delicately between her fingers, "these are from home." Home was a small village in the French countryside, the kind of place that existed in her stories, filled with lilac trees, whitewashed cottages, and fields that danced with cornflowers in spring. Her parents, who had never left that village until the outset of War, were taken by it, their voices becoming echoes in her memories. She didn't speak of it often, but when she did, it was through her hands. Through these simple, sacred rituals that turned grief to grace.

The wreath was how she remembered them, not with sorrow, but with life. She would never say, "We make this because I miss them." Instead, she'd smile and say, "They'd want the doorway to look nice."

At the kitchen table, we'd lay out our foraged treasures. The wreath base itself was an old willow hoop she had kept for years, softened and shaped by her hands. She would begin by anchoring the rosemary and bay, their greens twining like old friends. The holly came next, its fierce beauty tempered by sprigs of dried lavender, their soft purple heads peeking shyly through the leaves.

We would bind the bundles with lengths of red and gold thread, never glue, never wire, "It must breathe," she insisted. The cornflowers were always placed near the top, clustered together like a small, defiant patch of summer refusing to be forgotten. She called them her "blue-eyed blessings," or "Des yeux bleus qui portent bonheur."

As we worked, the kitchen filled with the mingled scents of resinous pine, sweet lavender, and the faint citrus from the dried orange slices we had prepared earlier in the week, strung up to dry on the old clothes horse near the Aga. "A little sun for the dark days," she'd wink, nestling them into the greenery.

It wasn't a fast process. Threads would tangle, the holly would prick, and there was always a moment when the entire wreath threatened to fall apart because we'd gotten overconfident with our layering. Grandmother would simply chuckle, reset the base, and remind me that "Making something beautiful is supposed to be messy. Life's a bit like that."

Then there was the final touch, the cloves. She would press them gently into the dried orange slices, their warm, spicy scent spiralling through the room. "to remind the house it's loved." I asked her once why she didn't use more flashy things, like glitter or shiny bows (I was little don't forget). She gave me a look. "Because darling, this is an old kind of magic. The quiet kind. It doesn't need to shout to work."

By the time we finished, the wreath was perfectly wonky, with a rebellious twig or two sticking out as if waving to the neighbours. But it *felt* alive. It felt like it had a story.

Hanging the wreath on the front door was an event. She would make me step onto the old wooden chair, the one from the study that wobbled alarmingly but which she refused to replace, and with a small, proud nod, the wreath was in its place. She'd help me down, step back, hands on her hips, and announce, "There. Now the house knows it's blessed."

I realise now, as I craft my own wreaths with my children, that it wasn't about the wreath itself. It was about *what she put into it*, memory, intention, and a refusal to let sorrow have the final say. The lavender, the thyme, the cornflowers, they weren't just plants. They were stories. Connections. A thread that tied her to her past and, through her, tied me to it as well.

In my home, we still make wreaths. The children have taken to it with their usual blend of wild creativity and accidental sabotage. My son insists on including "epic sticks" that invariably poke someone in the eye. My youngest daughter thinks every wreath needs a unicorn charm. The Cat is a repeat offender in stealing the ribbon spool, It's absolute mayhem. But it's our mayhem. In the middle of it all, I find myself, every year, tucking a small bundle of lavender and a tiny cluster of blue cornflowers into the wreath. For her. For the stories. For the spell that says, "We remember, and we're still here."

A wreath is never just a decoration. It's a doorway blessing, a circle of life, a quiet spell that greets every visitor, every passer-by, with a silent but potent message: *This home holds light, even in the dark.*

CHAPTER TEN

The Wild Wood

A Place Where Your Hair Will Inevitably Frizz

Footprints in Frost – Reading Animal Tracks as Nature's Messages

Winter has a way of quieting the world. The rustle of leaves becomes a soft crunch, the hum of insects fades into memory, and suddenly, you can hear your own footsteps as clearly as your thoughts. It's in this quiet that the land begins to whisper back. Nowhere is that whisper more literal than in the tracks left behind by the wild things.

My son, bless him, believes himself to be a Red Indian scout whenever we head out for a winter walk. Not in the problematic, costumed way of old television, but in the deeply earnest, utterly devoted spirit of a child who is convinced the world is sending him secret messages through paw prints and disturbed moss. He crouches low to the ground, nose practically brushing the frost, finger tracing the outline of a footprint with the same reverence an archaeologist might reserve for an ancient tomb.

"Fox," he declares, as if delivering intelligence from the front lines. "Heading north. Probably looking for rabbits."

Never mind that the track is barely distinguishable from a particularly determined pigeon. He has *decided* it's a fox, and therefore, it is. The dog, eager to contribute, barrels past him in a flurry of enthusiasm, snuffling at a completely unrelated spot, tail wagging as if to say, "I've found something! Probably a sandwich!"

Our winter walks are less about distance and more about discovery. We don't stride out with the aim of reaching a destination. We meander. We pause. We huddle around patches of disturbed mud or frost-laced grass, examining them like detectives at a crime scene, piecing together the stories that have been left behind.

Tracks in the frost are like nature's postcards. Little messages stamped into the earth, saying, "I was here. I passed this way." A delicate chain of bird prints skimming across the path becomes a tale of early morning breakfast hunts. A series of deep, bold paw prints tells us that one of the neighbourhood cats has been patrolling its kingdom. Sometimes, if we're lucky, we do find the clear, sharp imprints of a fox, walking with the quiet confidence of something that knows it belongs.

There's a particular patch of woodland near our home that becomes a winter wonderland of tracks. The mud there holds stories like no other place. One morning, after a particularly crisp frost, we found a trail that looked like a miniature dinosaur had gone for a morning jog. My son was thrilled. "Badger," he announced with authority. "Chasing a dragonfly." The fact that it was December, and dragonflies were but a summer memory, was entirely irrelevant.

But that's the thing about tracking. It isn't just about identification. It's about imagination. About connection. The track itself is only part of the story. The rest is built in the mind, filled in with wonder.

Even the humble hedgehog leaves behind a trail of delight. Tiny prints, often in a wonky line, as if the little creature is navigating by stubbornness rather than sight. I always picture them, nose down, determinedly plodding along, oblivious to the chaos of the wider world. Their tracks often lead nowhere in particular, which feels like a lesson in itself.

The children love to guess where tracks lead. My eldest, ever the practical one, will follow a line of deer tracks to the edge of a clearing and surmise, correctly, that the deer have moved on to quieter pastures. My youngest, however, will insist that a series of small, erratic prints is evidence of a squirrel dance party. Who am I to argue?

For me, tracking is a kind of moving meditation. It slows you down. You stop thinking about your phone, your to-do list, the email you forgot to send. You start noticing the curl of a leaf, the way frost outlines the veins like delicate lace. You see where the land has been touched, marked, traversed by beings who ask nothing more than to exist.

It's not about finding rare or exotic tracks. Most days, we see the same familiar prints: pigeons, robins, a fox or two, the neighbour's overconfident tabby. But every print is a story. Every trail is a thread that ties us back to the land. It's a reminder that we share this space, this winter, with countless unseen lives.

One of my favourite memories is from a walk last January. We were halfway through the woods when my son suddenly dropped to his knees, face inches from the ground. "Look!" he whispered, as if the track might scurry away. There, in the muddy frost, was a perfect imprint of a fox's paw, clear enough that you could see the pads, the fine edge of the claw marks.

It had been a wet couple of weeks before the frost arrived so we were able to follow the trail for ten minutes, weaving through trees, over ditches, through bramble patches. The dog, utterly convinced he was on a grand adventure, was beside himself with excitement. Eventually, the tracks disappeared into a dense thicket, and we stood there, the three of us, peering into the shadows as if the fox might peek back out and say hello.

"He's gone home now," my son said, with a small, satisfied nod.

It wasn't just a walk. It was a moment of connection. With the land. With the unseen wild. With each other.

I often think of those tracks as little spells left behind. Not crafted by human hands, but by nature itself. A charm against forgetting. A charm that says, "Pay attention."

Even the act of bending down to examine a print feels ritualistic. You're bowing to the earth. You're engaging with the world on its terms. In those moments, the frost becomes a scrying mirror, and the tracks are the whispers that float to the surface.

Of course, the dog never gets it quite right. He's more interested in smells than stories. He'll follow a scent trail with wild enthusiasm, only to abandon it halfway through because a suspiciously interesting stick has appeared. The cat, in contrast, prefers to watch from the windowsill, tail flicking, entirely unimpressed with our muddy expeditions.

But that's the thing about tracking in winter. It's not about expertise. It's about presence. You don't need to know the difference between a badger print and a large dog paw to enjoy the wonder of it. The magic is in the noticing.

So many of us rush through the colder months, heads down, shoulders hunched, waiting for spring to arrive and give us permission to look up again. But winter has its own stories, its own quiet miracles. They're just written in subtler ink. A track in the frost. A feather caught in a bramble. The hush of a branch that shifts under the weight of something unseen.

When we follow these signs, we remember that we are part of the wild. Not visitors. Not intruders. Part of the same pulse, the same breath that moves through fur and feather.

There is such joy in that. Even when the trail leads nowhere in particular.

Especially then.

The Green of Winter – Working with Evergreen Magic

Winter has a reputation for being grey and brown and altogether rather dismal, but that's only if you're not paying attention. Look closer, and you'll find that winter is laced with green. Not the brazen greens of summer, but the deep, quiet greens of evergreens, the ones who hold the line while the rest of the world sleeps.

I have a fondness for evergreens. They are, in many ways, the old souls of the plant world. They don't shout about their presence. They simply endure. Standing tall, holding their colour with quiet defiance as if to say, "We are still here."

There is magic in these plants. Ancient magic. Our ancestors knew it; it's why we bring evergreens into our homes at Yule, weaving their strength into garlands and wreaths, reminding the hearth that life persists. Holly protects. Ivy binds and weaves connections. Pine cleanses. These are not just decorations; they are living spells.

One year, after a particularly enthusiastic winter ramble, we decided to craft what we called 'Nature Charms.' Small bundles of evergreen sprigs tied with red thread, infused with whispered blessings and left at strategic points on our walk in the woods so others could follow, but also leading back to the garden gate, our front door, even the dog's favourite digging spot by the fence. The dog, naturally, thought these were gifts for him and proudly carried a bundle into his bed. The cat, in contrast, merely inspected the charms with a disdainful flick of her tail, as if critiquing our choice of ribbon.

The act of crafting these charms became a spell in itself. There was something deeply grounding about sitting around the kitchen table, fingers sticky with pine resin, tying tiny sprigs together, and speaking aloud what we wanted these charms to hold. Protection. Health. Joy. They were not complicated. But they were heartfelt.

Evergreens, I told the children, are the guardians of winter. They teach us resilience. They remind us that even when everything seems barren and still, life is quietly enduring. They don't need applause. They don't need to bloom in grand displays. Their magic is in their constancy.

It isn't just in the crafting. Standing beneath an ancient pine tree in the hush of a winter morning, you can feel it. That deep, slow pulse. A kind of wisdom that doesn't come in words but in presence. It's a moment of connection that humbles you, roots you, and somehow, at the same time, lifts you up.

On one walk, we found a holly bush so magnificent it stopped us in our tracks. It stood alone at the edge of the wood, its leaves glistening like polished jade, berries clustered like tiny lanterns. The children circled it, hands outstretched, as if it were a long-lost friend. We left a small offering at its base, a few seeds, a strand of ribbon. Not because we had to, but because it felt right. A simple thank you for holding the green when everything else had let go.

Evergreens aren't just symbols. They're companions. They keep the wheel turning through the dark half of the year. They are nature's promise that life, even when unseen, continues.

So, when you see that ivy climbing an old stone wall, or a stubborn little pine sapling pushing through the frost, take a moment. Acknowledge them. Maybe even whisper a blessing back. After all, they've been holding the line for us all winter long.

Tree Magic and Whispered Names – Honouring the Winter Woods

There is a hush in the winter woods that you don't find in any other season. Summer is a chatterbox, with birdsong and buzzing and the constant rustle of green. Autumn is all bravado, with its crackling leaves and gusts of wind that send branches dancing. But winter? Winter is a quiet conversation. It doesn't shout. It whispers.

I think I remember the first time I realised trees could have personalities, although there is something itching in the back of my head from my own childhood even earlier. We were on one of our meandering winter walks, the kind where you cover very little ground but see an entire world. We rounded a bend and found ourselves face to face with a truly ancient oak.

It was magnificent. Its trunk was so wide that even with all three children stretched hand-to-hand, they couldn't quite wrap their arms around it. Its bark was a tapestry of lines and whorls, each groove a chapter of stories we'd never read. It stood, bare-limbed and bold, like an old guardian who'd seen too many winters to be impressed by yet another.

Serious as always, my eldest pressed her palm to the bark and declared, "This tree's name is Old Grump."… and just like that, the tree had a name.

Naming trees became a family tradition from that moment on. We never forced it; we waited to see which trees would offer up their names to us. There was "The Listening Birch," slender and quiet, with branches that swayed in a way that made you lean in and whisper.

"Queen Ivy," a grand old ash tree draped in cascading ivy cloaks, and "The Juggler," a gangly rowan whose branches looked forever poised to toss the next snowball. In a way it's like spotting shapes in the clouds, laying on your back in the meadow, but this is winter and we are finding the shapes or personalities in the trees instead.

To the untrained eye, winter trees can seem lifeless, skeletal. But once you start paying attention, you realise they are anything but. Without the distraction of leaves, you can see their true shape. Their bones. Their posture. You start to notice how each species holds itself, the steadfast, muscular stance of oaks, the graceful sway of birches, the ancient, sacred hush of yews.

I teach my children that every tree carries a particular kind of magic. Oaks for endurance and strength. Birch for new beginnings and purification. Yew for transformation, holding within its dark green needles the mysteries of life, death, and rebirth. Hazel for wisdom. Hawthorn for protection.

And while we don't do grand rituals in the middle of the woods (it's hard to be solemn when someone is always trying to climb a tree or the dog has found something unspeakable to roll in), we do have our quiet gestures. A touch of the bark, a whispered thank-you, a small offering of a seed or a song. It's simple, heartfelt, and in many ways, more powerful than any elaborate rite.

One winter, we visited a grove of silver birches after a fresh snowfall. The children immediately ran ahead, leaving their prints in the untouched blanket of white, but I lingered. There was something about the way the sunlight filtered through those bare, white trunks, the way the snow clung to their bases, that made the air feel thick with presence. As if the trees were listening. Breathing.

I laid my hand on the nearest trunk and closed my eyes. For a moment, there was nothing but stillness. Then a thought, or maybe a feeling, bubbled up: "Let it go." It wasn't a voice. Not really. But it was clear as anything I'd ever heard. And it was exactly what I needed to hear.

That's the thing about trees. They don't give you answers. They give you space. They don't fix your problems, but they remind you to breathe through them.

We often think of magic as something loud, flashy, spellbooks and wands. But the magic of trees, especially in winter, is slow. Patient. It doesn't demand attention. It simply waits for you to notice.

When we name a tree, when we pause to acknowledge its presence, we are creating a relationship. We are saying, "I see you." And in doing so, we step back into the rhythm of the land, where time moves in rings and cycles, not in rushes and deadlines.

Now, whenever we walk through the winter woods, there's a kind of reverence woven into the adventure. The children still run and climb and bicker over who spotted the first squirrel, but they also stop, now and then, to pat a familiar tree or whisper a new name to a young sapling just brave enough to poke its head above the frost.

... and I? I stand among them, beneath the bare branches reaching into the winter sky, and I listen. To the hush. To the stories etched in bark. To the silent, steadfast magic of trees that wait, patiently, for spring.

Also by Bea St. Clair – Paperback ISBN: 9781916989078

ABOUT THE AUTHOR

Bea St. Clair is a witch with a fondness for cinnamon, overstuffed bookshelves, and the kind of candles that drip everywhere no matter what the label promises. An English witch who lives in a crooked little cottage with a beautiful garden that looks suspiciously like it might talk back if you listen closely. Her love of plants, and the curious science behind their magic, inspired her first book, *The Witch's Botanical Apothecary*. When she isn't brewing potions from herbs she grew herself (or ones that mysteriously appeared in the hedge), or foraging for odd-looking twigs that *"absolutely have magical potential"*, she can be found with soil under her nails, a teapot within reach, and at least one cat staging a coup on the keyboard. She writes with equal parts candlelight, laughter, and cake crumbs, firmly believing that magic is best when it's shared, and ideally when it smells faintly of rosemary and freshly baked bread. *A Witchy Christmas* is her love letter to the season, where enchantment and humour meet holly, pudding, and the occasional pine needle in your socks.

Printed in Dunstable, United Kingdom

76219951R00157